MUTANT EMPIRE

BOOK 2

SANCTUARY

MUTANT EMPIRE

BOOK 2

SANCTUARY

CHRISTOPHER GOLDEN

ILLUSTRATIONS BY
RICK LEONARDI AND TERRY AUSTIN

BYRON PREISS MULTIMEDIA COMPANY, INC.

NEW YORK

BOULEVARD BOOKS, NEW YORK

Special thanks to Ginjer Buchanan, Steve Roman, Lara Stein, Stacy
Gittelman, and the gang at Marvel Creative Services.

X-MEN: MUTANT EMPIRE
BOOK 2: SANCTUARY

A Boulevard Book
A Byron Preiss Multimedia Company, Inc. Book

PRINTING HISTORY
Boulevard paperback edition / November 1996

Check out the Byron Preiss Multimedia site
on the World Wide Web:
http://www.byronpreiss.com

The Putnam Berkley World Wide Web site address is
http://www.berkley.com/berkley

Make sure to check out PB Plug, the science
fiction/fantasy newsletter, at
http://www.pbplug.com

ISBN 1-57297-180-0

BOULEVARD
Boulevard Books are published by
The Berkley Publishing Group
200 Madison Avenue, New York, New York 10016
BOULEVARD and the "B" design
are trademarks belonging to Berkley Publishing Corporation

PRINTED IN THE UNITED STATES OF AMERICA

10 9 8 7 6 5 4 3 2 1

For my son,

Daniel John Christopher Golden,

who came into the world while this book was being written,
and reminded me why we all,
like Charles Xavier,
dream of the future.

PROLOGUE

Scott Summers stood in the cockpit of the *Starjammer* and watched his father with growing dismay. Even as they had escaped through an Imperial stargate, the ship had been crippled in its battle with an armada of Shi'ar star cruisers. Now the *Starjammer* was dead, adrift near Earth's sun. Auxiliary power and life support systems were the only thing between the ship's passengers and the fatal vacuum of space.

As his fellow Starjammers, Raza and Ch'od, worked furiously to repair the hyperburn engines in the rear of the ship, Major Christopher Summers, known as Corsair, attempted to get their communications rig up and running. Watching his father work, Scott admired the man's hope, dignity, and courage. Corsair's brow furrowed in concentration, then his right hand slipped and his knuckles rapped on the comm board. He swore, and set right back to work.

Scott looked out at the vastness of space that stretched before them. One side of the viewport was lit up with blinding peripheral sunlight, but Scott could still see the field of sable and stars to the other side. He could not help but wonder if the infinite dark beyond the viewport would soon become a crypt to hold nearly all that remained of the Summers family.

If they didn't make it, there would be no funeral, no grave, no marker of any kind that would enable people to know they had existed, had lived and died. Though he'd done his best to stave it off, doubt was beginning to creep up on him. More than that. It was threatening to overwhelm him. The realization unnerved him.

As Cyclops, the leader of the X-Men, Scott had been in more tight spots, close calls, and rough scrapes than any five career soldiers. But there had nearly always been the possibility of retreat, if it came to that.

There was no retreat here. If they were lucky, they would live. If not, they would die. A chillingly simple formula.

Slowly, however, Scott began to realize that his growing fear was not for his own life. He had regrets, certainly. Though he had never been overzealous in showing his passions, those whom he loved were aware of his feelings. That was vital. But there was so much more to life, and death. There were those left behind on Earth who would mourn him, and he grieved for their loss in advance.

The worst of it, however, was that there were far too many people he cared about on board the *Starjammer*, sharing his fate: Corsair, Raza, Ch'od, and the fourth Starjammer, his father's lover Hepzibah, who was injured in their battle on Hala, the Kree homeworld. That would be hard enough. But there were four other X-Men on board as well. Rogue, who always made him smile, was tending to the injured Gambit. Warren Worthington, whose field name was Archangel, was one of Scott's oldest friends in the world.

Then there was Jean Grey. Scott had loved her from the moment, all those years earlier, when he had first seen her standing in the foyer of Charles Xavier's mansion. To his neverending astonishment, she had loved him in return, and still did. They were part of a greater family, a group of Earth-born mutants fighting for harmony between their race and humanity. They gave of themselves every day as X-Men, to the dream of their mentor Charles Xavier, and to each other. They had risked their lives on a quest to rescue his father from execution. And they had succeeded.

But if the cost was an ignoble death while lost in space, and grieving loved ones on Earth who would never really know what happened to them . . . it was too great. The others had come because they cared for him, and now they would all die because of it. Because of him. As Cyclops, the leader of the X-Men, they looked to him for answers. He wasn't about to let them down.

"Scott?" Corsair asked quietly. "What is it, son?"

Scott turned toward his father, taking a deep, cleansing breath, and then he chuckled. He thought about telling Corsair about the weight of space and hopelessness that had pressed down on him, about his fears, and his new determination to see them through this, no matter what. But he didn't. They just never had that kind of relationship.

"Nothing," he finally answered. "Just trying to figure out if we have some kind of alternate power source."

"Not unless you want to hang your head out the loading bay and use your optic beams to give us some momentum," Corsair laughed. "Your head would explode after the first millisecond or so, but at least we'd be pointed in the right direction."

Scott pretended to think about it, then declined. He shared a laugh with his father that cleared the last cobweb of trepidation from his mind. That was for the best. He needed all his wits about him, now more than ever.

"How's it coming with the comm-rig?" he asked.

Corsair grimaced, then stood, brushing himself off.

"It's totally fried," he answered glumly. "We could be here for months, if we lived that long, and never fix it. If we're going to get home, we're going to have to do it on our own.'' Then his eyes widened, and he tilted his head slightly as he said, ''Unless . . .''

''Unless?'' Scott asked.

Corsair leaned over the communications board that he had dismantled and rummaged around in its guts for a moment.

''Yes,'' he said, almost to himself, ''I think it might work.''

He pressed his lips tightly together as he spliced two charred wires together.

''What is it?'' Scott persisted. ''Have you fixed it?''

''No,'' Corsair said finally, looking up with a wry grin. ''But at least I've got the emergency call beacon going. There isn't much interstellar travel in this sector other than would-be world conquerors, but you never know. Maybe we'll get lucky.''

''Better than nothing, I suppose,'' Scott answered. ''I'm going to go back and look in on the others. Are you through here?''

''No, but you go ahead,'' Corsair waved his son on. ''I'm going to see if the navigational computers are in any better shape than the comm-rig. I don't want to drain what little auxiliary power we have, but it would be good to keep some kind of flight path to Earth logged in, just in case we actually do repair the warp drive, or even the hyperburners.''

''Sounds sensible to me,'' Scott answered. He took a last look at his father, deep in concentration again, and realized that he had never seen Corsair more serious. Even when he was a boy, and Major Christopher Summers was one of America's greatest test pilots. Those times were long ago, but there were moments, looking at his father, when they were fresh as yesterday.

• • •

Archangel hated to be confined. No matter that there was plenty of room for them all in the main cabin of the *Starjammer*. The simple knowledge that he could not spread his bio-metallic wings and take to the air was stifling. When he considered that there was no air beyond the ship's hull in which to soar, the atmosphere became oppressive.

Even as a boy, Warren Worthington III had been a little claustrophobic. Not enough to affect his life, merely enough to unnerve him in cramped quarters, or bustling crowds. When he had reached puberty, and his original, natural wings had quickly grown from his back, he had at first been repulsed. But he quickly realized that his wings gave him freedom, that flight provided an ecstasy which was the complete antithesis of his claustrophobia.

The wings were a mutation, of course. All of the X-Men were mutants, *homo superior*, the next stage in human evolution. They were made so by an unknown variable, an x-factor, in their genetic constitution. Mutants were like snowflakes, the x-factor never creating the same variant mutation twice, save for rare cases when genetic heritage played a role.

The greatest scientific minds on Earth had never been able to discover precisely what influenced the x-factor, what defined a specific mutation. His own, angelic wings, had been in his genetic makeup from conception. While he had once believed the wings were a response to his need for freedom, Warren had realized that it was more likely that his claustrophobia was an awareness, on a cellular level, that he was not meant to be confined.

SANCTUARY

That he was meant to soar the blue skies, above the world.

Though his natural wings had been mutilated and amputated, and replaced with the deadly bio-metallic, razor-feathered appendages that now sprouted from his back, he still felt that urge. Confinement aboard the dead spacecraft gnawed at him. His muscles tensed, unable to relax, and Warren began to wonder exactly what the real symptoms of "cabin fever" were.

The cabin was still pressurized, they still had artificial gravity, but his body felt lighter, and chilly. He wondered if that was the first sign that the life support systems were going to give out.

"Jesus," he hissed under his breath. "Get a grip, man."

He stood and began to pace the cabin. Rogue sat on the edge of her seat next to a medi-slab, upon which Gambit lay unconscious. The Cajun had been electrocuted in battle with the Shi'ar Imperial Guard, and they had not yet been able to ascertain the extent of his injuries. He was still out like a light though, and Warren figured that could only be bad. Jean Grey was on the other side of the medi-slab, her hand on Gambit's pallid forehead. Her eyes were closed as she psi-scanned him, and Warren envied her calm.

He breathed deeply, methodically, and pushed the suffocating atmosphere of the ship from his mind. After a moment, he stepped to where Rogue kept her vigil. It had been no secret amongst the X-Men that she and Gambit had been semi-involved for some time, but Warren had always wondered how serious it was. The terror, pain, and nausea visible on her face revealed that her feelings were very serious indeed.

"How is he?" Warren asked, as he slid into the seat next to Rogue.

She looked up, a little lost at first. Or maybe shell-shocked, Warren thought. Then Rogue smiled, grateful for the question, and the respite from the silence, and the worry.

"Hi, Warren," she said in a library whisper, her southern belle accent even raspier than usual. "Remy's okay, as far as we can tell. Jean's scannin' him again, seein' if she can find anything else wrong. He needs medical attention, that's for sure. But if we can't get movin' again, it ain't gonna matter one little bit."

She leaned against the wall behind her and pushed her hands up through her auburn hair, and the white skunk-streak that ran through it. They were only friends, no doubt, but at that moment Warren could not help but notice how tragically beautiful she was. Rogue was a good, strong, decent woman. Once, she had been terribly misguided, trapped in her fear and the manipulations of others. Warren refused to believe that she had come out of all of that, that he had overcome his emotions regarding his own transformation, that they had all come so far together, only to die in the middle of nowhere.

But it looked like Rogue needed a bit of reassurance.

"Listen, lady," Warren began, "the Starjammers have been in tighter spots than this. So have the X-Men. Before we start panicking, why don't we see what Ch'od and Raza have to say about the hyperburn engines? Besides, we've got enough to worry about just making sure Gambit and Hepzibah are okay."

Rogue looked at the prone form of Gambit, then glanced over at where Hepzibah slept soundly. Raza had sedated her in order to facilitate her recuperation, and

Warren was surprised at how peaceful she looked, despite the bloody bandages over the wound on her arm.

"Yer right," Rogue agreed. "I just feel so damn useless."

"Tell me about it," Warren said. "But don't worry, I've a feeling we'll get our turn. We always do."

There was silence for a moment, then Jean opened her eyes abruptly and turned to them.

"Well?" Rogue asked.

"There doesn't seem to be any lasting damage," Jean said. "Still, we've got to keep an eye on him. His heart has taken an incredible strain, and it isn't out of the realm of possibility for him to have cardiac failure at this point."

"A heart attack?" Warren asked, astonished.

"I'm not saying it's going to happen," Jean answered, her green eyes intense. "Only that it's possible. We've got to watch him."

"Thanks, Jean," Rogue said earnestly. "And you, too, Warren. When you spend so much time fighting the kind of war we're in, sometimes you forget that not all problems are solved with force. I appreciate y'all bein' here."

"Well," Warren said magnanimously, "you're welcome, Rogue—but it's not like we have a choice."

Jean smiled, and Rogue actually chuckled. In the cold confinement of the cabin, it was a welcome sound indeed.

"Well, you all seem to be taking our predicament rather well," Cyclops said, as he emerged from the cockpit.

* * *

Jean stood and crossed the cabin to meet Scott. They shared a psychic bond, a special rapport boosted by Jean's telepathic abilities. Without a word, they greeted one another, then embraced for a long moment. When she released Scott from her arms, Jean looked up at his face, at the ruby quartz visor that covered Scott's eyes, allowing him to control the devastating optic blasts that were his mutant "gift."

The barest hint of his eyes was visible behind their red shield, but Jean wished, as she often did, that she could truly see them. She yearned to look upon the face of the man she loved unimpeded. The eyes were the window to the soul, or so it was said. Jean consoled herself with the knowledge that no facial expression could ever tell her as much about her lover as their psionic bond. It told her more about his love for her than any look of longing.

But, somehow, it was still a poor substitute for gazing into his eyes.

"Is Corsair having any luck with the comm-rig?" Jean asked, reluctantly bringing them all back to their imminent danger.

"We're broadcasting some kind of S.O.S. pattern, but that's all we're going to get. He's working on the navigational systems now," Scott answered.

"I just wish I was as confident as the rest of you," Rogue said, her powerful fingers still holding Gambit's limp hand. "I don't know as we've got a chance in hell of gettin' out of this alive."

"Not to worry, Rogue," Scott responded. "We'll make it home in one piece."

"In all seriousness, Scott," Archangel said, standing up, "besides wracking our brains hoping for some kind

SANCTUARY

of inspiration, can you think of anything we can do to help?''

Scott paused a moment, then shook his head.

''Come on, folks,'' Jean said, exasperated. ''Have a little faith, will you? Even if the Starjammers can't get this ship repaired, both Professor Xavier and Lilandra know we were en route to Earth, and how we were traveling. As soon as they speak, it will be only a matter of time before they come looking for us. And now Scott tells us we're broadcasting an S.O.S.''

''You make it sound so simple, Jean,'' Warren argued. ''But Lilandra isn't going to send anyone after us, and the Professor doesn't have any space-faring vessels.''

''So he borrows a spacecraft from Starcore or Stark Enterprises,'' Scott said, and Jean wanted to kiss him for the way he made it sound like it wasn't a big deal, when they all knew that it was.

''Point bein', if I ain't mistaken, that we all gotta stay alive until then,'' Rogue finished.

''Exactly!'' Jean said. ''And maybe we won't have to wait. Ch'od and Raza have been holding this ship together with spit and bubble gum for years. I'd be surprised if they were unable to fix it.''

A sudden clamor arose from the back of the ship, and then there was the pounding of heavy footfalls through the cargo hold, approaching the main cabin.

''What the—?'' Scott began.

''Fire in the hole!'' Ch'od yelled as he and Raza burst into the cabin and dove for the floor.

Immediately, Jean followed their example, confident that the other X-Men would do the same. For good measure, she instinctively threw a telekinetic force shield over all of them.

The back of the ship exploded, shooting a fireball into the cabin and rocking the ship so hard that they were all tossed to the starboard side. Only when it had subsided, and Ch'od and Raza were already up and running for the cargo hold with some kind of firefighting equipment in hand, did Jean realize that the aft section of the ship hadn't been vaporized in the blast. Of course, if it had, they would all have been dead. But the concussion had stunned her so badly that being alive wasn't a factor in her thought process at the moment.

"What are we waiting for, people?" Scott asked, the crisis pushing him into leader-mode. "Let's make ourselves useful!"

The four of them ran for the back of the ship, though Rogue stayed behind a moment to see that Gambit and Hepzibah had not been further injured by the blast.

"He may be a wiseguy," Archangel said as they came upon Raza and Ch'od fighting a fire in the hatchway to the engine room, "but I wish Bobby was here now."

"Yeah," Jean agreed, "there's never an Iceman around when you need one."

Archangel laughed, and the two of them followed Raza and Ch'od into the engine room. Warren beat his wings to clear the acrid chemical smoke from the room, even as Jean surrounded the blazing hyperburn engines with a telekinetic field, and then mentally forced all oxygen from within the bubble of power.

In seconds, the flames were out.

Scott stood behind her, looking relieved and a bit awkward. Then he bent forward and kissed her on the temple.

"I don't know what I'd do without you, Jean," he said.

"Now we know why they call them hyperburners," Archangel said, still reaching for levity to alleviate the tension of their situation.

"Now what?" Rogue asked, and it was the first time Jean had even noticed her in the room. She looked a little panicked, and Raza and Ch'od both looked up at the edgy tone of her voice.

"I'm dead serious," she continued. "Now what do we do? Those *were* the hyperburn engines, right? Well they burn pretty good. But now what are we gonna do? I could take this ship apart with my bare hands, but I can't do a damn thing to keep us alive."

She looked directly at Jean, who wondered for a moment if Rogue was going to lose it. But then the woman took a deep breath, let it out slow, and shook her head with a sigh.

"Okay, okay, I know. I'm not helping," she said, then turned to Ch'od. "But really, what now?"

"As I'm sure you all have guessed, the hyperburners are now completely useless," Ch'od answered, his yellow eyes calming despite the alarmingly savage appearance of his huge reptilian face. As he moved, the scales on his body rippled, and the webbed ears that poked from the sides of his head seemed to contract and expand like tiny Oriental fans. "What this means is that the warp drive is our only hope of getting this ship moving under its own power again. The good news is that Raza and I both feel this is possible."

"And the bad news would be—?" Scott began, then waited for one of the Starjammers to finish.

Ch'od and Raza looked at one another, and in their

moment of silence, Jean reflected that there were probably not two more dissimilar comrades in the galaxy. While Ch'od's huge, reptilian body was frightening, he was an eternally hopeful, amiable creature. Raza was a Shi'ar cyborg who had an air of intelligence about him. He was arrogant, ill-humored, and often even hostile. Still, they were both unfailingly loyal to each other and to the other Starjammers as well.

"In truth," Raza finally answered, "Ch'od and I hath discerned that yon warp drive canst not be repaired from within."

"Y'all are sayin' you have to fix the drive from outside the ship?" Rogue asked, incredulous.

"Indeed," Raza responded. "And we hath not the ability to effect such repairs without aid."

"Marvelous," Archangel mumbled.

"You'll have whatever help you need," Scott quickly assured them.

"We're all in this together," Jean added. "All of our lives are at risk, either when the life support systems shut down, or in some kind of accident outside the *Starjammer*. We've got nothing to lose."

"There are spacesuits, of course," Ch'od said. "As long as we take our time, and take great care with our movements, all should be well."

A moment before he entered, Jean sensed Corsair in the cargo hold just outside the engine room. She did not try to read people's thoughts or emotions without their permission, but he was so deeply troubled that it was impossible not to pick up on his distress.

"You may have to move a little faster than you'd like," Corsair said as he entered the engine room, his face betraying his apprehension as clearly as his thoughts had.

"What's the problem, Corsair?" Scott asked, and Jean noted how infrequently he called the man "Dad" in the presence of others.

"Whatever you're going to do, you've got to do quickly," Corsair said. "It's going to get pretty hot in here, and I don't even want to think about what the temperature will be like on the outside."

"You've got the navigational computer working," Scott realized aloud.

"Sure do," Corsair confirmed. "Just as we thought, people, we're drifting through space. Only problem is, we're not drifting aimlessly. We've gotten too close to the sun. We've been snagged by its gravitational pull."

"Oh my God," Jean whispered.

"It may take a bit, but if we don't get out of here, we're going to be roasted alive in this tin can."

CHAPTER 1

The constant thrumming vibration aboard the news helicopter began to give Trish Tilby a headache. The slashing sound of the rotors slicing through the air made easy communication with her camera crew impossible. None of that mattered. She was there to get the story. It was her job. She was good at it, and she loved it. The story was all that was important.

In her relatively brief career, Trish had been more like a rocket than a rising star. From the courthouse beat, she'd begged to get a few crime stories. A couple of times, she'd been in the right place at the right time to report on the mutant crisis, the hottest topic in America. She quickly became New York's most visible reporter on the subject, and more recently, the co-anchor of the local network affiliate's evening newscast.

Though she sympathized with the plight of mutants in America, the country's sentiments were overwhelmingly at odds with her own. But it wasn't her place to editorialize or offer her own opinions. She didn't make the news, she just reported it. Trish had seen the anti-mutant attitudes in America grow into near hysteria.

Now this. The biggest story of her career, and the one that could turn hysteria into anarchy. After what had happened in the past few hours, Trish realized, even those as liberal-minded as she was would be hard put not to join the anti-mutant cause.

After all, even in this day and age, it wasn't every day an entire city was held hostage.

The copter had taken off from the helipad at the affiliate's Bronx offices. Now, the pilot was navigating them straight down the East River, then around the Battery and up the Hudson River, making a circuit of Manhattan. She didn't know what she expected to find. Riots, looting, the kind of insanity that took over South Central Los Angeles a few years back. They had seen several fires burning, but had not yet dared fly directly over the island.

"Oh my God," she gasped as they reached the George Washington Bridge. "Kevin, are you getting this?"

The cameraman grunted behind her, recording it all. Beneath them, in the brilliant glow of the city and the subtle shine of the moon, people moved across the bridge in a solid wave. Where Trish might have expected chaos, however, this was an orderly exodus, the largest marching band in history.

"They've all got suitcases or other bags," Kevin said, and Trish envied him the telescoping capabilities of his camera. "Crying, frightened, but most of 'em look relieved."

"I just can't believe they're not running," Trish said, still awed by the sight.

"Magneto wants things orderly, I guess," Kevin noted, then pointed to the spot he had just focused his camera. At the Manhattan side of the bridge stood a Sentinel, its operating lights glowing in the darkness.

It was true, then, Trish realized. All true. Magneto had somehow commandeered an entire fleet of Sentinels from the U.S. government, and was using them to claim Manhattan island as a haven for mutants. The mutant outlaw, wanted in nearly every civilized nation for his crimes, had interrupted all broadcasts to announce the establishment of this haven, and to detail the rules for residency. Mutants were now the ruling class on Manhattan, and all mutants were welcome. Humans were invited to stay as long as they could live within the new hierarchy. If not, they could take their things and leave, on foot, calmly and without incident.

Magneto and his mutant Acolytes would see that his instructions were obeyed, and the island's perimeter would be patrolled by the stolen Sentinels. Trish had never seen one before, and she knew the sight would be with her always. It was colossal, at least eight stories high, and its robotic eyes burned with a cold, artificial intelligence. She had been stunned to see the orderly exodus on the bridge. No longer. She understood completely how intimidated those people must be.

"The hell with this waiting around," Trish snapped, suddenly angry. "Magneto didn't say the media couldn't enter the city. We're going in."

"You sure you wanna do that, Trish?" Kevin asked, obviously against the idea.

"Look, it may look all hunky dory down there, but there are fires burning, so obviously not everyone is meekly cooperating with this mutant terrorist's orders. I mean, the guy stole a city. We've got to cover it," she decided, and turned to Billy, the pilot.

"We go in," she ordered, and Billy nodded in response.

Immediately, the helicopter lurched as it rose quickly over the buildings. Seconds later, they were flying south over Manhattan's Upper West Side, trying to glimpse whatever activity might be taking place in the great steel canyons below. There were people milling about, but from what Trish could see, very little by way of chaos. It certainly wasn't any riot, or mass destruction.

As they approached the south end of Central Park,

they saw the fire at the park's southeast corner. She was going to instruct Billy to head for it, but he was already maneuvering them in that direction.

"Ya gotta be kiddin' me," Kevin hissed, then uttered a small, incredulous laugh.

"What is it?" Trish asked, trying to figure out what it was that was burning.

"F.A.O. Schwartz," he responded, the disbelief evident in his voice. "Who the hell would want to burn down a toy store?"

"This is it," Trish said. "Billy, set it down in the park, over by the skating rink."

"Set it down?"

"We're not going to get a story from up here, and the park's the only open space you're going to find," she reasoned. "Set it down and we'll find out what's happening here."

Billy shrugged, and Trish wished she could tell him how strongly she shared his reluctance. She was afraid. Not only of Magneto and the Acolytes and the Sentinels, but afraid of anarchy. If Magneto was truly in complete control, they might actually be safer than if there were resistance. And after all, this was New York City. Chances were pretty good that there would be heavy resistance, much of it armed.

Then there were the apathetic vultures who would use any situation to gain something, to pick off the corpse of a barely dead America. Trish figured that, somehow, looters and anarchists were responsible for the fire at F.A.O. Schwarz, and she wished she were far away from Manhattan. But she wasn't. If there was danger, that was part of the job. The only way to face it, she decided, was to wade right in.

She only hoped she wasn't going to get herself and her crew killed in the meantime.

* * *

The crowd in Washington Square Park was surpisingly orderly. A man dressed in preacher's garb addressed the people from atop a park bench not far from the park's familiar arch.

"Brother and sister humans, flee if you must," the man said with impassioned cadence. "But before you do, just think! Remember how the city was run when traditional bureaucracy was in charge! Were your needs attended to then? No!

"Perhaps the mutants are the next step in human evolution. If so, it is only right that they should rule. But even if they aren't, we're certain to get better treatment at their hands than at those of our previous leaders, whose only concerns were for their own pocketbooks, rather than their people's welfare.

"Go, if you must!" the preacher yelled, waving his hands in a grand gesture of suffering. "But if we stay, we become citizens of the most powerful sovereign state in the world!"

The preacher's audience mumbled amongst themselves, but there were none of the catcalls such an address normally drew. Amelia Voght was amazed. As one of Magneto's inner circle of Acolytes, perhaps the closest to a confidante the new emperor of Manhattan had, even she had not expected such a reaction.

Certainly, there had been those who resisted. Hundreds of thousands, in fact. Most were in the midst of an orderly exodus from the city, across bridges and through tunnels, shepherded by Magneto's fleet of Sentinels. Still, there had been far more incidents of looting, pillaging, mass destruction, and violence than Magneto would have liked. But Voght thought it was going remarkably well.

There had been very few individuals willing to stand up to him. Certainly the mayor and the police commissioner had been a problem, but Magneto had ordered Amelia to simply teleport them to New Jersey, and that's what she had done. She cherished the look on the mayor's face as he began to dematerialize.

It seemed that most New Yorkers were either so afraid that they would not leave their homes, or else they simply didn't care. Magneto had guaranteed that, despite the changeover in sovereignty, businesses would continue to function. People would still have jobs and income, and be able to travel to the mainland when absolutely necessary. For a lot of humans, that was apparently all the reassurance they needed.

Amelia had lived in Manhattan for a time, and she thought she could see a pattern in who stayed and who went. The majority of the city's transplants were moving out. But native New Yorkers, and the very wealthy, weren't going anywhere. Both groups thought of the island as "their" city. Which worked fine for Magneto's purposes. Not only had he created a sovereign state from nothing, but it had come complete with subjects.

Magneto had had them working all night. It was nearly dawn now, and things were starting to calm down. There had been an armed insurrection on the Upper West Side, and a spate of looting in the fashion and diamond districts, but the Acolytes had ended them all promptly.

Amelia was certain things would get a bit hairier once

the mutants began to show up. Magneto had issued an open invitation. That meant that the immigrants to Manhattan would include mutants who truly needed a place to go, but also every lowlife loser and scum looking for a way to escape the authorities. Not to mention a place where they were guaranteed the status of feudal lords.

Things may have been going smoothly, but the plan definitely had its drawbacks. Still, when it came down to it, Amelia had to admit Magneto had scored a huge victory for mutantkind. There had been a time, in her younger days, when Amelia Voght took Charles Xavier as her lover. Xavier was the founder of the X-Men. He was both Magneto's oldest friend and his greatest enemy. The two men were on opposite sides of a war with the same goal: peace. Magneto felt that it could only be achieved if mutants ruled humanity. Xavier felt the two human races could live in harmony.

Even though she long ago left her feelings for Xavier behind, and despite that she had become one of Magneto's Acolytes, Amelia had often wondered if either man was correct. Now, it seemed, the truth had come to light. Magneto was right all along. He'd won.

A low buzz like the distant shaking of a tambourine filled her ears, and Amelia looked over her left shoulder to see the shimmering holographic image of Scanner, a fellow Acolyte, appear behind her. Humans spread out, in fear of some attack, but Amelia raised her arms to calm them.

"Please, citizens, relax. You have nothing to fear," she said. "I am Voght, and this is Scanner. We are Acolytes of Magneto. Go about your business and you will not be harmed."

Amelia did not fail to register the terror that filled so

many of the faces around her, but the humans did as they were instructed. For the majority of them, that was how it had always been. They merely answered to a different authority now.

"Scanner," she snapped. "You frightened these people. What do you want?"

"My apologies, Amelia," Scanner's image responded. "There is a disturbance on Fifth Avenue at Central Park South. Lord Magneto has asked that you meet Senyaka there and attend to it."

"It will be done," Amelia responded formally.

As Scanner's image disappeared, leaving bright spots on her retina, Amelia sighed. Perhaps, she mused, she had been hasty in her optimism. After all, it would take quite some time to convince hardened criminals and opinionated cynics alike that there was no place in the new world for disobedience. Magneto's word was law, and the Acolytes were his punishing hand.

In a brilliant flash, Amelia disappeared from Washington Square. Her teleportation was the duration of an eyeblink, and when it was through she was standing on Fifth Avenue in front of the Trump Towers, just south of Central Park.

Smoke and flames shot high into the sky up ahead. The looters were everywhere. And why not? Fifth Avenue had all the most expensive stores, the best that Manhattan had to offer. Jewelry, fashion, furs. Yet, as Amelia walked further north, the looters ignoring her in their ecstatic frenzy, she realized what was burning. A toy store. Who, she wondered, would want to burn a toy store?

A large crowd of humans had gathered in front of the burning store, and in the flickering firelight, even from two blocks away, she could see the fervor on their faces. Several of them were armed, and some actually had torches! Amelia almost laughed, thinking about the terrified villagers in the first *Frankenstein* movie.

Then she saw Senyaka. Her fellow Acolyte was doing his best to keep the crowd at bay, cracking his psionic energy whip at them like a lion tamer. But he wouldn't be able to keep it up for long. Not against those numbers. Not if bullets started to fly.

"This is our city, mutie!" one man yelled, as he tossed an orange metal mesh city trash can in Senyaka's direction.

"We don't want you here, mutant scum!" another man shouted. "Your kind got no place in a human city. An' we ain't takin' orders from your murderin' boss, Magneto, neither!"

The man, a brawny thug with too much belly and not enough brains, was about to launch into a further tirade when Senyaka stepped forward and lashed his whip around the man's throat.

"Back, human dog!" Senyaka screamed, even as the man choked and tried to pull the whip from his searing flesh. The man fell to the ground, and though they could have pressed an attack then, the crowd was too appalled by the agony of their comrade to move. In seconds, the man was dead.

Amelia had never been taken by the near-religious fervor with which the other Acolytes followed Magneto. And so she could not withhold a shudder as the man expired. Needless death had always disturbed her.

"You flatscans had better learn to live under mutant rule, or you will die under it!" Senyaka declared, and lifted his whip as an invitation to further challenge.

SANCTUARY

It should have ended there, with Amelia just to one side of the crowd, unobtrusive in the night. But this was New York, a city whose people were known around the world for their hostility. Amelia had never believed it was worse in that respect than any other city, but there was no questioning the fury of the gathered crowd. The taunts had ended. In angry silence, they advanced upon Senyaka. Then, finally, one young woman snarled, "C'mon, guys, he can't take us all."

Even as the crowd surged forward, Amelia 'ported the few feet to Senyaka's side.

"Enough!" she commanded, and her sudden appearance was enough to startle the crowd to a momentary stop.

"Another mutie!" someone yelled.

"So? We can take her down, too! We gotta take 'em all down!"

"Your arrival is well timed, Amelia," Senyaka said, his expression hidden behind the linen cowl that covered his face. Still, she thought he meant it. Unusual, for one so proud.

"I try," she said quietly, then turned to the crowd. "Apparently, many of you have failed to grasp your new situation as citizens of the new sovereign state of Manhattan," she announced. "Perhaps you feel that because the Sentinels patrol the shores of this island, and Magneto can only be in one place at a time, that you are still free to do as you please.

"You are wrong."

"Mutie freak!" a man screamed, then jumped into a crouch, pistol leveled at Amelia and Senyaka.

Before either of them could move, he squeezed off several rounds. Her reaction was immediate and instinctive, self-preservation skills she had honed over years as the object of humanity's hatred. Without conscious thought, Amelia teleported the bullets away, then brought them back headed in the opposite direction. The gunman did a little three-step jig as his own bullets caught him in the chest and abdomen.

The crowd gasped in horror and astonishment, and drew more tightly together, an unconscious defense mechanism.

"You're nothing but monsters!" the same young woman shouted. "This is our city, and we don't want your kind here."

"Your city, is it?" Amelia said acidly. "It's so nice to see how well you take care of what is yours."

With the fire, and the looting, all around them, Amelia was still uncertain if the people would understand the irony of the situation. She did not regret the death of the gunman. That, after all, had been self defense. But if they did not disperse immediately, she knew she would have to do something that she would regret.

"Return to your homes," Amelia said loudly. "If you wish to leave, pack your things and go. There is still time. If you want to stay, you must live by Magneto's law. For as of now, there is no other."

"We're not going anywhere, bitch," the young woman said, then stepped to the fore of the crowd and produced a long knife from within the folds of her knee length leather jacket.

"That will do," Amelia said, exasperated. They could not play at this all night. She had no choice.

Amelia lifted her right hand and made a gesture which helped focus her mind. The young woman dematerialized instantly, her knife clattering to the pavement.

Someone in the crowd whispered a prayer.

"Bring her back, mutie," a wiry dark-skinned man said ominously. "Bring her back or you're dead."

"If you could have killed me," Amelia responded. "I'm quite sure you would have done so already. But, you wish me to bring back the shrill harpy who was standing here threatening me with a blade? Indeed, if that is your wish, I will be happy to oblige.

"Look up, if you will," Amelia said, and pointed to a spot in the sky.

At first, though she knew precisely what she was doing, even Amelia could not see through the blanket of darkness that hung over the city. Then the woman started screaming, several hundred feet above them. It was easy to spot her after that, plummeting through the air, firelight flickering off her black leather jacket, and her pale, terrified face. She screamed all the way down, and when she struck the pavement, nobody looked. Not even Senyaka.

But Amelia watched. It was her doing. Her responsibility. She would have to live with what she had done. Though she knew that her cause was just, and that this one death might save dozens of other lives, it would haunt her. Killing always did.

"Now," she said to the silenced crowd. "You can disperse immediately, and return to your homes, or I can do precisely the same thing to you. And if you doubt my ability to teleport you all simultaneously, I would be more than happy to prove you wrong."

Amid muttered curses, prayers, fearful glances, and vows of vengeance, the humans began to slowly drift away. They watched her carefully as they departed, and she watched them back. Though it was there in her heart,

Amelia showed them no remorse. She needed them to know that she would kill them if she had to, and feel nothing for their deaths. It was a useful deceit.

"A masterful peformance," a soft voice said above her, and Amelia looked up to see their master, Magneto, hovering in the air, regal in his crimson and magenta uniform.

"Lord Magneto," Senyaka said with hushed reverence, and fell to his knees. "I live to serve you."

"Yes," Magneto said, as he lowered himself to the ground beside them. "Yes, you do."

"I was almost frightened myself, Amelia," Magneto said, turning to her with a smile. Amelia was pleased with the warmth that existed between them, but knew that such special attentions would not endear her to the other Acolytes. Senyaka was spiteful, and was certain to report Magneto's preferential treatment of Amelia to the others. Still, there was nothing she could do about it. And they would not dare to harm her, knowing that she was "teacher's pet."

"Come," Magneto commanded. "There are other fires to put out before dawn breaks on the Mutant Empire."

"Where would you like me to transport us, Lord?" she asked.

Amelia looked into Magneto's face, awaiting his response, but then his manner changed. His smile at first disappeared, and then returned, brighter than ever.

"Well!" he exclaimed. "It appears that not all the humans were frightened away by your performance after all."

Amelia and Senyaka both spun to see what Magneto was referring to. Amelia thought she had seen it all, believed that she had witnessed the limits of human audacity. But at that moment, those limits were redrawn in her mind. For there, at the edge of the park, stood a human news crew, camera and all, recording all of the events that had just occurred, and were even now occurring.

Incredibly, Magneto was elated. For some reason, that bothered Amelia more than his anger.

* * *

"This is Annelise Dwyer at the CNN newsdesk. If you're just joining us, we're continuing live, uninterrupted coverage of the Crisis in Manhattan. Several hours ago, a band of mutant terrorists led by Eric Magnus Lehnsherr, known and feared throughout the world as Magneto, infiltrated and attacked New York, using robots known as Sentinels, to conquer Manhattan. Magneto has declared the city a safe haven for mutants, and a sovereign state with himself in place as ruler.

"This is not the first time that Sentinels have flown over the skies of Manhattan, but it is the first time they have been on the side of mutants. First created by Dr. Bolivar Trask, the Sentinels were mandated to combat the so-called mutant menace. However, Magneto has apparently reprogrammed these Sentinels to serve mutants rather than hunt them. Some CNN sources have suggested that these new Sentinels were created by the U.S. government, but so far, Washington denies any knowledge of the robots.

"According to official sources, half a million people have already fled Manhattan on foot, and more are pouring through every tunnel and over every bridge as we speak. We take you now, live, to Jersey City at the mouth of the Holland Tunnel, where Steve Williams has recent footage of this mass exodus, and an interview with the governor of New York, in just a moment. First, though, Steve, tell us about this exodus. What are people saying? Are their friends and families trapped in Manhattan, or have they stayed by choice?''

* * *

On the TV screen, thousands of people fled in terror from the Holland Tunnel. The reporter discussed concerns about the safety of people walking through tunnels and PATH underground train railways as well. He reported on the taking of hostages, the anti-mutant backlash, and the fact that, already, various mutants had been seen flying or levitating over the river to get into the city, to accept Magneto's offer of sanctuary.

Wolverine sat in the darkened den, the flickering TV screen all the light available, and more than he needed to see the room in perfect detail. His eyes were slitted, brows knitted together, and his lips curled back in a low, unconscious growl. He was getting itchy.

He'd been screwed by the system dozens of times. His mind had been sifted and fried so often that he still had a hard time separating the real memories from the implanted ones. And there was so much he had forgotten, so much he'd been made to forget. Nearly every time Wolverine had worked within the system, he'd been betrayed. It chewed people up and spit them out, or made them its own. He'd lost friends to it. Not their lives, though he'd lost plenty that way as well. No, he'd lost them to its philosophies, its twisted malice.

There was no love in Wolverine's heart for government or authority. He was a loner by nature, answering to none but himself. But then, what was that old saying, "We get the government we deserve?" True. People, at least in America, voted for their government. They had the ability to do something to remove those they did not approve of. Free will, freedom of choice, freedom period, that's what Wolverine believed in. For better or worse.

But in Manhattan, Magneto had taken that away. Wolverine understood why. Sometimes he wished he didn't. He understood the frustration when Charles Xavier's dream of harmony between humans and mutants seemed so far away as to be almost impossible. He understood better than most what it was like to be hounded for what you were. But Magneto was doing the exact same thing, with the tables turned.

Magneto had gone way overboard, this time. It was too much. Not only had he taken away the rights of the people in Manhattan, but the rights of everyone they cared for, of the entire nation, the world. Wolverine didn't care one whit for the businesses that would suffer because of his actions, but the people, that was different.

While their lord was not known for wanton killing, the Acolytes had established a reputation as murderers. There was no telling how many people had already died in this "occupation." And there would be more. Follow Magneto's law, or else. That was clearly the message. While it was a swift brand of justice that seemed almost admirable in light of the recent failings of the U.S. court system, it was simply wrong.

With one fell swoop, Magneto had placed himself as some medieval king over Manhattan island, allowed some of the cruelest mutants alive to take the place of feudal lords, and relegated every human to the status of peasantry.

Wolverine hated the system, but what Magneto had done in New York was infinitely worse. As he watched the terrified faces that filled the TV screen, the growl deep in his throat became louder, the itch in his soul to go to the city and take it back grew almost uncontainable.

Bishop's arrival couldn't have been better timed. A true warrior, the man walked in silence. Even Wolverine's hyper-sensitive ears might have had trouble picking up the noise of Bishop's footfalls, but there was no disguising the individual human scent, which Wolverine picked up long before he reached the den.

"About time, Bishop," Wolverine said without turning around, even as Bishop stepped into the room.

"We are nearly ready to depart, Logan," Bishop began, with a military stiffness that had been drilled into him long before he joined the X-Men. "Professor Xavier has asked that we all join him in the ready room immediately."

"Like I said," Wolverine replied, "it's about time."

The two men walked together down the marble corridor of the Xavier Institute, and Wolverine could not help but notice his teammate's sullenness. Nor could he blame him. Though all the X-Men had cause to fear Magneto's actions, to fear the deployment of the Sentinels—even though they were being used against humans rather than mutants, as was their original intent—none had more cause than Bishop.

Though the most recent addition to the team, in a way Bishop had been an X-Man his entire life. For, in truth, his life had not yet begun. He was a man of the future, born in a time when the X-Men were the stuff of legend and the Sentinels had first destroyed the modern society that the X-Men knew, and then ruled what was left of the world. When Magneto had fled the Colorado site of Project: Wideawake with the Sentinels earlier that day, Bishop had begun living a waking nightmare. His face had the haunted look of a holocaust survivor, for in many ways, that was the truth of it.

Wolverine wanted to reach out to Bishop, to offer support. But, except in very extreme circumstances, it was not in his nature, just as it was not in Bishop's nature to request, or accept, such support.

They walked in silence to the ready room, where the others had already gathered. Fully half the team was away, on a mission to save Cyclops's father, Corsair, from execution, but the others remained. Not much of a force to contend with what Magneto had put together, but it would have to do.

"Logan, Bishop, please be seated," Storm said. "The Professor ought to be with us momentarily."

Wolverine nodded and slid into a chair. They all seemed preoccupied, even Storm, who shared field leadership duties with Cyclops, and was therefore the current leader of the team.

"I'm getting a little tired of waiting around," Iceman said, unusually somber. "If we had stopped Magneto in Colorado, none of this would be happening now."

"There it is, then," Professor Xavier said as he glided into the room in his hoverchair. Though he was forced to use a wheelchair in public, Wolverine had observed that he spent more and more time in the hoverchair while at the Institute. And who could blame him? For a man who couldn't walk, floating was far easier than manipulating a wheelchair.

"I'm sorry, Professor," Storm responded, eyebrows raised, "but where is what?"

"What Bobby said, about stopping Magneto in Colorado," the Professor explained. "It's been haunting all of you. I may be the most powerful telepath in the world, but you don't need to read minds to see how it has affected you."

The Professor hovered at the head of the table. Wolverine felt Xavier's gaze fall on him, then move on, to each of the gathered X-Men. Storm was to Xavier's left, and the usually verbose Henry McCoy, a.k.a. the Beast, to his right. Wolverine sat opposite him, with Iceman to one side, and Bishop to the other. That was it. The six of them against Magneto, the Acolytes, and an army of Sentinels. Or five, really, since the Professor was not likely to take part in the actual battle unless absolutely necessary. The world still did not know that he was a mutant, and it had always served the team's purposes for things to remain that way.

But Bobby was right. If they had stopped Magneto in Colorado . . .

"Stop it," Xavier said curtly. "You cannot blame yourself. Not only because you are not responsible, but because it will affect your performance in the battle to come. I have yet to receive any communication from Cyclops's team. It's up to you."

"Charles," the Beast spoke up. "In light of the odds stacked so precipitously against us, I trust you will permit me a trifling inquiry as to our strategy. That is, do we have one?"

SANCTUARY

Xavier grimaced, looked around the table slowly, then back at the Beast.

"I'm working on it, Hank," he said finally. "I'm working on it."

CHAPTER 2

"Jesus, Trish," Kevin hissed at her side, "he's seen us!"

"Just keep rolling tape, Kev," she responded in a whisper. "Don't let me down."

Less than fifty yards from where Trish Tilby stood, the Acolytes had just murdered two people. Their leader, Magneto, one of the most feared men in the world, had then joined them. Almost immediately, Magneto had seen her and Kevin at the edge of the park. Now Trish waited, not breathing, for Magneto to act. She expected pain, some form of swift retribution. Perhaps even death.

What she did not expect was the way he smiled, and the charming little laugh he gave as he used the magnetic force of the Earth to lift himself from the ground and float toward where she and Kevin stood paralyzed with fear. The two Acolytes, one of whom Trish recognized as a woman named Amelia Voght, followed on foot, obviously awaiting their leader's instructions as to how to deal with the presence of the media.

"You really got us in it deep, this time, Tilby," Kevin whispered to her through clenched teeth. And she couldn't argue.

"Well, well," Magneto began, "what have we here?"

Trish flashed back, for a moment, to old man Gaines, who ran the country store in the small New England town where she'd grown up. Magneto's manner and tone were eerily reminiscent of the pleasant old fellow, long since passed away. Mr. Gaines would smile brightly at her whenever she came in with her Dad. He would pat her on the head and give her a piece of licorice and then, instead of turning to business with her father, he'd spend a few minutes actually conversing with her. She'd never forgotten it, that paternal curiosity and kindness.

Connecting Magneto with Mr. Gaines made Trish want to puke. But she couldn't help it.

"I knew it was only a matter of time before some intrepid member of our media tracked me down," Magneto said happily. "With a city as devoted to news and entertainment as New York, you would have thought some of the press would have stuck around to cover the story. But if they're here, they're not looking for an interview."

The other Acolyte, the cowled man Trish now remembered was called Senyaka, remained with his head slightly bowed. Their friendliness was disarming. Even more so, it was disturbing.

"Wait just a minute," Magneto said, eyebrows raised. "I've seen you before, haven't I? You are one of the locals, the woman who covers the so-called mutant crisis. Perfect. What was your name again, Ms.—?"

"Tilby," she said calmly, coldly. She wasn't going to let the man's strength of character overwhelm her. Though she finally understood the expression, "cult of personality."

"Of course," Magneto said effusively. "Trish, isn't it? Trish Tilby?"

Trish stared right into the man's face, past the handsome features and the winter white hair, locking her gaze on the blue-gray eyes but ignoring the distinguished way they crinkled into tiny crow's feet at the edges. She pretended not to notice his regal bearing, the almost armorlike quality of the crimson and deep purple uniform he wore.

"That's right," she answered. "And you are?"

She heard Kevin's sharp intake of breath behind her as the mutant conqueror's smile disappeared. The warmth leeched from Magneto's face in an instant, like a glaring light that had not been turned off, but burnt out. He licked his lips, and Trish felt the strength of his personality in another way. There was a real, tangible danger in every breath this man drew.

"And I am?" he asked slowly, no mockery in his tone, but certainly in his manner. "Not amused, to begin with. Not amused at all."

Trish looked past Magneto to see that Senyaka was glaring at her with hatred for her affront. The red-headed woman, Voght, was shaking her head in bemused astonishment.

"I had imagined you a relatively intelligent woman, Ms. Tilby," Magneto said. "If I was mistaken, perhaps you would care to leave the city immediately. On foot, like the rest of the human cattle whom I have allowed to depart."

She almost turned around then. Almost ran screaming in terror, the fear of death driving her to take whatever risk was necessary to escape. Though he was not pulling at her physically, Trish could imagine the mental urging that Kevin must have been focusing on her at that moment. But after a second, she knew she wouldn't run. It was the story. Sadly, her job defined her life, and getting the story would define her job. But there was more to it than that. She couldn't run from such malevolent actions.

"You'll have to bear with me, Magneto," she said, lifting her chin. "I'm afraid I'm not really used to dealing with tyrants whose thugs murder innocent civilians before my eyes. Maybe that's par for the course for international war correspondents, but it's just not been part of my experience up to now. I suppose I'll have to get used to witnessing atrocities.''

Magneto's right eye twitched with barely controlled fury and he seemed about to scream, or strike out at her. Then he let out a long breath, half sigh and half deflation, and nodded pensively.

''You shame me, Ms. Tilby,'' Magneto admitted, and Trish didn't know whether to be stunned or incredulous. ''What do you know of my history?'' he asked.

It took her a moment to realize what Magneto was referring to, and then it hit her. He was a Jew. As a child, Magneto had seen his entire family destroyed by the Holocaust. She remembered that from Magneto's abortive appearance before the World Court.

''I've read your dossier,'' she answered. ''Your past gives me even greater reason to be—''

''I have seen more atrocity in my life than any one man should ever have to endure,'' he said. ''When I was but a child, my family was murdered, because we were Jews. Throughout my adult life, I have been persecuted because I am a mutant.

''I will not allow it to continue,'' he said, leaning forward and staring at her with those intense slate eyes.

''I do not condone murder,'' he said, more calmly. ''Even in self defense, or in the pursuit of greater justice, the taking of life, even human life, sickens me.''

Magneto laid a fatherly hand on Amelia Voght's shoulder, though the woman did not look at him. For a moment, Trish wondered whether the gesture was as paternal as she'd thought, or if there was some romantic involvement there.

''But this is war, Ms. Tilby,'' he continued. ''There

are casualties in war. I believe I have been more than fair in my edicts. No one who conforms to my law will be harmed in any way. In point of fact, the quality of life for those who remain within the city will likely improve. Those who do not want to live under my rule are free to leave.''

Magneto took his hand from Voght's shoulder and leaned his head back, looking regally down on Trish. She could almost feel the arrogance that emanated from him, and yet, she also sensed that there was every reason for him to be arrogant.

''You are free to leave as well,'' Magneto said. ''Or, you may stay and get the 'scoop' of your career. You and your cameraman may record anything you wish, and I will see that it is taken by courier to your employers for broadcast.''

Trish looked at Kevin, trying to gauge what was going through his head. The cameraman had never been as career-oriented as she, but surely he could see the possibilities. At the same time, they both had to recognize the dangers involved.

''How about it, Kev?'' she asked, and he did a double take, as if he was startled she would even ask.

''Trish, if you think for a moment I'm gonna back your action here, you've gotta be—'' Kevin began.

''Before you continue,'' Magneto interrupted, ''I should mention that, if you decide to leave, you will not be allowed to do so the same way you came. For humans, Manhattan is a no-fly zone. That you were able to get past the Sentinels' perimeter at all is a minor miracle. No, if you're leaving, you'll be on foot like all the other human emigrants.''

Magneto raised a hand and looked past them, then.

Trish followed his gestures, turning to see that their helicopter had lifted above the trees of the park several hundred yards north and was now moving slowly toward them. It was not in flight. It was being moved by Magneto's power.

"No!" Kevin said suddenly, and Trish held up a hand to stop him from saying or doing anything rash.

"Our pilot, Billy, is probably still on board," Trish said, by way of explanation. "If you detest murder as much as you claim, you won't kill him as part of a simple exercise."

Magneto nodded, turned his right hand in the air, and the helicopter flipped on its side in the air. After a moment, the door popped open and Billy slid his legs out, then quickly dropped, cursing, to the park below.

"Holy—," Kevin hissed angrily.

Then they watched in astonishment as the helicopter seemed to implode, crushed into a ball of screeching metal like an empty beer can in a huge invisible hand. A ways away from where Billy had leapt out, the helicopter thudded to the ground.

Speechless, Trish turned to Magneto, who stood imperiously awaiting her reply. Without consulting Kevin again, she gave the only answer she could think of.

"We'll stay."

"Excellent," Magneto said, smiling again. "Now go and see that your friend is unharmed, and if he wishes to remain with you. Then return here and we will all move on. There is much to be done before daybreak."

With an enormous relief that they were to be allowed out of Magneto's presence, even for a few minutes, Trish turned to follow Kevin back into the park, searching for Billy.

"Just a moment," Magneto said, and her stomach lurched. "The camera."

Kevin handed it over, as silent as Magneto's two Acolytes, who had quietly observed the proceedings without comment. They were well trained, or very frightened of their leader.

Magneto passed a hand over the film cartridge, then returned it to Kevin.

"You might want to rewind and start again," he said. "The tape is now blank."

"What?" Kevin asked, obviously pissed off.

"You said we could record anything we wished," Trish reminded him.

Magneto's face remained impassive.

"*Almost* anything."

●   ●   ●

During her years as a member of the X-Men, Ororo Munroe had established a reputation for extraordinary calm during battle. That was part of the reason that Charles Xavier had made her co-leader of the team. Ororo, also called Storm, had learned patience as a child thief on the streets of Cairo, Egypt. Now, though, her patience was wearing very thin.

And clearly, she wasn't the only one.

"What is all this waiting?" Bishop snapped, pacing across the room with military stride, as he'd been doing for nearly twenty minutes. "What does Professor Xavier expect to gain from speaking with the government? It is their hatred of us that caused this crisis to begin with!"

"Bishop," Storm said, "we're all on edge here, but let's not forget that those Sentinels would still be sitting in a silo in Colorado if Magneto hadn't hijacked them."

Bishop turned to her angrily, about to issue some sharp retort she was sure, but then his features softened and he shook his head. Storm knew that look. It said that she didn't understand, that none of them would ever understand. And she knew, as well, that it was true.

"You're right, of course," Bishop said. "But for how long, Ororo? For how long?"

The room was quiet for a moment. At the window, Wolverine stood looking out at the night. He didn't tap his fingers, or his feet. He didn't hum. He didn't pace. Wolverine was a hunter, and though he lacked patience, and might voice his annoyance, he would never physically give himself away.

Bobby Drake was his opposite. He still sat at the table where they had met with Professor Xavier, but he was rapid-fire-drumming the Lone Ranger theme on the table with the fingers of both hands. From time to time, he would sigh, or mutter to himself. Storm couldn't help but smile as she watched him in her peripheral vision. For Bobby, this behavior was amazingly restrained.

Hank McCoy, was another story entirely.

"No matter what the government concludes, we cannot linger here," Hank said hurriedly as he bounded from his chair to stand beside Storm. "The longer we tarry, the more mutants enter Manhattan, the stronger the opposition grows. Time is of the essence, Ororo."

"Do not think for a moment that I disagree, Hank," Storm said. "But without the Professor's approval, I don't think we should go anywhere."

"Indeed," the Beast said, obviously frustrated but not arguing. He reached to an intercom switch on the wall, and snapped it on.

"Time is wasting, Charles," he said without preamble. "We must depart at once."

"I'll be right there," Xavier's voice came back, filtered into the room through the speaker, and the Beast looked back to Storm with an apologetic shrug.

"I am aware that this assemblage has never been a democracy," he said. "But at times, there are certain imperatives of logic that must be addressed."

When the door hissed open to allow Professor Xavier entrance, Storm could not have been more relieved.

"Finally!" Bishop exclaimed, as they all gathered round the table once more.

"What news, Charles?" Storm asked, and Xavier hesitated only a moment before answering.

"None, I'm afraid," he began, and held up a hand to forestall interruption. "Valerie Cooper is meeting with the President as we speak, attempting to get authorization to officially work with the X-Men for the duration of this crisis."

"Come on, Professor!" Bobby said angrily, leaping to his feet. "There's no way in hell our old buddy Gyrich is gonna let that happen. Yeah, maybe we're feeling pretty down about what went on in Colorado. But this is a whole new scenario. Every minute that ticks by just makes it harder to put an end to this thing."

"Bobby is correct, Charles," the Beast said emphatically. "You must do whatever you may, secure what reinforcements you can, just as Valerie is doing what she may within the parameters the government has contrived for her. But we cannot delay."

After a silent moment, Storm said calmly, "They are right, Professor. Though we stand very little chance of succeeding, we must go."

SANCTUARY

"Don't talk that way darlin'," Wolverine snarled before Xavier even had a chance to respond. "We'll take it to 'em hard, guerilla style. They won't even know we're they're until it's all over for 'em. Trust the ol' Canucklehead, will ya? They've got way too much ground to secure. We leave now, we can have New York back in the hands of the thieves who've been running the place by first light."

Wolverine looked at Professor Xavier, then, and Storm could almost hear the words before they came out of his mouth.

"Whaddaya say, Charley?" Wolverine asked, and Xavier winced. He had asked Logan dozens of times not to call him by that name. Storm suspected that Wolverine did it on purpose, just a little way to shake the balance of a man to whom equilibrium was everything.

"Storm," Charles asked, "are you prepared for this suicide run?"

"Completely," she answered. "The *Blackbird* is ready to go, as are the X-Men. This may be the decisive battle in the war for your dream of harmony, Professor. It must be fought, though we are sadly outnumbered and outgunned."

Professor Xavier nodded.

"With the *Blackbird*'s VTOL abilities, you should have no trouble landing in Central Park," Xavier said. "As you are all mutants, the Sentinels will not stop you. However, they may be programmed to notify Magneto if they detect you. There will be nothing you can do about this. Attacking the Sentinels openly is not an option.

"I will be in Jersey City, doing as much spin control as I can with CNN and the major networks. When I do reach Valerie, we'll try to figure out if the X-Men and the government can work together. I've left a message for Scott and the others. If they return to Earth in time, we'll need them desperately.''

He paused a moment, then gave the mission his final blessing in a mental message that entered the minds of each member of the team in the ready room.

What are you waiting for? Xavier's voice said in Storm's mind. *Get moving, X-Men.*

In seconds, they were racing down a corridor, boots slapping marble, toward the Institute's hangar bay. Storm was grim, determined. The *Blackbird* had already been fueled and readied, and they were aboard with the engines fired up only minutes after their meeting had concluded.

Bishop took the stick, with the Beast in the co-pilot's chair. Storm sat in back with Iceman and Wolverine. They lifted off in hover-mode, using the Vertical Take-Off and Landing mechanism the Professor had mentioned, and when they were clear of the Institute, they blasted south toward Manhattan. The trip would take only minutes, but urgency made the journey ahead seem much greater to Storm.

Aboard the *Blackbird*, the X-Men sat in somber, uncharacteristic silence. An arduous day had become a tense, dangerous night. Even on the hardest nights she had spent in Cairo, Ororo reflected, there had always been morning to look forward to. Tonight was different.

Dawn had never seemed such a distant dream.

• • •

"Gyrich, are you out of your damned mind?" the President of the United States shouted, red-faced, as he stormed over to the door of the Oval Office and slammed it shut.

The President spun on his heel and stared, and Valerie Cooper was pleased to notice that her rival, Henry Peter Gyrich, squirmed slightly in his seat. The Secretary sat just to Gyrich's left. As the Director of Operation: Wide-awake, he was immediate superior to both Gyrich and Cooper. Like Gyrich, he looked uncomfortable as hell.

Val felt fine, strong, almost smug. But she didn't know why. It wasn't like she wouldn't get her ass kicked along with her comrades'.

"Mr. President," Gyrich fumbled, "it's the only way, sir."

"No, Gyrich," the President said stiffly, cutting the Secretary out of the conversation all together. "There's got to be another way. I am not about to tell the American people that we've got a full scale war in the middle of New York City! The place is filled with civilians who've decided not to evacuate, not to mention those still in the process of doing so."

"Mr. President, if I may, those who've stayed in New York could easily be construed to be traitors to our country. Just as the Confederate soldiers were during the Civil War," Gyrich explained. "Same principle, sir."

The President's face went from red to purple, and Val expected him to explode in a tirade. Instead, he seemed almost to snarl as he bit down on every word.

"At this time, we will move troops and armaments to all logistically reasonable locations, where they will remain on standby. They are the *final* solution, and only on my specific instructions. I will not have a war on Manhattan island!" he hissed. "Do we understand each other, Gyrich?'' The President leaned over Gyrich, who now looked very small in his chair.

"Mr. President, I—" Gyrich began.

Then the President did explode, shouting in Gyrich's face. Flecks of spittle flew from his mouth.

"Do you understand what I have said, Gyrich?" he shouted.

"Y-y-yes, sir. Absolutely," Gyrich said, stammering. Val was astounded. She had never seen Gyrich stammer. Had never even allowed herself the pleasure of imagining that it was possible.

Then the President turned to face the Secretary, still leaning over threateningly, though his tone had softened. He and the Secretary had known one another for years. The President had put him in the Cabinet, given him Operation: Wideawake to play with, and listened to his advice more often than not. Not today.

"You and your pit bull are still in charge of this one, Bob," the President said. "Don't mess it up. Keep him on a very short leash."

"Yes, Mr. President," was all the Secretary managed to say.

Relaxing somewhat, the President walked around his desk and sat down to face them. After glaring half a moment at Gyrich, he turned to Val and his face softened. She didn't let it fool her. He was a tough bastard, and he'd take her head off in a heartbeat if he had to.

"Now, Ms. Cooper," he said slowly. "Seems to me you're the only one whose brain is half-functioning in this room at the moment. Barring full invasion or bombing the hell out of Manhattan, what have you got for me?"

"Yes, well, first, Mr. President, I'd like to note that I

don't believe either of those two options would work to begin with," Val said confidently. "Unless you're prepared to raze the city to the ground, forcing Magneto to simply find another to occupy, which would not solve the problem at all. The difficulty is the Sentinels. Correct me if I'm wrong, but we don't have the capacity to do limited, contained nuke strikes on one of them, never mind all of them simultaneously."

The President didn't smile, and Val took a mental step backward, cautioning herself not to be smug. He definitely wasn't in the mood for smug.

"Go on," he said, and Val nodded.

"The only chance we have of ending this thing without either giving up Manhattan or absolutely destroying it in an all-out war, is to get the Sentinels' original programming back online," Val concluded.

The President leaned back in his chair.

"Now we're talking,". he said. "What's the hold-up?"

"Well, sir," Val said, realizing the President didn't understand what she was getting at, "the only way we can do that is at the source. Somebody has to get inside the brain of the Alpha Sentinel, and change the programming from the computer core."

"Wait just a minute," the President said sharply, getting angry again, this time at all of them. "You mean to tell me that there is no remote override capacity built into these monsters?"

"No sir, there isn't," the Secretary spoke up, much to Val's relief. "It was thought that such an override would jeopardize the whole project. If anyone got hold of the code, they'd have been able to remotely hijack the whole Sentinel program."

"Which they did anyway!" the President cried in exasperation. "Good God, you don't know how grateful I am that the previous administration put this project together. I sure as hell don't believe we can keep the damn robots' origins a secret. But if we can solve this peaceably, it'll be a hell of a coup.

"So, Cooper," the President said, leaning toward her and resting his palms on his desk. "What do we do now? Obviously, we need to send a team in there, and we can't wait for X-Factor to get back from Genosha. Do we have anyone else with any experience with this kind of thing?"

"Well, sir, that's another problem," Val said, mentally crossing her fingers as she waded into the most difficult part of her pitch. But she knew she had to succeed. It was the only way. Eventually, they'd all have to realize that.

"Any human being directly approaching one of the Sentinels will be warned off," she said quickly. "And if they don't respond, they'll be incinerated."

"Cooper!" Gyrich shouted, leaping to his feet as he realized what she was about to propose. "You can't be serious! Even you've got to see that these are the monsters responsible! We can't possibly trust—"

Gyrich sputtered to a halt when he realized that the President and the Secretary were glaring at him in incredulous anger. He began to explain himself, but the President stopped him.

"Mr. Gyrich," the President began calmly. "You sit your ass down in that seat, and you don't speak again until I ask you a question. And don't you ever raise your voice in the Oval Office again."

Gyrich sat down hard and began to sulk.

"Please proceed, Ms. Cooper."

"Yes, sir, well, what I was about to say is that the only people who can get close enough to the Alpha Sentinel and distract it enough to get into the computer core are mutants. And with X-Factor unavailable, the only mutants we have any contact with that I know would be capable of the job, if anyone is, are the X-Men."

The President rolled his eyes and cupped his forehead in his left hand as if massaging a headache.

"Ms. Cooper," the Secretary said quickly, "don't you realize the public opinion regarding mutants at this time? The American people would be appalled to learn that we were working with mutants to overcome Magneto. The President would likely be accused of being a mutant himself, and there goes the election. The people don't trust any mutant, no matter how benevolent. And I don't have to remind you, the X-Men have not exactly earned a reputation for benevolence."

"Mr. Secretary, whatever their reputation, the X-Men have saved our collective asses more times than I can count," Val countered. "We've got a number of instances in the video archives, should you care to take a look. And they're the only ones who've ever had any tangible success against Magneto."

Valerie turned to the President then, and was surprised to see the nearly pleading look on his face. He was at a loss.

"Damned if you do, damned if you don't," he said quietly, almost to himself, and despite the man's bluster, she felt for him.

"Mr. President, when it comes down to it, it doesn't really matter what any of us think of the X-Men, or what the American public will think," Val said finally. "Short of full-scale war, they're our only hope."

"Bob, cut to the chase," the President said, turning to his old friend and advisor. "No politics now, no diplomacy. Is she right? Is this truly our one realistic shot?"

Gyrich seemed about to speak, but then clearly thought better of it. Val assumed he had remembered the President's warning. The Secretary seemed to weigh his words carefully, apparently searching for some answer other than the truth. Finally, he relented.

"Yes, sir, Ms. Cooper is correct," the Secretary said. "God help us all."

"All right then," the President said, sitting back in his chair. "Cooper, track down the X-Men and get them into action. It's your ball, woman. Don't drop it or we're all screwed. Not to mention all the people in Manhattan who'll die if you blow it.

"Bob, you're to stay here and coordinate this thing for me, and the pit bull here is going to be on location with the troops," he continued. "You'll answer to me, but coordinate it all for me, including Cooper's little infiltration unit. Gyrich is still number two man on this job, but Cooper reports directly to you, Bob. Any problem with that, Gyrich?" the President asked.

Gyrich shook his head.

"Good," the President said. "'Cause if Cooper does blow it, there's only one failsafe left before we launch an assault and end up leveling the damn city. That's you. If Cooper's plan doesn't work, you're to be prepared with a sanction team to go into New York and terminate Magneto."

Gyrich grinned. It gave Val the chills.

"Sir, don't you know how many times that's been tried?" she said, unable to stop herself.

"Whatever it takes, Ms. Cooper," the President said. "If you do your job, it won't come to that, and we'll never have to find out if it would have worked this time.

"Now, you're all dismissed. Get to work," he said.

They stood and walked to the door of the Oval Office. The President pressed something under his desk that buzzed the door's security locks open, and Gyrich feigned enough courtesy to hold the door for the Secretary and for Val.

"One last thing, Ms. Cooper," the President said, just as she was about to pull the door shut behind her.

"Yes, sir?" she asked.

"Don't ever question me, again," he said coldly. "I'm the Commander-in-Chief of this country. You'd do well to remember that."

CHAPTER 3

The temperature had already begun to rise aboard the *Starjammer*. It was not yet truly uncomfortable, but it was noticeably warmer inside the ship. And if they could feel the difference inside, Scott considered, how much warmer would it be outside the *Starjammer*?

He'd find out soon enough. Raza and Ch'od were planning a spacewalk to repair the warp drive externally. Scott and Rogue were supposed to be their backup team, making certain they remained tethered to the ship and coordinating their tools. It was by no means his first time in space, but Scott did not think he would ever be able to venture out into that infinite void without some trepidation. It wasn't fear, though he was not so foolish as to deny fear when he felt it. Rather, it was an almost overwhelming respect, awe. In the immensity of what surrounded them, what difference did it make whether they survived or not?

Thing was, it did make a difference. No matter how insignificant they might be in the grand design, their tiny lives meant something. When he was a boy, looking up at the stars would put things in a different perspective for him. Compared to them, nothing that he did or said, nothing that happened to him was important. As an adult, that perspective had been dramatically altered. Everyone mattered to someone. Every action had an impact.

Scott was determined to see the Starjammers and the X-Men returned safely to Earth, no matter what the cost. He would revel in the beauty of the infinite, in his awe of space, but he would not fear it, or be intimidated by it. He was a human being, with a mind and a heart. Both of which he had freely given to another. That was all the perspective he would ever need.

You're drifting again, Scott, Jean said telepathically, even as she helped him secure the deep space pressure suit that he would need to wear for the walk.

"Sorry, sweetheart," he answered out loud. "I guess I'll just never get over all of this. Space, I mean."

"I know," she nodded. "No matter what wonders, or horrors, we've faced on Earth, it's still such a small portion of . . . well, everything. We're very fortunate to have been able to experience space travel, Scott. And further than any authorized mission has ever traveled.

"If people on Earth ever realized just how vastly populated our galaxy is—" she continued, but Scott cut her off.

"It would frighten them to death," he said, with a hint of a smile.

"Still, we are very fortunate," Jean said, returning the smile.

Scott turned to her, and was struck once more by how beautiful she was. As long as he lived, he didn't think he would ever tire of simply looking at her. So good and kind, intelligent and noble, and so intimidatingly gorgeous that in another age, songs would have been written about her. Her hair was fire red and her eyes a brilliant, emerald green, but Scott's visor kept him from seeing those shades without a reddish tint. It didn't matter.

Jean had a way with a look, the crinkle of her nose or narrowing of her eyes, the twitch of her lip that was barely a smile. She could speak volumes without opening her mouth, without using an ounce of her incredible psi talent. Scott didn't ever want to be without her.

They'd been through that once, and he didn't want to even consider what it might do to him to lose her again. And yet, be that as it may, he was extraordinarily grateful to have her with him then. Whatever dangers they faced, they should do so together.

"Scott," she said in a hushed voice, her face reddening, "you're embarrassing me."

"Oh, come on, honey," Scott laughed. "Can't a man gush over his lady once in a while? Besides, they were just thoughts. There isn't even anybody else in here, and nobody on the ship has psi talents but you."

"Still," she said, in a girlish way that was uncommon for her. It enticed him more, the way she was always so full of surprises.

They had the secondary passenger cabin to themselves for the moment, as the other X-Men and Starjammers were busy elsewhere, preparing for the space walk. Scott was glad. Their predicament had put a thought in his mind that he had not been able to shake from it. He knew it would nag at him until he addressed it, until he discussed it with Jean.

Scott, she asked in his mind, sensing his distress, *what is it?*

"It's Nathan," he answered, his own feelings so conflicted that he was sure Jean wouldn't be able to get a clear reading of them. Hell, he didn't even know what he was really feeling. But he wanted to sort it out.

It was extraordinarily complicated. So much so that it hurt Scott's head to think about it. But he had a son. A son grown to adulthood in the distant future, without the benefit of his father's experience and wisdom. Now his son, Nathan, was back, and technically older than Scott himself. It was both bizarre and heartwrenching. They'd lost so much, the two of them.

But Scott felt that Jean had lost something as well. She'd been thought dead when Scott had met and married Nathan's mother. That was a whole other story, but the real point here was Jean. And Nathan.

"Forget about it," Scott said quickly. "I'm not even sure what's happening in my head now. I just want us all home safe as soon as possible."

That wasn't completely true, though. There were things he wanted to say to Jean. Why was it, he thought in frustration, that he could never come right out and say what was on his mind?

"Scott . . ." Jean began.

"Okay, let me see," Scott said, realizing that he had to talk, just to sort it out, just to let her know. "I'm trying to deal with the fact that Nathan is my son. Not only what I lost in the years he was gone, everything I missed, but also the fact that he's my son and not yours."

Scott paused a moment, unsure how to continue.

"You know Nathan and I are close, Scott," she said, and though they shared an extraordinary psychic bond, Scott knew that Jean was striving to understand, just as he was.

"That's not it," he said. "I can't escape the feeling that Nathan should have been our baby. That we should have children of our own."

Jean smiled. "Wow," she said.

"What's funny?" he asked defensively.

"You are," Jean answered, touching his hand, letting him know with the gesture and the soothing psychobabble of her thoughts in his head that she loved him deeply. "I understand what you're saying, what you're feeling. We're staring death in the face again, and maybe this time it's a little more real than before. Maybe because we have time, too much time, to think about life and death and consequences."

She stroked his hair lightly, then shook her head slowly, that little smile still on her face.

"Scott, honey, putting aside the dangers we face every day, the dangers our children would face," Jean said slowly, "did it ever occur to you that I might not want children right now? Or even anytime soon?"

Scott's eyes widened and his head moved backward almost imperceptibly. He couldn't think of a single thing to say.

"No," Jean said, smiling even more widely now, "no, I can see that it hadn't."

"Do you ever?" he asked, tentatively.

"Sure," she answered. "If we're ever going to have a normal life, I definitely want kids to be a part of that. But it's a long way off."

"I suppose," he said. "I was just thinking about you and me and Nathan and started to think something was missing."

"Maybe it is," she answered. "But that's our life right now. Somewhere down the line, I would love to have children with you. But as Logan said to me once, 'There's a lot o' miles between here and there, darlin', and it's gonna be hard travelin'.' "

Scott snorted laughter.

"Your Wolverine impression is improving, Jean," he said, then grew quiet again. After a moment, he asked, "Do you remember *Excalibur*?"

"I assume you mean the movie and not Nightcrawler's team in England,'' Jean answered drily. ''Sure, why?''

''There's that scene, when Arthur is going off for his final battle, and he goes to see Guinevere in the convent?'' Scott began.

''I remember,'' Jean said.

''I'll never forget what he says to her then, when he's going off to die,'' Scott continued, reaching out to hold Jean's hand in his, unable to feel much through the thick pressure suit gloves. ''Arthur says, very matter-of-factly, 'I have often thought that in the hereafter of our lives, when we owe no more to the future, you will come to me and claim me as your husband. It is a dream I have,' '' Scott quoted. ''It's an incredible moment, and horribly sad to think that these two people will have to die before they can find peace together.''

The two of them were silent then, contemplating his words.

I pray that's not us, Scott thought clearly, knowing Jean would pick up the words.

It's not, Scott, her words whispered in his mind. *I promise you it's not.*

They embraced, and Scott was distracted by the odd crinkle of his pressure suit. Sweat trickled down his back, the heat of the ship only magnified by the additional layers.

''Come on, Jean,'' he said finally. ''Help me get the helmet on, so I can make sure the Personal Atmosphere Unit is functioning properly. In fact, everybody should probably get into these suits, just in case something really goes wrong while we're outside. If the life support systems were to fail, you all need to be ready.''

''Excellent plan, Scott,'' Corsair said from the open

hatchway, and Scott bit back the urge to ask how long his father had been standing there.

"Everybody set, Corsair?" he asked instead, and his father shot him the thumbs up sign. Back to business, now. No room there for "son" and "dad." But, Scott thought, it was pleasant while it lasted.

"Roger that," Corsair said, nodding. "Raza and Ch'od are all suited up. Now if we can just tear Rogue away from Gambit's side for a moment, we might actually be able to keep this ship from melting into slag around us."

Corsair was smiling, but Scott could see the worry in his father's eyes, about their predicament, and about Rogue's reliability. Scott made it his policy not to delve too deeply into the personal lives of the X-Men, particularly those relatively new to the team, but Scott also thought he was a fairly observant guy. How it happened, he had no idea, and he wasn't certain about the rest of the team, but he hadn't even noticed the relationship between Gambit and Rogue developing. One day it just seemed to appear to him, full bloom, and then a lot of little things had begun to make sense.

Now, though, his job was to make sure that the relationship between his two teammates didn't compromise their job. In the end, he didn't think it would. All of their lives were at stake, and Rogue, headstrong though she unquestionably was, had always come through in a pinch before.

"You want me to speak with her, Scott?" Jean asked, beside him, obviously sensing his hesitation.

"Thanks, but no," he answered. "Part of the job. I need you to focus fully on backing us up while we're out there. Anything goes wrong, you're our only safety measure.''

"You got it," Jean said, nearly in a whisper, and leaned forward to kiss him lightly on the cheek.

She helped snap his helmet into place. It was constructed of an expanding mesh alloy of Shi'ar design. Rather than the traditional face plate, the helmet's front section was wide open. When the final latch was closed, and the Personal Atmosphere Unit began to function, a force shield materialized in front of Scott's face. It was impervious to solids, and yet it allowed Scott's exhaled carbon dioxide to leave the suit even as it processed oxygen in from the depths of space. Fortunately, it would also allow his solar-based optic beams to pass through without breaching the containment of the suit. No matter how often he was exposed to it, Scott could only marvel at the technology of the Shi'ar.

Scott, Jean, and Corsair made their way toward the main cabin. They passed Raza and Ch'od, who were moving to the back of the ship to get at the airlocks. Hushed words were exchanged between the two Starjammers and their captain, then Corsair smiled at Scott and Jean, and they continued on.

In the main cabin, Archangel paced nervously, bobbing his head slightly with pent up energy. Scott wasn't sure if Warren was even aware of the way his bio-metallic wings ruffled, spreading slightly, when he was on edge. Back when he was just called the Angel, Scott recalled, Warren's real, natural wings had done the same thing. It was comforting, yet at the same time, disturbing, that the wings, which often seemed to have some kind of sentience, were so closely tied to Warren's psyche.

"Hey," Scott said, quietly enough so that only Archangel could hear. "You okay, Warren?"

"Little cabin fever is all, Slim," Archangel answered, using Scott's old nickname from their early days with the X-Men. "I'm trying to chill out, but I'm not doing such a great job."

"Try to focus, Warren," Scott said, still in a hush. "You're needed, here. You've got to make sure nothing happens to Gambit."

"Remy?" Archangel asked. "But what else would—"

Scott turned away from Archangel and moved to where Rogue held vigil over the unconscious Gambit. On the other medi-slab, Hepzibah was recovering well but was being kept sedated to speed her healing. But Gambit had simply never revived from the shock of his electrocution. Looking at Rogue now, Scott didn't know how he had ever failed to see the flowering of the relationship between the two.

"Rogue," Scott began, "we need to talk."

"No," Rogue said quickly. "No we don't."

Scott was surprised. He was about to launch into a speech about responsibility, to make her see that they all needed her, that Gambit would die anyway if she didn't help. Then Rogue got to her feet and looked down at him. Her auburn hair flowed around her shoulders like a mane, its white streak only adding to her unique beauty. She was a relatively tall woman, but very petite. Still, the power within her was unmistakable.

"Let's go," she said simply.

"But I thought—" he began, stumbling in a manner that was unusual for him.

"Seein' Remy like this is tearin' me apart, Cyclops," Rogue admitted. "I'm not gonna lie to ya about it. It kills me to leave his side. But you don't grow up as hard as I did without learnin' when it's time for action. The time is now. Just let me suit up, and I'll be with you.''

"As Scott already pointed out, we all need to suit up," Corsair said. "Anything happens to this ship, we'll need more than our uniforms to keep us alive.''

"You go on ahead," Archangel urged. "I'll keep an eye on our little sick bay until you get back.''

Rogue walked to where Archangel stood, sentinel over Gambit and Hepzibah. She squeezed his shoulder.

"I know you've never been real fond of Remy, Warren," Rogue said. "But I really care for him. Watch over him for me, will ya?''

"We're X-Men," Archangel said, smiling warmly, "we take care of our own.''

Scott could have hugged Warren for that endorsement. He needed Rogue completely together on their space walk, and Archangel's reassurance was more valuable than he could possibly know. After all, with Corsair keeping watch over Hepzibah and the ship's heat shields, and Jean making sure the space walk went off without a hitch, Archangel was the only one who could watch Gambit. Rogue needed to know that Warren was committed to that duty.

The relief on her face showed very clearly how much weight had been lifted from her.

"Y'know, Warren, they all said that when you got your new wings, your personality changed too," Rogue said. "I don't know 'bout any of that, but it seems to me that, wherever the real you, the person inside, went away to . . . well, it seems like you're back now. I'm glad.''

"Me too," Archangel said slowly, brow furrowing.

"I only wish everyone else could see it as clearly. Thanks, Rogue."

"Thank you," she said, and finally turned to walk from the cabin.

There was so much on his mind that Scott didn't really have time to digest their exchange. But somehow, some way, he felt like he'd let Warren down. He promised to himself that, if they survived this, he would try to figure out how, and rectify his mistake.

But then, first things first. Survival.

* * *

He'd always thought of it as the cold expanse of space. Scott supposed that, nearly anywhere else, that would be about right. But this was different. This was death on the horizon. The irony was not lost on him. The sun was vital to all life on Earth, and the battery that powered his own optic beams. It was the symbol of life, growth, power. But move too close, and it became a voracious inferno, consuming all.

Sweat trickled down Scott's forehead, underneath the lip of his ruby quartz visor, and he blinked it away. There was sweat on his back as well, and he could feel the disorienting fatigue that extreme heat always seemed to bring on. He wondered for a fleeting moment if his face would blister, even through the force shield, this close to the sun.

He didn't intend to find out. They'd been very careful to make certain none of them would have to discover the effects of such exposure. Twenty minutes of complex navigational maneuvers, without the real power to make them, combined with brute force to allow them to turn the *Starjammer* so that the area where they would be working was not directly in the path of the sun's burning glare.

An additional half hour had passed, and they toiled away in the shade provided by the *Starjammer* itself. Tethered together like mountain climbers, with Raza tethered to the ship itself, they used their respective knowledge and skills to make what repairs were possible to the hull and warp drive of the vessel.

"Cyclops," Ch'od's voice slithered into his ears from the comm-link in their suits. "Raza and I seem to be doing fine here, perhaps you and Rogue ought to attempt to repair some of the more serious structural damage."

"You're sure you don't need the backup?" he asked, doubtful.

"You are out here, if we really need the help," Ch'od asked. "That is enough. While you are repairing, you should also look for any stress points that look as if they might lead to a pressure breach."

"You got it," Cyclops said, listening to the tinny sound of his own voice filtered back to him. "Rogue, you catch that?"

"Sure did, Cyke," she said. "I s'pose it's time for a little spot-weldin', huh?"

Cyclops was floating free of the ship, drifting along with it, secured only by his tether to the others. The slightest motion was magnified by the gravity-free environment of space, so Scott was very careful and measured with his actions. He had dealt with anti-gravity in other situations as well, and not just in space.

Rather than kick his feet as if he were in a swimming pool, which had been his inclination the first time he'd experienced the sensation, he performed a slow, forward somersault. A few moments later, he came around to face Rogue only a few feet from the *Starjammer*'s hull. As he had expected, she reached out a hand to arrest his motion, and reeled him in.

"This ain't the time for showin' off, Cyclops," Rogue admonished, and Scott smiled despite their plight.

She might not be able to conduct herself as though this were all business as usual—not that anyone could have—but at least she was trying. Scott had to give her credit for that.

Together, they examined the section of the hull that had experienced the worst damage.

* * *

Rogue felt particularly parched. Dehydration was no fun, but she knew they wouldn't get a break until they'd finished what they'd come on their little space walk to do. It was hard for her to deal with their situation. Not merely the danger of it, but the entire reality of space travel, space walking. Of course, the danger was there too, helping keep her mind off of Remy.

She didn't want to think about it. Couldn't. Rogue kept telling herself that if they could just get home, get back to Earth, that Gambit would be okay. She kept reassuring herself, but a little voice inside her head called her a liar every time. Truth was, she didn't know if he'd be okay or not. It was all in God's hands, now, she figured. Rogue had never been much for prayer, but she'd always believed in God. She figured, out there in the middle of space they had to be closer to him than ever, and hoped that meant he'd hear the prayers that were screaming through her head right then.

"Watch it, Rogue!" Cyclops snapped at her side, and she looked up to see the warning in his eyes, then back down at what she was doing. They'd been working together, her trying to bend back into shape portions of the hull that had been damaged, so that Cyclops could attempt to weld these breaches closed with his optic blasts. But when she looked down, she pulled her hands quickly from the ship with a frightened gasp.

The material of her pressure suit around her hands had been too near a sharp edge of metal hull. Had she continued to press, distractedly, on the torn section, she might well have ripped a hole in her suit. Back on Earth, Rogue thought herself nearly invulnerable to injury. But without the pressure suit, she guessed that she'd be dead just as quickly as any of them.

"Thanks a lot," she said, sighing in relief, then grabbed hold of the hull yet again.

"No problem," Cyclops answered. "I know you're tired. We all are. And you've got a lot on your mind. But let's just be careful, okay? We can't afford any accidents out here."

"You said it," she agreed.

She finished reshaping a small hull breach, and pulled herself along the surface of the ship so Cyclops could move into place. While his optic beams were normally concussive in nature, when tightly focused, they could burn as hot as the nastiest laser. And with the sun so close, Cyclops seemed to be brimming with nearly inexhaustible power. A reddish glow filled the inside of his helmet, and a small cloud of energy was constantly flowing through it, only to dissipate in space.

"It's a wonder your head doesn't explode with all that energy you got stored up in there," she said in amazement.

"Well I suppose there should be some benefits to being so close to the sun other than working on our tans,'' Cyclops responded, keeping his attention on the job at hand.

"My goodness," Jean's voice filtered into Rogue's helmet on the comm-link. "Did Scott Summers just make a joke?''

"I try," Cyclops said in response, and Rogue was warmed by their exchange. Though Jean was inside, the communications setup that linked them all reassured her that their resident psi would be on hand if anything went wrong. Not that it was likely to. The work had reached the point where it was almost boring.

"I feel like an egg fryin' on the sidewalk in July," Rogue said, then lapsed into silence as she watched Cyclops at work again.

His optic beam melted the metal edges of the hole together like a soldering iron. Rogue was reminded of the time Fred Dukes, a mutant who called himself the Blob, had bragged one too many times about his invulnerability. Nothing could hurt him, Dukes had boasted. Cyclops, usually the picture of calm, had used that tight focus beam to burn a hole right through Dukes' shoulder. Far as she could tell, Cyclops had felt guilty about it later, but Rogue still chuckled as she remembered the look on the Blob's face. Served him right.

When Cyclops finished, they moved on to the largest hull breach. Rogue did what she could, but when she was through the hole that remained, it was too large for Cyclops to simply weld closed. Rogue looked around the ship's hull for something to use as a "band-aid," but didn't see anything immediately.

"Ch'od," she said on her comm-unit. "I need somethin' to patch this dang hole. Any ideas?"

"Give me just a minute, Rogue," Ch'od said, and the sound of his voice made Rogue realize that all this time he and Raza had been working together in near absolute silence. After years as Starjammers together, it seemed they had reached the point where they functioned together as smoothly as clockwork without having to ever say anything

That was the X-Men at their best. Apparently, the same applied to the Starjammers. No wonder, she thought, since both teams were led by men of the Summers clan. Even if she hadn't been involved with Gambit, Cyclops would never have been Rogue's type. Too squeaky clean, straight and narrow for her tastes. Yet those same traits made her admire him greatly.

"Now, Rogue, what was it you wanted?" Ch'od asked on the comm-link.

Rogue boosted herself up lightly to see where Ch'od had turned away from the warp drive to address her directly, though their voices did not carry in space. The *Starjammer* had two enormous "legs," each of which ended with an engine well, similar to the turbines on a jet airplane. Those were the hyperburners, she knew, the *Starjammer*'s main propulsion system. With them out of commission, they were forced to rely on warp drive. She guessed that, with it fixed, they could warp into an appropriate navigational pattern, come out of warp just above Earth's atmosphere, shut down the ship and let momentum take over.

If they could get the warp drive fixed.

Raza and Ch'od worked at the burnt and shattered casing of the warp system, further up on the starboard leg from where Rogue and Cyclops labored. While she and Ch'od spoke, Raza continued to work, a greenish glow from the broken casing reflected off the force field that covered his face.

"I got a major breach here, and I gotta patch it," she repeated.

"That certainly is a problem," Ch'od answered. "I'll have a look."

Ch'od pushed away from the ship in a movement calculated to bring him directly to where Rogue clung to the ship's hull. As she watched him, her peripheral vision picked up movement beyond him. Raza's head snapped back in a defensive motion as sparks flew from the drive system, alighting on his suit. He shook his head, obviously annoyed, and brushed them away. Rogue almost looked back at Ch'od then, her mind consumed with the need to finish with their repairs and get back inside the ship, to see if they could get home.

She didn't turn away, however. Instead, she saw Raza lower his head once more over the shattered casing, only to draw it back again, more slowly this time.

"Sharra and Ky'thri," Raza's astonished voice whispered in Rogue's ears.

"Raza?" Ch'od began, turning toward his friend clumsily, losing the careful control of his motion. "What is—"

The warp system seemed to explode in Raza's face, blasting him backward as his tether snapped like a whip and slammed him against the ship's hull. Simultaneously, blue flames shot from the engine well just behind Rogue and the ship began to spin with extraordinary speed. The misfiring of one half of the warp drive lasted only a moment, but it set the *Starjammer* moving like a maniac top, trailing Ch'od, Cyclops, and Rogue behind it—

—directly into the trail of the engine blast. Their tethers were incinerated immediately, and had they been wearing anything other than the Shi'ar pressure suits Corsair had given them, their bodies would have fared no better.

With a burst of power, Rogue lashed out with her left arm at a silver flash of hull that whipped past her peripheral vision. She snagged the ship and, with her extraordinary strength, dug in to the *Starjammer*'s hull, hanging on for dear life as the ship continued to spin. It was already slowing, but it was all Rogue could do to keep from vomiting inside her helmet.

When she regained her equilibrium, though the ship still moved, she began to look around for the others. Raza was still tethered to the *Starjammer*, but his unmoving form was being towed along behind the ship as it turned. Rogue assumed the force of the explosion had knocked him unconscious. Anything else was unthinkable.

But what of Cyclops and Ch'od? As the ship's rotation slowed further, nearing a stop, Rogue frantically searched for some sign of them. Her last image of them was that of the moment the warp engine blasted all three of them, destroying their lifelines. She had been lucky enough to grab hold of the vessel to keep from being shot out into space.

Now there was no sign of either of the others. Ch'od and Cyclops were, quite simply, gone.

Chapter 4

"**B**race yourselves, people," Bishop said from the cockpit of the *Blackbird*. "We've just crossed into Manhattan."

There were no more words. There didn't have to be. The five X-Men on board the plane went on immediate alert. The Sentinels were supposed to guard the city's perimeter, but Magneto had claimed all mutants would be allowed entry into this new "sanctuary" he had carved out of one of North America's largest cities.

Question was, did that hospitality extend to the X-Men, or had the Sentinels been given specific programming to keep them out? They'd know in a minute, Wolverine thought. Some part of him hoped the answer was yes. If they were attacked upon entering Manhattan, they'd get down to the nitty gritty all the quicker.

That's what he was here for. To fight. To win. The politics of it just bored him. It didn't matter to Wolverine whether the government sanctioned their presence or not—and so far they'd had no word one way or the other. In any case, there was a job to be done, and the faster they got around to this latest fracas with Magneto, the better.

After what happened in Colorado, Wolverine was looking forward to throwing down with the Acolytes again. He didn't want to think about the combined resources of Magneto and the Sentinels—one thing at a time.

There was no way he was going to let Magneto win. New York would turn into the tyrant's private playground only over Wolverine's dead body. If that was what it took, that's what it took. As the tension grew aboard the *Blackbird*, he could feel the low growl building in his throat. Not loud enough for the others to hear, but loud enough for him to feel it in every fiber of his being.

"Well?" Iceman finally broke the silence. "Any sign of them?"

"No visuals," the Beast said from the cockpit. "Bishop, have you got anything on radar?"

"Nothing," Bishop answered. "Apparently we're as welcome as the next mutant."

"Let's not get carried away," Storm cautioned. "Simply because we were not stopped at the 'door' doesn't mean we are welcome. It could very well be that Magneto would rather have us in here, where he can keep an eye on us."

"Then he's a hell of a lot dumber than I gave 'im credit for up 'til now," Wolverine snarled. "Magneto oughta know better than to think he can cage the X-Men. I ain't exactly a domesticated beast."

"I, on the other hand, am entirely house-broken, thank you very much," the Beast said from up front.

"Laugh it up, McCoy," Wolverine said grimly. "It ain't gonna be a party down there, though."

"True enough, Logan," the Beast acknowledged. "But humor is oftimes all that distinguishes man from savage animal. It serves me well as a reminder that I am, head to toe, human first. Mutant, second."

"Ah, Hank," Storm said wistfully, "if only the world could see that."

They were quiet again, then, and Wolverine could not help thinking of Hank's words. He was not without a sense of humor. In fact, he could be quite a practical joker in his own right, given the chance. But there was a time for that kind of thing, and as far as Wolverine was concerned, this wasn't it. Still, if that was what the Beast needed to deal with the scenario, Logan figured he'd best leave his teammate to it. There were things he needed, ways he had to feel, to get by as well.

But for Wolverine, those feelings were quite a bit more hostile.

"Central Park below, team," Bishop said quietly.

"Bobby, is that mini-Cerebro tracker functioning properly?" Storm asked.

Iceman picked up a small black metal and plastic unit that looked more like a hand held video game to Wolverine than any useful technology. Looks could be deceiving, however. In truth, it was a much smaller version of Cerebro, the computer that Professor Xavier used in the Institute's efforts to find developing mutants and keep track of those they were already aware of.

"It's lit up like a Christmas tree," Iceman said, then turned the tracker unit so both Wolverine and Storm could see the green dots that filled the grid on its face. At the bottom of the grid were a group of dots that were enveloped in a red, warning glow.

"It can't pinpoint Magneto specifically," Iceman explained, "but it can point us in the right direction. From here, we go south."

"The ol' Canucklehead is right on your tail, Bobby," Wolverine said, his voice even more guttural than usual. "Time to take Magneto down a peg. He's gone way over the line this time."

Retro-thrusters on the VTOL unit kicked in, and the *Blackbird* seemed to rise a moment as if cresting an ocean wave. Then the plane dropped. There was no hesitation, nothing gentle about it. The *Blackbird* wasn't built as a comfort vessel. It was made for action. Wolverine admired that in people and things alike.

The quick-drop hatch opened out of the belly of the *Blackbird*, even before the plane touched down on Central Park's Sheep Meadow. With the Beast at his side, Wolverine leaped from the hatch and landed in a crouch on the grass, which was buffeted by the *Blackbird*'s retros.

The whole park, Wolverine thought, was a lark, a foolish dream. There in the middle of the city, Central Park pretended to be peaceful countryside, just as the city dwellers pretended when they escaped to the park. It may have been a jungle at night, predators stalking the wood, but the falsehood of it insulted Wolverine. Even if his senses had not been so far superior to the average human's, it would have been impossible not to smell the stench of the city infiltrating the park.

"Fire," the Beast said as he touched down next to Wolverine.

"Got it," Logan responded. "Southeast, less than half a mile."

"Spread out," Storm commanded from the air, even as Bishop piloted the *Blackbird* to a final stop in the park. "Logan, Hank, I can see flames from here. Scout one hundred yards south, and return. Bobby, do a perimeter check with me on flyover."

Bishop emerged from the ship just as they were moving to comply with Storm's orders.

"Bishop, lock the *Blackbird* up tight, all defenses armed," she added. "It wouldn't do to have our exit destroyed. All rendezvous back here in five minutes."

It was a fast five minutes. Wolverine melted into the woods with predatory silence. He could hear the Beast off to the west, making little attempt to mask his passage. Hank might have the look of an animal, but that didn't mean he had the primal instincts.

He moved in the direction of the fire, alert to any sign of offensive movement. It felt foolish, surreal. Manhattan island had suddenly become a war zone. Indeed, if all they found were masses of hysterical civilians, it wouldn't surprise Wolverine at all. But there was a chance that they had been detected and that an ambush would be waiting. He wasn't about to let that happen.

The fire filled his nostrils, though still several hundred yards away. Then he detected something else. Something human. It was a dense, sour smell, mixed with alcohol. Even before the homeless man cut and run from the brush up ahead, Logan had spotted him with nothing more than moonlight to see by. The poor man, perhaps fifty, took off like a startled deer. Though not nearly as quick, of course. It might have taken Wolverine twenty seconds to down a startled deer.

This guy took five.

Up close, he stank to high heaven, his odor so powerful Wolverine could barely smell the fire anymore.

"God, no, please, don't kill me," the man squealed. "Please, no, I ain't got nothin' in this world. I just don't wanna die."

"Stop squirming!" Wolverine snarled, bringing the man up to his full height by tugging on his loose shirt-front. "I ain't gonna hurt you. Relax, will ya? Stop jabbering!"

There was a tone that he allowed into his voice at certain times. Wolverine wasn't sure he liked the tone, or what it said about him, but it was there, and it worked. The homeless man responded immediately, and Wolverine finally got a good look at him. He wasn't at all glad that he did. The man was shabby looking, his clothes stained and tattered, and he looked as though he hadn't shaved or had his hair cut in a decade. He was sick. Smelled sick, now that Wolverine could scent anything beyond the man's stink. But he wasn't more than thirty.

He only moved like he was fifty.

"I'm not going to hurt you," he said, more softly, almost kindly, to the wide-eyed man, then let go of the poor soul's shirt.

"But," the man began, "you're a mutie, aren't—I mean, a mutant, aren't you? You guys are takin' over, that's what Bernie says."

"There are some mutants trying to take over the city," Wolverine admitted. "We're here to stop them. I don't suppose you've seen anything that could help us track 'em down."

The homeless man suddenly snapped to attention, in a salute of surprising quality. A military man, then, maybe Gulf War. Not so long ago and already come to this. For a moment, Wolverine had to wonder if the guy would be better off with Magneto in charge.

"Yes sir," the man said then, obviously disappointed to see that his salute had not been returned. "Me an' Bernie were down right where that fire was, where the people burned down the toy store, you know, the one with all the letters? Well, we seen them muties ... I mean, mutants ... well, we seen 'em killing people. They're gonna murder us all, man. That's what Bernie says."

"Where's Bernie now?" Wolverine asked, surprised that he didn't smell anyone else out in the Park.

"I don't know," the homeless man said, then lowered

his head, ashamed. "I kind of, well, I ran away. To get help, see. That's it, to get help. Only I didn't find any."

Wolverine put a hand on the man's shoulder, and their eyes met. Despite his mad talk, there seemed to be some kind of awareness in there.

"Sure you did," Wolverine said. "You found me, didn't you?"

"Yeah, that's right," the man happily agreed. "I ran to find help, and I found you."

"What's your name, bub?" Wolverine asked.

"Jerry," he answered. "Name's Jerry. What's yours?"

"Logan."

"Pleased to meet you, Mr. Logan," Jerry said, sort of bouncing on the balls of his feet now that he'd made a new friend. "Mr. Logan, you going to want to look at that chopper now?"

"Chopper?"

"Yeah, the all-scrunched-up one."

• • •

The X-Men stood around the news helicopter in silence. Jerry had led them there at his own request, but now Wolverine was wondering if that had been a mistake. The broadcast affiliate's call letters had been stencilled on the side of the chopper, and the Beast recognized them immediately.

"Lord, no," Hank said. "Trish?"

"There's nobody inside," Wolverine said quickly, sensing the Beast's distress.

"There was a man," Jerry insisted. "He jumped out right before it got crushed, at least that's what he said."

Jerry hung back away from the X-Men slightly, and

Wolverine couldn't blame him. The man was clearly not in his right mind, and while the whole team looked fairly intimidating, Beast and Iceman were clearly non-human. And, after all, Jerry's buddy Bernie had told him that the "muties" were going to kill him.

"What man?" the Beast asked. "Where did he go?"

"Walked right out of the park," Jerry answered. "Said he was going to get out of the city." Jerry snorted in derision, then added, "Yeah, I'm sure he made it, too."

"Hank, we don't know that Trish was covering this story," Storm reasoned, but the Beast was having none of it.

"In the midst of this crisis, in the hour of need, with her notoriety on mutant issues, where else would she be, Ororo?" the Beast asked grimly. "Our relationship may have ended, but I still care for her very much."

Wolverine couldn't hold back any longer. They had wasted too much time. And the Beast deserved the truth.

"She was here, Hank," Wolverine said. "I picked up her scent in the woods before, but I didn't recognize it 'til we found the chopper."

"See, buddy," Iceman said with his usual enthusiasm. "She's okay."

"Just because she walked away from this disaster, doesn't mean she's okay," Bishop chimed in. "We're in the middle of a genocidal civil war, Drake. It isn't that simple."

Silence descended upon the group as Bishop's words sank in. Far to one side, Iceman crossed the several steps to where Bishop stood and whispered, though not so low that Wolverine could not hear his words.

"You are one cold son of a bitch," Iceman said, and

there was an anger, and a danger, in his voice that Wolverine could not recall ever hearing there before.

"You can abuse me and insult me all you like, pal," Iceman continued, "but Hank McCoy is the best of us, bar none. You show him the respect he deserves."

There was a challenge growing in Bishop's face as the man listened to Iceman speak. Wolverine saw it there, rising, about to be unleashed. It was to be expected. Bishop was a hard man to hurt, even harder to kill, and Bobby Drake was so lighthearted it was difficult to imagine what his implied threat might actually entail. Wolverine waited for the challenge, the "or else?" that he knew would come from Bishop at any moment.

But it didn't.

After a moment, Bishop merely nodded slightly. A lesson had been learned. None of the others was close enough to have heard Bobby's words, not even the Beast, and Wolverine was not about to discuss it. Not with Iceman, or with Bishop, or anybody else. He knew, also, that he would never forget it. Bobby Drake had been the class clown all his life, the butt of jokes. But if he'd been a different person, he would have been an extraordinarily dangerous man. The potential was there.

"Logan," the Beast asked, the moment of reflection ended. "Which way did they go?"

"All roads lead to Rome," Wolverine said, and pointed to where firelight still turned the black sky a sickly yellow to the southeast. "Everything around here seems to be pointin' to that fire, and that's definitely the direction Trish was headed."

Without another word, the Beast set off in the same direction.

SANCTUARY

"Bobby," Storm asked quietly, "what do you read on that mini-tracker?"

"Same deal, Storm," Iceman responded. "Bunch of green dots all around, but a big concentration to the south. And the red dots are south as well."

"Thank the goddess for small favors," Ororo said. "Let's go."

They moved quietly into the woods after the Beast, all except Wolverine. He hung back a moment with Jerry, who had seemed to disappear when things got tense, though he never left their sight. Somehow, he had learned how not to be seen. Or—and Wolverine hoped this wasn't the case—they had simply learned how not to see Jerry, and those like him.

"Listen, bub," Wolverine said. "You stay here until this is all over, okay? Until you know that things are back to normal, you stay in the park. And if your friend Bernie shows up, keep him here with you. It isn't safe for you to be in the city."

"It isn't safe anywhere, Mr. Logan," Jerry said grimly, and there was a flash of intelligence, of sanity and wisdom in the homeless man's face that made Wolverine wonder exactly how crazy Jerry was.

The look stayed with him as he caught up with the X-Men, and the words rang in his head as they emerged from the park several minutes later to find that utter chaos reigned supreme.

Screams and gunshots echoed in the distance, and Wolverine could see the light of other fires on the night-time clouds far to the south. The city had become a madhouse, a maelstrom of frustrated and terrified people who had either locked up their homes or decided to vent their fears with violence.

As the X-Men stepped into the street, two teenagers shot past, screaming with rapacious delight before throwing a Molotov cocktail through the window of a movie theater. The restored woodwork and beams in the lobby as well as the ticket booth burst into flames. Down Fifth Avenue, Wolverine could see looters pillaging the most expensive stores in the city.

"Wolverine," Bishop said to his left, "we've got media coverage."

In the fifth story window of a Fifth Avenue building half a block away from the burning F.A.O. Schwartz, fire reflected off the lens of a video camera. It might have been an amateur if not for the boom microphone that hung out the window beside it. The Beast had noticed it as well, and started to move forward excitedly. Wolverine stopped him.

"It's not Trish, Hank," Wolverine said.

"Come now, Logan," the Beast responded. "It is not even conceivable that you might be able to tell her scent from here."

"You're right," Wolverine admitted. "But I still say it ain't her. That camera's got us dead in its sights. There's no way, no matter what the danger, that Trish Tilby wouldn't identify herself to us if we ran into her in the middle of a crisis like this. Think about it."

The Beast seemed to deflate slightly, then simply nodded.

"We'll find her, Hank," Logan insisted, and he meant it. No matter how bad a situation was, Wolverine had never been the type to offer false assurances. There was no benefit to it. Fear, desperation, rage, reckless abandon; in a hopeless situation, sometimes those things and the sheer force of will were the only things that could tip the scales. Hope was for children and dreamers, Wolverine often said. Though, in truth, he had relied on it more than once. Still, he tried to stay away from it. Not real healthy in his line of work.

"Beast, Wolverine, Bishop, see if you can calm the locals, find out what you can about Magneto's whereabouts, if possible, and if any other mutants have yet been sighted with the Acolytes," Storm ordered, and then allowed the winds she commanded to lift her from the pavement and carry her aloft.

"Iceman, put out the flames in that theater, then come help me with this larger blaze," she added. "We can't have this spreading uncontrolled, or it could take down the whole city."

Then she was gone, rising up into the darkness. Wolverine watched as Bobby raced to the theater, lifted his hands, and, in seconds, buried the entire façade in a heavy, moist mixture of ice and snow. He turned back toward F.A.O. Schwartz, held his hands beneath him and began freezing the air there, building an ice ramp below him and adding to it so rapidly that he propelled himself along it toward the blazing building.

Thunder rumbled above them, and then the sky simply opened up above F.A.O. Schwartz in an uncommonly severe downpour specifically directed at the blazing structure. As it fell, Bobby began to turn it to ice, which would not only douse the flames, but help keep the crumbling structure from toppling onto the people below.

"Well, gentlemen . . ." the Beast began, but then was cut off by a shriek that tore aside the veil of surreality that had hung over the chaotic scene.

"There," Bishop said, and pointed south a block and a half.

Wolverine had already seen it, though. Five men stood around a figure, probably female, who crouched on the ground, cowering in terror. They were pounding on her with their fists, and as she fell to the ground, they began kicking.

Logan was made for hunting, for sliding in stealth through a tree-lined ridge or an urban jungle alley. He was made for the consummation of the hunt, for the fracas, the brawl, the life and death combat, the taking of life up close and personal. But there were things about the hunter most people forgot. One of them was speed. Wolverine was faster than he looked. Bishop lagged slightly behind, but the Beast kept pace with him as he raced toward the helpless woman and her attackers.

"Muties," he heard someone exclaim as they raced past.

"More of 'em," somebody else said.

"I seen 'em on TV," a woman cried. "They're the X-Men!"

The tone of each voice was identical. Not relief. Not the tone of someone about to be rescued, not the relief of the oppressed when the cavalry finally arrived. Disgust, hate, fear—especially fear. But Wolverine was used to it, it was always the same. Maybe in the wilds of Canada, in the backwater towns where most people thought mutants were a myth, maybe there he was just another hunter. Just another guy who'd watch your back and buy you a beer, as long as you didn't get up in his face.

But this was America. Land of the free. Home of the brave. A nation of diversity whose own nature filled its people with self-loathing. A nation where unrealistic expectations forced citizens to look for someone to blame because they aren't what the "dream" says they should be. Someone, anyone. Any color, or religion, or sex, or age, or birthplace. But, especially, mutants. After all, hating mutants was something they could all agree on. It wasn't even considered politically incorrect to hate mutants.

It wasn't everyone. Wolverine knew that. But as he ran past looters cowering in shadows, and angry citizens too stunned to decide whether to flee or attack, as he approached five young street toughs battering and kicking a defenseless woman, it became harder and harder to remember it. They were there to stop Magneto, to save humanity from the most feared mutant the world had ever known. Maybe they could do that. But Logan knew there was no way to save humanity from itself.

"Enough!" Wolverine growled, hauling two of the woman's attackers away and throwing them to the ground.

A third rounded on him.

"Hey, man, whatcha doin'?" the man snapped, looking at his friends in astonishment before looking up at Wolverine. "She's a goddamn mutie freak! She deserves to get . . ."

The punk's eyes bugged out when he saw who it was he was talking to. Wolverine grabbed him by the front of his muscle shirt and pulled him close. Logan wasn't tall, and he had to haul the man down to look at him eye to eye. But size didn't matter in the end. The man was terrified.

"So am I," Wolverine snarled. "You want to give me what I deserve?"

The Beast took down the last of the woman's attackers, and Bishop knelt by her battered form.

"Ma'am, are you all right?" he asked softly. "Are you badly injured?"

"Oh my God!" the woman shouted as she looked up at him. "You're them! You're X-Men!"

"We are," Bishop agreed, reaching out to move her hair from a gushing wound on the side of her head. "That looks pretty bad. Here, let me . . ."

"Don't touch me, you mutie freak!" she howled, and leaped from the ground, backing away from Bishop like a cornered animal. "I'm not one of you, hear me? I'm just a normal human being! I'm not some freak like you!"

She turned and ran, as best she could.

"I wish we had time to teach these miscreants a lesson," the Beast said, holding his two captives off the ground.

"Me too," Wolverine snarled. "But we don't."

"Man, I thought she was a mutant," one of the punks on the ground whispered to the other. "I can't believe we did that."

Wolverine dropped the man he'd been threatening and pulled the other one from the ground. His face was badly scraped from his impact with the pavement when Wolverine tossed him, and Wolverine slapped his hand away as he tried to wipe the blood from his face.

"So now you're filled with regret 'cause she turned out to be human, huh, bub?" he snapped. "But if she'd been a mutant after all, then it would have been okay to stomp her like that?"

The man snarled back, his lip curling in hatred as he blinked away the blood on his face.

"Damn right," he said coldly.

Wolverine could feel it happening inside his head, the

berserker rage that had overcome him often in days long past. He fought it down, fought the red haze that threatened to blind him the same way the blood was blinding the ignorant cuss in his hands. Barely in control, he held his right fist up to the man's face and popped his claws.

"You and the rest of your little Nazi party can go in a minute. All we want to know is where Magneto and the Acolytes have shown up. I'm sure the word's on the street, and you're about as low to the street as can be," he said grimly.

"Why don't you—" the bigot started to say, but swallowed his words when Wolverine held the tips of his claws level with the man's eyes.

"He was here," the man said quickly. "We'd pinned down a couple of his freak soldiers. We was gonna show 'em what happened to muties who get too big for their britches. They killed a couple of people, murderin' freaks. Then Magneto shows up, sends everybody runnin', and turns around and takes off with that lady from the news."

In his peripheral vision, Wolverine saw the Beast snap to attention.

"What woman?" Logan asked. "Trish Tilby?"

"That's the one," one of the other punks said. "Damn mutie lover."

Wolverine watched the anger pass like a wave over the Beast's face, then disappear.

"Get out of here," Hank said coldly, and they ran in terror, calling threats back to the X-Men they did not have the courage or the ability to fulfill.

"No good will come of this race war," the Beast said.

"Apparently, none of you have been listening,"

Bishop snapped. "I've told you all exactly what is going to come of it, but you aren't paying attention."

"Say what you want, Bishop," Wolverine replied. "I know where you're from. I know what you went through. But just because it happened for you, doesn't mean it has to happen for us. The future is always uncertain."

Bishop kept silent after that, but Wolverine found himself reminded of an old Doors song. The lyrics were disturbing. *The future's uncertain*, the song said, just as he'd told Bishop. But the song went on from there. *And the end is always near*. It wasn't something he wanted to think about.

"I suppose we should try to do something about these looters," Wolverine said.

"At least until Storm and Iceman finish putting out that fire," Bishop agreed.

The glint of the video camera caught Wolverine's eye again, and he glanced up toward the window, half a block away, where the camera was pointed down at them.

"And the media coverage ain't gonna hurt," he said cynically. "Let people know that not all mutants are followers of Magneto."

"Let us take action, then," the Beast agreed. "But I am compelled to speculate if the presence of the camera has influenced this judgment. We must find Magneto with all due haste, and yet we interrupt that pursuit for petty looting and raging fires we might customarily forbear. I would hate to conclude that we were performing to garner support, instead of pursuing the most direct course to the termination of this fiasco."

SANCTUARY

"We'll head after Magneto as soon as Ororo and Bobby are through," Wolverine said. "For now, though, let's forget about the cameras. We do what has to be done. 'Cause we can. Simple as that."

"I hope you're right, Logan," the Beast answered slowly. "I do hope you're right."

There was a crash to the left, and then a plate glass window shattered as a chair burst through it and smashed to the street. A short man wearing a long coat leaped through the jagged remnants of the window and started off down the street, gold and diamond necklaces and bracelets stuffed in his pockets, a trail of rings, earrings, and coins falling behind him like bread crumbs in a fairy tale.

"Halt!" Bishop shouted.

"My stuff, man!" the thief shouted. "It's my stuff!"

"I doubt that," the Beast said, and in three bounds, he tackled the man about the waist. Hank hauled him up by the jacket and carried him back to the jewelry store. An aging Asian woman stood just inside the shattered glass. There were tears in her eyes as the Beast handed over the thief's jacket.

"Thank you so much," the woman said softly. "I . . . I don't suppose it will be long until someone tries again, though."

"Ma'am, is there a secure site where you might remain hidden until this crisis has passed?" the Beast asked.

"Upstairs," she nodded. "I think I will be safe upstairs."

"Go there," Hank said, holding the woman's small hands in his own, his blue fur looking not at all out of place in that moment. "We shall endeavor to conclude all of this as expediently as possible."

"Do you think you can stop them, then?" the woman asked, and Wolverine thought she sounded skeptical.

"Indeed," the Beast said, then turned back toward Wolverine and Bishop. "Indeed."

In that moment, Wolverine knew without a doubt that there was always room for hope. Sometimes, he realized, it was all you had.

Chapter 5

Jean Grey put her hand to her forehead and smeared sticky wetness down one cheek. There was blood on her head and on her fingers, and she didn't know why. She was lying down on a cool metal surface, disoriented, still somewhat dizzy, and slightly nauseous.

"Jean!" someone shouted nearby, and she wished they would stop. "Jean, you've got to snap out of it! Scott needs you! Scott's going to die if you can't help him!"

Scott? she thought, confused.

Then she heard his voice, his mind in hers, speaking to her. Thinking his thoughts inside her own mind.

Jean! Jean, you've got to help us!

It hit her hard and fast, Scott's mental voice triggering her return to reality. The explosion, the *Starjammer* spinning out of control, Scott and Ch'od . . . lost. Untethered. Somewhere in space.

"Jean?" Corsair asked, above her, holding out a hand to help her up.

She took it, rising immediately to her feet and then using his shoulders, strong like his son's, to steady herself.

"How long?" she asked.

"Just a few seconds," he answered, his words just as curt, just as hurried. "Jean, can you . . ."

"Quiet, Corsair," she snapped unintentionally. "I've got to concentrate, search space just to find them. Then, we'll see if I've got the strength it's going to take to pull them back."

Corsair's mouth snapped shut. He squeezed her arm once, gently, and helped her sit in the pilot's seat. As much as she tried to focus all of her thoughts on her search for Scott, there was still a part of her left disoriented by the injury to her head. She had banged it pretty good on something there in the cockpit, and couldn't even recall what it had been. In the few seconds she had been semi-conscious, her mind had heard and recorded much, only some of which was beginning to register with her. Raza had been injured, rather badly. Rogue was bringing him into the *Starjammer* and she and Corsair would rush to treat the cyborg's wounds. That made three wounded, not including herself, and two possibly . . .

No. She would not allow herself even to think it. Dead, lost in space, it meant the same thing. There was no way that Jean Grey was going to give up on the love of her life. No matter how vital the X-Men were, how important Professor Xavier's dream was to the world, none of it meant anything to Jean without Scott Summers by her side.

Scott! she thought, sending the alarmed voice of her mind out into the ether of space. It was a wave of power from her brain, a huge net that she hoped would capture something, anything. She had heard his voice before, she was certain of it. So he had to be out there. But where, and how far? Would she be able to . . .

"Jean, is that necessary?" Archangel said from the cockpit hatch behind her. She turned to see that he was clutching his head with both hands. Blood flowed from his nose.

"Only if you don't want Scott to die out there, Warren," she snapped, perhaps more harshly than she wished.

Archangel only nodded and moved back into the cabin. Jean knew it was going to hurt them, all of them.

But she had to try at least one more wide-spectrum mental sending, to try and get Scott to respond. She could sense him out there, in space. Knew that he was still alive. But she couldn't locate him. She would need real communication to do that.

Scott, answer me, please! she sent, and heard a groan from the main cabin behind her.

Silence. Several painful seconds ticked by, and then Scott's voice returned to her mind.

Jean, thank God! he said. *Can you get us back?*

She didn't respond for a moment, spending the time instead tracking his mental voice back to its source. Then she had him. Had both of them. Scott and Ch'od were still hurtling away from the ship. Already they were more than a mile distant. On Earth, it would have been impossible for her to use her telekinesis over such a distance. But this was different. The same rules hardly applied. There was nothing separating them but the hull of the *Starjammer*, nothing interfering with her powers. She thought, or rather, she hoped, it would be possible. But she would have to combine her telekinesis with her telepathy.

Scott, listen, she thought, sending it as a narrowly focused mental signal that would not affect the others on board the ship. *You've got to get hold of Ch'od. If I can catch you, it'll be a whole lot easier if I don't have to worry about two objects that need to be halted. Grab him and hold on tight.*

Their minds linked and clear once again, Jean could sense the struggle Scott went through, reaching out for and latching on to the amphibious alien. She knew his hates and fears, knew that his first inclination would be some act of selflessness, some way to help Ch'od even at his own expense.

Don't even think it, her mental voice called to him. *Just hold on tight, and be ready for the impact. If I can stop your momentum at this distance, it might be a heck of a tug.*

Whatever it takes, Scott's mind responded. *Got him!*

All right, prepare yourself, she thought. Jean Grey reached out her mind again. She felt more than ever the dichotomous nature of her mutant mental abilities. It was, in that moment, as if her telepathy was one arm, pinpointing and targeting Cyclops and Ch'od at that great distance, and her telekinesis was another arm, the fingers of which gently wrapped around the two, closing into a protective fist around them.

Then, with that mental fist, she simply pulled.

Jean Grey cried out in pain.

''Jean!'' Corsair called, instantly at her side in the cockpit. ''Are you okay? What's happening?''

She waved him away without even opening her eyes, still focused on Scott and Ch'od, on the strain she felt as she tried to halt their motion. It felt as though someone were tearing her skull apart, some savage animal worrying at it to get to her mind.

Finally, she let go.

Scott, I think I could pull you back here if you didn't have so much momentum, she sent, certain he would read the despair in her heart. *But I can't stop it, honey. God, I'm sorry. I can't slow you down.*

There was silence then, out in space, and through their rapport she could sense Scott's mind churning, searching for an answer, a solution. When he found it, she felt that as well.

What is it? she asked, before he'd had time even to call her name.

It's a long shot, Jean, but it's all we've got, he said. *Ch'od's going to hold on to me, tight, from behind. With all the power I've leeched from our proximity to the sun, if I can let off every ounce of that in one optic blast, in the direction we are moving, it should act like a retro-thruster. It should stop us, and it might even start us back toward the* Starjammer.

But you'll never be able to stay conscious, she thought, and felt despair creeping up on her, familiar as her shadow.

True, he responded. *But Ch'od will. As long as he can hold on to me while I try this stunt, you can pull us both in by locking on to him.*

It might work, Jean thought. Then, in unison, their mental voices said, *It has to.*

* * *

Cyclops explained his plan to Ch'od quickly. They had not a second to spare, as each moment moved them further from the *Starjammer*, and closer to the outer limits of Jean's power to retrieve them.

"Get around behind me," Scott barked, and, using the X-Man's body to guide himself, Ch'od spun around with startling speed and efficiency. Normally he was extremely congenial and inquisitive. But in an emergency, he was all business. Corsair had told Cyclops that many times, but this was the first time Scott had really seen it in action.

Ch'od wrapped his arms around Cyclops' chest, even as their legs twined together. It was as if he were giving the huge Timorian a piggyback ride, something that would have been physically impossible in normal gravity.

"Is this too tight?" Ch'od asked, ever courteous, even in the worst of times.

"A little uncomfortable," Cyclops admitted. "But I'll live. Whatever you do, don't let go. And don't squeeze too tight, or you'll have nothing left to hold on to. Just mold your body to mine. Do as I do, and brace yourself."

They were spinning, end over end, and Cyclops knew they were only going to get one chance at this. It had to be timed perfectly, and his aim was vital to their survival. In this he relied on a special talent that had nothing to do with his mutant abilities. For, ever since childhood, Scott Summers had had an innate skill that had always helped him during battle. Some kids were natural spellers. Scott had an almost uncanny knack for spatial geometry.

He prayed that extended to outer space. Jean had planted in his mind the direction of the *Starjammer*. She held onto him like a dog on a leash, so he knew where they needed to go. He tucked his legs under himself, and Ch'od did the same. Their roll brought them around one more time.

"Straighten your legs on my mark," he said. "Now!"

Cyclops and Ch'od shot their legs out simultaneously, so that their bodies lay on a flat plane parallel to the direction their momentum was pulling them. In that instant, Scott looked down along the line of his body, and, head cocked uncomfortably, let loose with every ounce of power he could summon to his optic beams. It was an extraordinary catharsis unlike anything he had ever experienced, a complete emptying of his reserves that he had never dreamed possible. His eyes burned and his mouth was dry. For some reason he thought he ought to have a headache, but he didn't.

He could feel their momentum slowing, the pull on their bodies was tangible, and he believed they actually began to move in the opposite direction.

Finally, the well ran dry. Suddenly spent, his eyes rolled up into his head and even the stars disappeared.

* * *

Corsair ran through the main cabin, careful not to stumble in the awkward pressure suit he wore. There were three medi-slabs laid out in the cabin now, one each for Gambit, Hepzibah, and now Raza. Raza's arm had been badly injured, and they had been forced to sedate him to speed the healing process, but both he and Hepzibah were likely to be up and around soon. Gambit, on the other hand, Corsair wasn't willing to take any bets on. None of them were certain how badly the Cajun X-Man had been injured. Only time would tell.

While Rogue stood by the medi-slab where Gambit lay, Archangel checked the instruments reading Raza's life signs. The *Starjammer* was in bad shape, and there was no telling what was working properly or not. All Corsair knew was that life support systems were slowly failing. They had two or three days at best, and then they'd be dead.

If the sun didn't torch them first.

"Rogue," he snapped into the comm-unit in his helmet. "Jean's bringing Scott and Ch'od into the airlock. I need your muscle."

She turned, startled out of her preoccupation, and blinked twice. Archangel looked at him as well, and it suddenly struck Corsair that each of them was with one of their wounded comrades, but his own lover, Hepzibah, was untended, alone. He knew he should be at her side, yearned to be there. But he was captain of the *Starjammer*. Survival had to be his priority. Silently, he sent her his love.

"Rogue," he snapped. "Let's go!"

"But Remy—" she began, and Corsair wondered if she was still disoriented from the explosion, not even five minutes ago.

"Archangel will watch Remy," Corsair said sternly. "We've got our friends to attend to."

He set off deeper into the ship, past the cargo hold and toward the airlock. Rogue fell into step behind him and kept pace all the way. They stopped short at the small window and instrument board that manually controlled the airlock. Hands on either side of the clear surface, Corsair peered into the small cubicle that separated the airlock door from the outer hull door.

That outer door was already open, waiting for Jean Grey to telekinetically reel Cyclops and Ch'od in from space. Corsair stared out at the stars, feeling helpless and frustrated. It wasn't enough that they were dead in space, that the ship was becoming a furnace where they might well be boiled alive by the heat of the sun. It wasn't enough that nearly half of them had some injury or other, some quite serious. No, that wasn't enough. The warp drive had to misfire, throwing Corsair's best friend and his eldest son out into the ether of space.

But as angry as he wanted to be at God, as much as he wanted to shout curses to the heavens, something he'd become quite proficient at over the years, Corsair couldn't quite bring himself to do it. It was only, after all, through the sheer will of a young woman named Jean and by the grace of God that Scott and Ch'od were alive.

Then they were there, growing quickly larger in the window, hurtling toward the *Starjammer* so fast that Corsair thought they might actually slam into the ship. At the last moment though, and with some reserve of strength that Corsair found incredible, Jean must have used her psi skills to slow them. Ch'od and Cyclops drifted into the airlock cubicle, the amphibious Starjammer clutching on to the unconscious leader of the X-Men even as he reached for some purchase within the small space.

"My Lord," Rogue said, and Corsair wasn't sure if the hushed words were a prayer or merely astonishment. "I don't guess I ever expected to see either of them again. Not in this life, anyway."

But Corsair's joy was short lived. He had ever been the pragmatist.

"Let's hope we haven't gotten them back just so we can all die together," he said, then slammed the button that would seal the outer hull door and cycle air into the cubicle. Moments later, the airlock hissed loudly as the inner hatch released, and Corsair slid it aside.

Ch'od, who had been using the door to brace his weary body, stumbled and fell to the deck of the *Starjammer* with Cyclops in his arms.

"Ch'od!" Corsair called, kneeling by his friend.

"Not to worry, Corsair," Ch'od said quickly, though still taking quick breaths within his pressure suit. "I shall be fine in a moment. Your son also, if I'm not sorely mistaken. Which is excellent news, for we don't have a lot of time to devise an alternate plan."

SANCTUARY

Corsair stared at Ch'od, then at Scott's unconscious form. It seemed surreal to him, Ch'od adapting so easily to the aftermath of such a trauma. But he was right, they had to move on, and quickly. Corsair even chuckled slightly, as Rogue helped Ch'od to his feet. He would never cease to be amazed by his friend's extraordinary constitution.

But what of his son?

"Scott?" he asked. "Can you hear me, son? Scott, are you awake?"

Behind the helmet of his suit, behind the ruby quartz of his visor, Corsair thought he saw his son's eyes flutter momentarily, opening slightly, and then they were closed again.

"You'll be all right, Scott," Corsair said softly. "We've had far too little time together, son. You have to be all right."

His arms and shoulders taut with the strain, Corsair lifted his son into his arms. For a moment, he was struck by a memory of Scott as an infant, crying with fever and unable to fall asleep unless his father held him. As much of a strain as being a new parent had been, as frustrating as it had been, there had been a certain joy in rocking his baby boy to sleep.

He felt that again, now, and it brought back the pain of his wife's death, and all the years he and Scott had spent apart. Ch'od rose to his feet, and steadied himself against the bulkhead.

"We have no time to lose," Ch'od said. "Corsair, we must try again to repair the warp drive. And now, or it may well prove too late."

Rogue moved to help Corsair with the burden of his son's weight, but he ignored her. The terror he had felt every moment since the explosion abated slowly, leaving him nearly breathless. After a moment, Scott groaned in a low, guttural voice, and lifted a hand to shield his eyes from the light that filtered through his helmet and visor.

"Scott," Corsair said. "You did it son. You're all right."

"For the moment, Dad," Scott answered. Like father, like son, ever the pragmatist.

"Corsair, did you not hear me?" Ch'od asked. "We've got to—"

"I heard you, Ch'od," Corsair answered. "And I'll join you on the hull, since Raza cannot. Scott's in no condition to—"

"I'm okay, Corsair," Scott said, sitting up. "You're going to need backup out there, and Rogue and I are all you've got."

Corsair did not fail to note the change in his son's tone. He merely nodded, resigned to their fate. His fear for Scott had never interfered with their ability to work or battle side by side in the past, and he would not allow it to do so even in this crisis.

"I'm happy to go back out there with y'all," Rogue said with a smile. "But this time, let's be a little more careful, okay?"

* * *

Jean lay in the cockpit, recovering, and Archangel found himself in the unusual role of duty nurse for the wounded members of the *Starjammer*'s crew. He wasn't terribly concerned for Hepzibah or Raza; when they awoke from their sedation they would be greatly weakened, and temporarily unable to use their injured limbs, but awaken they would.

SANCTUARY

Gambit was another story. The on-board Shi'ar medical computers could have done a simple diagnostic program, but the system had shorted and crashed, along with most of the *Starjammer*'s programming. If they were certain of the voltage, or even the nature, of electric current Gambit was hit with by Warstar of the Imperial Guard, they might be able to guess at what Remy was going through, and what the long term effects of his electrocution might be. But Warstar could have fried every synapse in Gambit's brain, and they wouldn't know it until they got him back to Earth.

If any of them got back.

A sobering thought, and one that Archangel had been trying to avoid. Dwelling on his "patients" had given him a momentary respite from their situation, and from his growing case of cabin fever. He was definitely getting a little stir crazy, cooped up in the ship. It helped a bit that he was the only person walking around in the main cabin, but that was a superficial improvement at best.

He felt that nervous energy building inside of him once again, and found, to his surprise, that he'd been tapping his foot for a while without realizing it. The cabin wasn't shrinking. Archangel wasn't delusional. But it certainly felt smaller. He closed his eyes a moment and he could feel it pressing in around him. The cabin, the ship, and space beyond.

A ruffle of fear went through his bio-metallic wings where they lay flat against his back beneath the pressure suit. Archangel felt the twinge of muscles that would spread them to their full span, and he mustered what control of them he had to keep them from tearing apart the Shi'ar space garb.

Turning away from Gambit's prone form, Archangel began to pace the cabin. He had never felt so completely useless. And not since his days with Apocalypse had he felt so close to the edge of losing control. But he wouldn't lose it. Absolutely would not. He had been twisted into something that just wasn't him, wasn't Warren Worthington, and it had been a long road back. He still had yet to completely convince his oldest and best friends in the X-Men that he had recovered, that he was flying high again.

"Just suck it up, Worthington," he muttered to himself, then took a long slow, breath and released it. He stretched, slowly, trying to relax the tension in his body.

" . . . no . . ."

The word was spoken very quietly, gruffly, with a dreamy quality that only the exhausted, the dying, or the feverish could muster. Archangel spun around, prepared to defend himself, though he suspected there would be no need. His suspicions proved correct a moment later, as he hurried to the medi-slab where Gambit lay, twitching as if in the grip of some horrid nightmare.

" . . . no . . ." Remy mumbled again, though more forcefully this time.

Then his face and his tone changed dramatically. Gambit's breath came faster, more frenetically, and his facial features contorted as if he were in pain, or adamant denial. Perhaps both, Archangel considered.

"No, Essex!" Gambit snarled, still less than conscious, his attitude reflecting a savagery that Archangel had never seen in him. "You wan' Gambit do a little t'ing for you, maybe dat seem okay before. But no more, Essex! You hear me, *homme*? Gambit not gon' let you hurt anybody, 'specially not . . ."

SANCTUARY

Remy LeBeau's entire body went slack then, his face draining of all color. Archangel thought in that instant that Gambit's heart might have simply stopped, so quickly did the Cajun's energy seem to leave him. Warren realized it would be impossible for him to check Gambit's temperature with both of them in pressure suits, but from the flush on Remy's cheeks and his delusional rambling, he had to assume the man's fever was extremely high.

Who in hell is Essex? he wondered to himself. "Gambit?" he ventured, moving his helmet closer to Gambit's own. "Remy, it's Warren. Are you awake? Can you hear me?"

Gambit's eyes snapped open, black and red light pulsing where pupils ought to have been, a mist of crimson energy seemed to spark inside his helmet.

Rage erupted on his face as he looked at Archangel, and he growled that unfamiliar name again, "Essex!"

Gambit reached up, faster than Warren had ever seen him move, and latched his fingers onto Archangel's helmet. Sparks flew and the helmet grew immediately hot.

Archangel cursed in a panic, fumbling for the latches of his helmet. "Gambit, what the—"

He didn't finish his question, too caught up in his struggle to be free of the helmet. Gambit had used his mutant power to charge Archangel's helmet with explosive energy. He had seconds to remove it, or it would explode, taking his head with it.

"Oh, man, oh, man, oh, man . . ." he chanted, until finally the snaps slid under his thumb, the entire helmet twisted sideways, and he whipped it off his head and across the cabin.

It hadn't hit the floor when it exploded. Archangel

shielded his eyes, and when he looked back, there was a huge black smear on the cabin floor. Gambit stood over him, glowering with righteous fury, feverishly unsteady on his feet.

"Back off, Gambit," he said, scrabbling backward and attempting to stand. Within the pressure suit, he felt weighted down by his wings for the first time. "You're not well, man. You shouldn't be up."

"I'm done wit' you, Essex," Gambit snarled, and took another menacing, shaky step toward Archangel. "You leave my family alone, now, *oui*?"

"Remy," Archangel said, standing now and reaching out his hands in a gesture of comfort. "It's me, Warren. Archangel. Snap out of it man, it's the fever talking. I'm not this Essex guy, okay?"

"You don' want to leave, you gonna have to die," Gambit said, slurring his words a bit.

Archangel barely dodged as Gambit aimed a high kick at his face—a fairly weak kick by Remy's usual standards. The Cajun followed through with a lunge at Warren's throat, a clumsy move he would never normally have attempted, and Archangel easily sidestepped and batted him aside. Gambit stumbled toward the medi-slab where Raza lay, and fell over the wounded cyborg. He lay across Raza for a moment before returning to his feet.

When Gambit wheeled on Warren, he held a Shi'ar medical probe that Corsair had used earlier. Already, the red-tinged energy was sparking in his hands. The probe glowed with the explosive charge of Gambit's mutant ability, and then the Cajun threw it like a dart at Warren's chest.

Instinct alone saved Archangel's life. Without conscious thought, his bio-metallic wings tore right through the pressure suit. They opened to their full span and wrapped themselves around Archangel in a heartbeat. The charged probe exploded upon impact with his wings, but Warren remained untouched.

He withdrew his wings, tucking them against his back, and Gambit was already rushing at him again.

"Remy, stop, dammit!" he shouted. "It's me, Warren."

Once more, he sidestepped, then slammed Gambit against the wall of the cabin. The Cajun fell to the ground, dazed by the impact. Archangel hoped that it might have shaken some of the fevered mania from the man.

"Come on, Gambit," he pleaded. "Don't make me hurt you worse than you already are."

Gambit bobbed his head up, and squinted as he tried to see clearly.

"That's it, man, look at me," Warren urged.

"Essex," Gambit breathed. "Time to die."

As he pulled himself up, Gambit reached for a long metal tube strapped to the wall. Archangel had seen Ch'od use it earlier to put out the fire; some kind of chemical fire extinguisher then. The contents of which were more than likely under pressure. Gambit's right hand was already glowing with volatile energy as he reached for the tube, and Archangel realized that Remy might very well blow a hole in the *Starjammer*'s hull with the combination of his power and that one metal cylinder.

Archangel couldn't allow that to happen. Gambit's hand was only inches from the cylinder when Warren's wings flashed out to their full span. He wasn't certain whether he commanded them or whether they simply intuited and precipitated his actions. It didn't matter. Only one thing did: stopping Gambit.

Wing knives flashed across the room and sliced through Gambit's pressure suit, imbedding themselves in his flesh. Immediately, Remy LeBeau slumped to the floor, paralyzed by the chemicals secreted by Warren's bio-metallic feathers.

Archangel rushed to his fallen teammate, lifted Gambit from the floor and put him back on the medi-slab. He tore away the pressure suit in a panic and began removing the wing-knives as carefully as he could. Normally, they were effective but ultimately not harmful. With Gambit's previous injuries, however, there was no way he could be certain.

"Corsair!" he shouted, hoping he would be heard. "Jean! Someone! I could use a little help in here!"

Silently, Archangel mumbled a prayer.

Chapter 6

Charles Xavier stood in the middle of Exchange Place in Jersey City, New Jersey as the maelstrom of anarchy swirled around him. In his youth, he had reined in the burgeoning power of his telepathy, closed out the billions of mental voices on Earth. It was effortless for him now, but even so, even with his nigh-impenetrable mental shields in place, there was a low hum in his brain. It was the babble of thousands upon thousands of panicked minds.

They climbed up from the PATH train station into the safety of Jersey City, a sea of human flesh, awash with a relief and a sorrow unmatched in their prior existences. The media swarmed around them, picking at their remains with the cold distance of carrion birds.

Beyond the PATH station, past the Hudson River, the twin towers of the World Trade Center were still beacons, the lights of Manhattan still made for a breathtaking panorama. But it was the view of another world now, the alien vista across a hostile border, where an invisible wall was imprinted with invisible words, something like, "Abandon hope, all ye who enter here."

"I'm sorry, Professor Xavier, did you say something?" Annelise Dwyer asked.

"What's that?" Charles Xavier responded, startled from his reverie.

"I thought you'd said something," the CNN anchor said, then shook her head. "Never mind, I must be hearing things."

They sat in an area cordoned off from the rest of the Exchange Place plaza, the entirety of which had become a media tent city. The scavengers descended upon the catastrophe of Magneto's ascendance with a savage grace. Yet, despite his usual antipathy for news people, Xavier found himself strangely attracted to Annelise Dwyer. The hopeless optimist within him wondered if she had been able to reach the much-envied position of CNN anchor without becoming as jaded as the majority of her peers. She certainly seemed to care.

It did not hurt that Xavier found her attractive, in an odd sort of way. But then, he had long since established a history of being attracted to powerful, odd women. Moira MacTaggart, Gabrielle Haller, Amelia Voght, Lilandra . . . and thoughts of Lilandra brought back his concern for Cyclops and his "away team," who had yet to arrive back on Earth. Quickly he sent a psi-probe out into the ether of Earth's atmosphere, hoping against hope that there would be some response from Jean Grey.

There was none. They were either not yet within the range of his mental scan, or they had not emerged from the Shi'ar stargate alive. Another crisis, for another time. Now, the situation at hand had to be dealt with.

"We're on in fifteen seconds, Professor," the newswoman said as she waved away a production assistant who was fooling with her hair. "I hope you can put some kind of positive spin on all of this. God knows, we need it."

Xavier smiled at that. He'd been right about the Dwyer woman. She still cared.

"I'll do my best, Ms. Dwyer," he answered.

"Please," she said, nodding her permission. "Call me Annelise."

"In five, Annelise," the production assistant said, holding up five fingers and counting them off with the seconds. "Three. Two. One."

Annelise introduced herself to the CNN audience, then greeted Xavier formally.

"Recently, you did a three way forum here on CNN with Senator Robert Kelly and Graydon Creed, Professor," she pointed out. "Though the men seemed, at least in that debate, to be at odds, both have held press conferences recently advocating the use of armed force to take Manhattan back. Creed has even gone so far as to call for the rounding up of all known mutants into detention centers, similar to those used to hold Japanese-Americans during World War II. Would you care to comment on any of their points?"

"Absolutely," Xavier said sternly, in his best administrative tone. "To begin with, I want to show my complete support of the President's policies in this matter. He wisely proceeds with caution over a course that is both new and treacherous. While Senator Kelly and Mr. Creed do have different motives—one makes choices informed by fear, the other by hatred—their advocacy of a military solution is, simply put, ignorant of the situation."

"That's a rather inflammatory statement, Professor," Annelise said, her surprise obviously genuine.

"Not at all," Xavier countered, looking directly at the camera now. "I am here, as you can see. Neither Senator Kelly or Graydon Creed is in Jersey City, or anywhere near New York at the moment. Obviously neither of them has studied the capacity of these Sentinels as I have. In short, no massive military onslaught has any hope of achieving anything but mass property damage and probably the deaths of a great number of innocent civilians."

"You have another solution, Professor?" Annelise

asked. "We can't just allow terrorists to claim our cities with impunity, can we?"

"Not at all, Annelise," Xavier agreed. "And I'm told the President does have a plan. Also, I'm not saying incisive use of force is unwarranted, only that a mass attack would be useless. But, on to an even more disturbing issue, Graydon Creed's detention center idea. This, as I'm sure you and all good Americans will realize, is nothing more than a concentration camp, though we should expect no less from a fascist whose communications on the Internet have revealed that he supports the idea of genetic cleansing through the genocide of mutants."

"That is a stunning charge, Professor," Annelise commented, though they had already discussed the point before broadcasting it.

"All supported by documentation available on the Internet, I assure you," Xavier answered.

"Well, Professor," she continued, "what of the media videotape of Magneto's Acolytes killing humans in cold blood, and of Magneto's abduction of local reporter Trish Tilby and her cameraman."

"Despicable events indeed," Xavier responded, treading carefully now. "Despite common opinion, however, Magneto is not a cold-blooded murderer. Fanatic he may be, terrorist, call him what you will, but he would not have committed the kind of cold-blooded murder we saw on that tape. Which seems to indicate that Ms. Tilby and her cameraman will be relatively safe so long as they accompany him. On the other hand," he continued cutting Annelise off before she could, understandably, object, "all moral guides indicate that Magneto must be held responsible for the murderous actions of those who act on his behalf. He had foreknowledge of his Acolytes' penchant for death when he became their leader.

"In addition, Annelise," he said, and turned to the camera again as he relaxed into a paternal role and voice. "The American people have also seen the heroic actions of the X-Men, a band of mutants largely considered outlaws who are obviously attempting to put an end to Magneto's 'Mutant Empire' before it really gets going."

"Now that you mention it, Professor," Annelise began, and seemed to hesitate a moment, as if unsure she wanted to pursue her question. "Well, what of your rumored connection to the X-Men? Is it true you are working with them?"

"Please, Annelise," Xavier said with an exasperated sigh. "It is true that I have, in my life, met several members of this group. In fact I know Dr. Henry McCoy, the renowned biochemist, quite well indeed. But I am, as you well know, among the foremost experts on mutation in the world. I understand how certain things might be misconstrued, however. It comes with the territory.

"But, listen," he said, and turned once more toward the camera with his best paternal manner, "what the American people need to know right now, more than anything, is that they are safe. For the time being, they need not be concerned that there will be some sudden mutant uprising. The majority of the world's mutants are law-abiding citizens. Those who aren't may very well be making their way to Manhattan even as we speak. And if that is the case, well, at least they won't cause any additional trouble.

"No, though Graydon Creed may attempt to foment some kind of genetic civil war, as long as the American people keep their wits about them, the only thing we have to worry about is how to get Magneto out of Manhattan.''

"Thank you, Professor Charles Xavier," Annelise said. "This is Annelise Dwyer, live in Jersey City, New Jersey. We go back to Greg Lombardi at CNN Center in Atlanta. Greg?"

Xavier sighed as Annelise pulled off the staid jacket she had donned for the broadcast. He felt slightly nauseous, and slumped back in his wheelchair a bit, trying to shake loose the tension that had drawn the muscles in his back tighter than guitar strings.

"Professor Xavier, are you all right?" Annelise asked.

"Please," he answered kindly, "call me Charles. And the answer to your question is that I am most definitely not all right. I feel quite ill, in fact."

"Is there anything I can do?" she offered.

"Certainly," he chuckled drily. "You can lie and tell me I didn't sound like a politician just now. That's the one thing I promised myself I would never be. Politics means compromising your beliefs and goals, Annelise. I hope to God I haven't come to that."

"Don't worry, Charles," she said softly, gently comforting him. "As long as you feel like throwing up every time you placate the masses, you haven't sold your soul yet."

* * *

As Charles Xavier wheeled himself away from the CNN remote setup, he scanned the rest of the media tent for Valerie Cooper. Upon his arrival, he'd had no time to even touch base with Val before CNN hustled him off for his interview. He knew that if there was a solution to their predicament beyond that espoused by Graydon Creed, it would lay either in the hands of his badly outnumbered X-Men, or in the product of Val's experience, knowledge, and skills combined with his own.

Even before he heard her call his name, Xavier felt the mental recognition of his presence in Val's mind. Some emotions were too powerful to screen out, and her volatile mix of relief and frustration was like a beacon. He turned to see her striding purposefully through the media circus, ignoring the pleas of desperate reporters alerted to her position of authority by the federal badge she wore. It allowed her entrance into any building or situation during this crisis, but it was also little better than a bull's-eye when dealing with the press.

"Professor Xavier," she said, with a pleasantness Xavier knew was forced. "How good to see you again. Do you have a moment? I'd love to hear your thoughts on this whole mess."

"Absolutely, Ms. Cooper," he answered, just as pleasantly. "Let's find a quiet place to chat, shall we?"

Xavier hated such falsehood, but every reporter around them, from the lowest viper to the most scrupulous journalist, was listening to their every word. They had to take their conversation elsewhere.

Though Xavier preferred not to rely on people to push him in his wheelchair, it was a welcome break when Val stepped behind him and began to do just that. When help was offered by anyone other than one of his X-Men, or someone equally close to him, he usually declined. In this case, however, he was glad that she had not asked. While at the Institute, he generally used the hoverchair that Lilandra had given him as a gift. But in public, he was forced to use the conventional chair.

SANCTUARY

It was really quite ironic, in a very cruel way. Xavier had been crippled as a young man, but later, in a miraculous series of events aided by the extraordinary technology of Lilandra's people, he had been given the ability to walk once more. For a time, he had lived in peace as Imperial Consort to Lilandra on the Shi'ar throneworld of Chandilar, for all intents and purposes married to the empress of a culture for whom marriage was the most sanctified of events.

But his heart had never been torn. He loved no other above Lilandra. Yet there was a growing crisis for mutants on the world of his birth. The X-Men needed him, desperately. And, in fact, he found that he needed them as well. He had responsibility, duty, and though they both hated to part, Lilandra understood the concept. It was the very thing which kept her from accompanying him to Earth. The very thing that was, even now, blanketing their relationship in a terrible chill that had nothing to do with distance and everything to do with philosophy.

So he had returned to Earth, to the X-Men, and almost immediately fate had stepped in, in the form of his old enemy Amahl Farouk, the Shadow King. One moment, he stood proud as any other man, strong and able. The next, he was crippled once more, his body cruelly twisted, and he was confined to a chair again.

Perhaps that was the price he paid for his dream. He had long since decided that the dream was worth any price, however. As long as it came true. He and Val Cooper had to make certain that Magneto's fantasies of empire did not get in the way. Though, Xavier thought, he would be fooling himself if he did not recognize how much damage had already been done.

"I think we're as alone as we're going to get, Val," Xavier said, looking around on Washington Street, around the corner from the PATH station and the media tent. They weren't far from the military encampment here, and Xavier could see a pair of Jeeps stopped parallel to one another, though facing opposite directions. Their passengers seemed in the midst of a heated debate, and Xavier knew it would not be the last on that day.

"Okay," Val answered. "What the hell is going on? I thought you people were going to wait to hear from me?"

"The team couldn't afford to wait," Xavier answered simply. "We didn't want Magneto to have the luxury of getting completely entrenched in his new 'sanctuary' without some kind of opposition."

"So they're taking the fight to him with no hope of winning," she snapped. "Does that make sense, Charles?"

"There is always hope," he said. "They've come through worse spots that this. We both know that."

"So where's the rest of the team?" she asked, sighing and glancing around in a pretense of distraction. "I didn't see Cyclops, Gambit, Rogue—you know what I mean. Where are the others?"

"I don't know," he answered honestly. "I'm not even sure they're alive."

The color drained from Valerie Cooper's face.

"If we're lucky," Xavier continued, "they're about to reenter Earth's atmosphere even now. But I haven't been able to reach them using any method."

"We need help," Val said softly, chewing her lip. "I got the President to approve my working with the X-Men on this, trying to get into the Alpha Sentinel with the override codes. But if I've got no X-Men . . .''

Her voice trailed off, and Xavier saw that Val was looking beyond him. She scowled, closed her eyes a moment and shook her head. When she finally spoke, he already knew what she would say.

"Here comes Gyrich," Val said, and the despair and hatred in her voice could not have been more clear.

"Ah, Professor Xavier," Henry Peter Gyrich crowed as he approached, "how nice to see you. Come to make a case study, have you?"

"As you well know, Mr. Gyrich," Cooper snapped, "the Professor has been brought in as an expert consultant for the duration of this crisis."

"Oh, yes, I'd forgotten," Gyrich sneered. "And what of the X-Men, Professor? How do they fare?"

"It's good to see you again, Mr. Gyrich," Xavier said stiffly. "Regarding the X-Men, I've no idea. Though the television says they're in Manhattan right now."

Gyrich tipped his head to one side and gave Xavier an odd smile. Charles was chilled to the bone. The problem with Gyrich was that he wasn't evil, or even "bad" per se. He was not an enemy that could be openly combatted. Rather, he was a bigoted patriot who would do anything for his country's benefit, even if his country did not specifically request it. Like Oliver North, he had his own ideas of what was good for America. But Gyrich also had some strong beliefs on the role that mutants did *not* play in the future of the nation.

Gyrich was not a villain, but he was an extremely dangerous man, just the same.

"So, what's the story, Ms. Cooper?" Gyrich asked after an uncomfortable silence. "What's your next move?"

"My next move, Mr. Gyrich, is to get the override codes for the Alpha Sentinel from you."

"You mean you don't already have them?" Gyrich asked, feigning astonishment with a caustic obviousness.

"You know I don't," Val snapped. "Given your position as part of Operation: Wideawake, it is implicitly your duty to provide those codes to me. I'm sure the President and the Director will see it that way."

"You're speaking out of school, Valerie," Gyrich said coldly, his eyes narrowed to slits as he glared at her and Xavier.

"Not at all, Henry," she said snidely, and Xavier realized for the first time that, in her own way, Val Cooper might be just as desperate to win at any cost as Gyrich was.

"Xavier has been cleared," she continued. "You know that. Give me the goddamn codes."

"There's no need for cursing," Gyrich chided. "I simply don't have the codes right now. I'll have to get them for you."

"Mr. Gyrich," Xavier interrupted, "I would caution you, at this juncture, not to impede Ms. Cooper's plan. It is, in truth, the only sure way to resolve this situation, and even then not without massive risk."

"Are you threatening me, Xavier?" Gyrich asked, in a tone that made it clear he was not unused to being threatened.

"Not at all," Xavier answered. "For I have nothing to threaten you with. I am, very simply, advising you as I was asked to do by the President himself. And my advice is, play ball. If Magneto's mutant empire succeeds due to your obfuscation and obstruction, I don't have to tell you that your employers would be sorely vexed.''

"Magneto will not succeed," Gyrich said, anger rising up behind his steely smile. "I will make certain of that. In any case," he continued, turning back to Val, "the X-Men are not here. Until they are here, your plan cannot go forward. Therefore, we have no choice but to proceed with Plan B, as it were.''

"And what, exactly, is Plan B?" Xavier asked.

"Sorry, Professor," Gyrich said. "That's classified to need-to-know. If Ms. Cooper's plan is not going to be enacted, then the pair of you simply do not need to know.''

"You're making a terrible mistake, Mr. Gyrich," Xavier said.

"The X-Men will be here," Val insisted. "You've got to give me more time.''

"Your time is up, Cooper," Gyrich said with a chuckle. "You and all your mutant sympathizing friends. Some of us actually want to stop Magneto. And the damned X-Men are probably signing up to be knights of his accursed round table right now.''

Gyrich turned stiffly and began to walk away in an arrogant manner Xavier couldn't help but think of as goosestepping.

"Mr. Gyrich," Xavier said, in a tone that made Gyrich hesitate, then turn to face them once more.

"What is it, Professor?" Gyrich asked wearily. "I have a mission to put together.''

"You're trying to take down Magneto, among the most powerful individual beings on the face of this planet. In some ways, perhaps *the* most powerful," Xavier said. "Maybe you've considered that. Maybe it doesn't disturb you. It is even possible that you've truly prepared for it.

"But don't forget that the Acolytes are there as well, not to mention whatever new Acolytes have joined him since this whole charade began. Finally, you'll have to contend with *them*."

Xavier pointed across the Hudson River to the sinister figure of a Sentinel that towered above the West Street entrance to the Holland Tunnel, outlined by its own running lights, eyes glowing red in the darkness. For a moment, he thought of Cerberus guarding the gates of hell. He pushed the thought away as he turned back toward Gyrich.

"They're not going to let you in," Xavier said calmly.

"We built them, Professor," Gyrich responded. "Why don't you let us worry about them, hmm?"

Gyrich walked quickly away, his every step a testament to efficiency.

"Perhaps he's actually figured out a way to do this," Xavier mused aloud, but beside him Val snorted derisively in response.

"Not without billions in collateral damage and a lot of casualties," she said. "The President won't let the military go in full force, but a small strike force, specifically designed to assassinate Magneto? They'll go for that."

"Do you think they actually believe it can be done?" Xavier asked, taken aback.

"They think they can do anything," Val responded. "They're invulnerable, unstoppable. They're the federal government, by God, and nobody tells them when to sit up or roll over."

"Fools," Xavier said quietly.

"Gyrich is right," Val said, "nobody is going to listen when I protest. It's going to be a massive cluster fu—"

"Val," Xavier interrupted. "I could contact the X-Men in Manhattan, as you well know."

"Via telepathy," Val said, nodding. "You could instruct them from there, at least to try to determine which is the Alpha Sentinel. But we'd still need those codes."

"True," Xavier said. "Likewise, I don't think it is in our best interests to pull them out of there right now. They're on Magneto's trail. If they can get close to him, engage him, then we still have a chance at this. Even Gyrich's plan may work if the X-Men keep Magneto busy long enough."

"You contact the X-Men," she decided. "If they run across the Alpha Sentinel, we need to know about it. In the meantime, I'll try to get those codes from Gyrich. Of course, if we end up helping Gyrich, we can't let him know we helped or he'll have confirmation of his suspicions regarding your connection to the X-Men."

"Let's do our best to avoid that," Xavier said, in that instant making a decision that brought home to him how truly dire their situation was.

"On the other hand," he said gravely, "considering the stakes here, we may all have to make sacrifices if we expect to prevail."

*   *   *

Gyrich was in his glory. Cooper had failed, plain and simple. Now it was his turn. There was no way his superiors would balk if he went forward now, with the X-Men unavailable. None of which meant that he had any intention of clearing his plan or getting authorization before moving ahead. He was the commander of this operation. He would take the fall if it went awry, and the credit if it succeeded.

And it would succeed.

It was very clear to Gyrich that the proper way to proceed was to first sanction Magneto. The Acolytes would not be a problem after that. Once opposition was eliminated, they would have to deal with the Sentinels. Without using mutants, which Gyrich was dead set against—after all, what was to stop them from commandeering the Sentinels for their own purposes?—the only way to take down the Sentinels might be through massive force. If they could be drawn out over the river, they might avoid some of the collateral damage. But it would be very messy, just the same.

Which was fine with Gyrich. While he was not prepared to allow Magneto his little empire, he was more than happy to take advantage of the terror created by the incident. The lasting memory of it, particularly if there was a lot of damage, even a few casualties, would allow him to operate with far greater freedom in his anti-mutant efforts. When it was all over, Gyrich intended to have a long talk with Graydon Creed of the Friends of Humanity, who was sounding more and more like a politician, and a potential candidate for public office, every day.

Gyrich hurried toward the entrance to the PATH station, where civilian evacuees were being shepherded quickly away by military personnel. The soldiers at the door saluted in deference to his position, but Gyrich did not return their gesture. He wasn't a soldier, after all. He was the boss.

SANCTUARY

He descended the down escalator into the depths of the station, barely noticing the stream of displaced New Yorkers on the up escalator. On the train platform, he was met by an army sergeant, who guided him down onto the tracks. They walked at a brisk clip, still parallel to the flood of humanity leaving their homes. Finally, they came to a doorway to one side of the tracks. A keycard unlocked the door, and Gyrich waited for the sergeant to move away before he opened it and entered.

Inside was a much smaller tunnel, ten feet high and perhaps twenty across. It was an access and maintenance area that ran alongside the PATH train tunnel all the way into Manhattan.

So much for getting past the Sentinels.

"Attention!" a harsh voice growled, and the nineteen soldiers inside snapped to. Their commander, Major Skolnick, stood rigid as he saluted Gyrich.

"Surgical ops unit one ready, sir," Major Skolnick announced. "Our gear will be delivered within one hour, sir. At which time, Operation: Carthage will be a go!"

"Excellent," Gyrich responded, a smile of anticipation creeping across his face. He had named the mission for the most malicious military action in history. The Roman government had determined that their ancient enemies in the north of Africa, Carthage, had to be utterly eliminated. They ordered the city razed to the ground, the soil sown with salt so that nothing could ever grow there again. They had done this with a very simple directive: "Carthage must be destroyed." It meant utter annihilation. Gyrich felt that same all-encompassing need for destruction as well.

No matter what else happened, Magneto must be destroyed.

CHAPTER 7

Word had spread like a virus down Fifth Avenue that the X-Men had come, and the looters scurried into their holes like frightened rabbits. It reminded Bishop of his days, now far in the future, with the XSE. Their name, and his own reputation, had been enough to send criminals fleeing in mortal terror. Here and now, in a time long before he was ever born, he had become part of a team, an institution he had previously considered little more than legend.

But the legend had a terrible ending. An ending where the legend died, where each and every member of the X-Men team was horribly slaughtered. Where the Sentinels ruled, at least for a time, and mutants became the hunted. His teammates knew of this; Bishop had told them. But he understood how difficult it was for them to really understand it, when they had not lived with the results of it.

His every muscle was tensed, body humming with energy, as they made their way down Fifth Avenue, Storm flying above them. Professor Xavier had contacted them mentally several minutes earlier, and given them instructions regarding the Alpha Sentinel, and Bishop had paid close attention. He understood how vital it was to take Magneto out of the game as quickly as possible, but in his own mind, the Sentinels were the greater threat. Still, Magneto's dream of domination might be exactly the thing that set events in motion leading to his disastrous future.

In any case, the X-Men had their orders. Take Magneto down first. And Bishop was a dedicated soldier in the war for Xavier's dream. He followed orders.

''Bishop,'' Wolverine growled low, appearing at his

side. "You gotta calm down, bub. You're running so hot I can smell it like burnt rubber. We're gonna need you frosty when things get tight."

"I appreciate your concern, Wolverine," Bishop said stiffly. "But I am fine. You do not need to worry about my performance."

"That's only part of it, pal," Wolverine responded. "The X-Men take care of our own. You're wired like a junkie in sore need of a fix. Gettin' crazy could get you killed."

"Thank you," Bishop said calmly, meeting Wolverine's eyes though he had to look down at the much shorter man. "Truly, thank you. But I will be fine."

"Okay, then, enough o' this military march crap," Wolverine said, raising his voice slightly to get the attention of the Beast and Iceman, who were just off to one side.

Bishop thought it interesting that with Storm in the air, it was Wolverine who took charge rather than Hank McCoy. Then again, though McCoy was one of the most brilliant men of his time, that did not make him an exceptional warrior. Something that Wolverine undoubtedly was. In truth, Bishop did not think he had ever met another so perfectly suited for the art of war than the man they all knew only as Logan.

"We're like the Earp brothers at the OK Corral walkin' down the street like this," Wolverine said, and Bishop nodded. It had been bothering him all along that they were so vulnerable, walking along the middle of the street the way they had been.

"Magneto probably knows we're coming, but there's no reason to let him know exactly when," Wolverine continued. "For starters, let's get off Fifth. We'll head west two blocks, then south on Seventh to Times Square. Hank, Bobby, take the west side of the street. Me 'n Bishop will take the east side. And stick to the shadows when you can. The X-Men usually come in with a bang, but this situation calls for a little caution, a little stealth."

"As you suggest, Wolverine," the Beast answered. "Bobby and I will continue to track Magneto, but all readings still indicate a southerly direction."

They began to move west at 47th Street, sticking close to the buildings as Wolverine had suggested. It was going to be a bit slower going, which Bishop found cause for concern, but there was nothing to be done about it. There were only the five of them against Magneto, the Acolytes, the Sentinels, and whatever other mutants had been in New York at the time of the takeover. They had to err on the side of caution.

Bishop knew they were only going to get one shot at this.

*　*　*

The silent, muscle-bound Inuit man made his way north from Times Square, staying to the right on Seventh Avenue. Behind him, several kids, barely in their teens, raced across the neon-lit expanse of the huge intersection brandishing pistols with an abandon that he envied. No one told them what to do. If you got in their way, you were the enemy. When they shot someone, more often than not, that person would die, or at least fall down. Things were not always so cut and dried, the large man knew.

But perhaps, with Magneto making his move at long last, things were about to attain a clarity they had not had previously. Perhaps there would be more to his life than obedience and death. Or, it was possible he would merely be trading one master for another, foregoing a life with direction for one with responsibility, as he had done for so long.

His massive form was sheathed in black kevlar body armor, with a light raincoat covering that, as well as the quarrel which held a large supply of slayspears, his own personal weaponry. As projectiles, they would have been deadly on their own. But when charged with his potent, killing energy, and thrown with his extraordinarily accurate aim, they became far more effective. The man carried the burden of death heavily on his back.

Half a block further ahead, he saw the blinking sign for a club that promised "Live Girls," and knew he had reached his destination. Even as he stepped through the entrance, he could see the shattered mirrors that lined the walls of the strip club, the bare runway whose blinking lights flashed without purpose now that the "live girls" had gone.

To the right was the bar. Three familiar figures sat there, backs to him, sipping shot glasses full of whiskey in silence. None of them looked up at first, but he recognized them all just the same. The woman was Arclight, a powerhouse of a female he had never expected to see again. There was another bruiser, a huge, grossly muscled man known as Blockbuster. Finally, the third, the man who had called him here: Scalphunter. His metallic armor was festooned with gleaming steel parts which could be put together to create more than one hundred different weapons, all deadly in his hands.

Scalphunter turned from the bar and offered a chilly smile.

"I'm glad you came, Harpoon," the gleaming killer

said. "I wasn't sure if you would. But then, it's not as if we have any place better to go these days, is it?"

Harpoon grimaced. Scalphunter was right, of course. None of them had any real purpose, nor had they had any contact—at least he had not been in contact with any of them—since Mr. Sinister had disbanded the Marauders. It had amused Harpoon at the time. After all, he was a criminal. They all were. Hardcore, at that. Murderers all around, and happy to do the job at the time. But they'd been fired. How did you fire a murderer? Not as if any of them would have dared go after Sinister. The man was far more dangerous, and unpredictable, that the lot of them combined.

"Hey, 'poon! How's it hanging?" a voice cried from the back of the bar.

Harpoon spun, on guard, but relaxed as soon as he saw the blur that was fast approaching. Piles of mirror glass shards swirled and eddied in one corner as a man-sized tornado moved toward him. Harpoon smiled, both at the comparison with the Tasmanian Devil that came to mind, and in greeting. The tornado had a name, Riptide. And Riptide was a friend. The only one of the Marauders that Harpoon was glad to see. Scalphunter was a stone cold killer, but Riptide was just out of his mind.

The tornado stopped, and there he stood. Riptide was a lanky six feet, dressed in a uniform thinly striped in black and white, nearly invisible pockets hiding a multitude of throwing weapons, from knives and *shuriken* to weighted razors. He was deadly, he was crazy. But Harpoon trusted him.

"Come on, pull up a chair," Riptide said. "You look like you could use a drink."

Harpoon nodded and allowed Scalphunter to pour him a glass of whiskey. Then, as usual, he listened.

"Look, man, I ain't gonna lie to ya," Riptide said, a manic grin splitting his face. "Nobody here has any intention of going straight. I mean, we got a good thing going, and there are always going to be contract hits to fulfill, human dogs to leash, know what I'm sayin'?"

Harpoon nodded. He enjoyed the hunt, and the kill, as much as the next guy. But terror and oppression for its own sake was not his style. He did not need to debase innocent bystanders to gain pleasure, and that was perhaps the widest gulf between himself and the other Marauders. He knew it didn't make him any more moral. What was morality anyway, he thought, but rules made by the prey to keep away the predators?

But Scalphunter and the others were cruel. They toyed with their victims. Harpoon believed in immediately killing his targets, finishing the job quick and clean. He was a hunter, nothing more or less. Still, these were his former comrades. He at least owed them the time it took to hear them out.

"I can tell you're skeptical, 'poon, but just listen up, okay?" Riptide said, and Harpoon gestured for him to continue.

"We wanna get the Marauders back together," Riptide said. "And we wanna pledge allegiance to the flag of Magneto, or whatever the hell the obnoxious windbag wants us to do."

Harpoon narrowed his eyes in confusion, and Scalphunter interrupted Riptide to elaborate.

"Quiet a second, Rip," Scalphunter said. "Look, Harpoon, I know you and I ain't always been the best of friends. Still, we're gonna have a sweet deal going here pretty soon and because you always played it straight as one of the Marauders, I figured we should give you a chance to get in on it.

"Here's how it is," he continued. "Magneto's setting up a nation right here in Manhattan. Mutants are the bosses, and humans are the grunts. That means we're nobility, get it? The humans, they've gotta do whatever we tell 'em, try to get through the day while we mutants live like kings. Tell him the best part, Arclight," Scalphunter said, and Harpoon turned to where Arclight and Blockbuster had sat, speaking quietly to each other as the other tried to recruit him.

Arclight was pretty. Perhaps not beautiful, but for Harpoon, pretty was good enough. He'd always had a thing for her, and she had known it, but never showed him any real affection other than that reserved for all her teammates.

"The best part," she said, and smiled at Harpoon in a way that reminded him just why he'd been attracted to her to begin with, "is that we can take all the contracts we like outside of Manhattan, slip out, do the job, slip back in, and even if the feds or Interpol find out we were behind it, there isn't a damn thing they can do about it. There's no way Magneto will let them extradite mutants from his new empire for prosecution."

Arclight was still smiling prettily. Scalphunter was sneering his perverse pleasure. Riptide was grinning madly.

Drily, quietly, Harpoon began to laugh.

* * *

Iceman and the Beast were already half a block ahead of them at the TKTS booth that lay at the beginning of the intersection between Broadway and Seventh Avenue. Wolverine watched as they crossed over to the west side of Broadway, then slid into the darkened entrance to a fast food restaurant. A moment later, they appeared again and began to move south once more. Wolverine was impressed. He had not expected either of them to be so proficient at this kind of work. Their past histories—both with the X-Men and with the other teams the pair of them had worked with over the years—indicated a tendency toward barrelling in with guns blazing. Perhaps Logan's presence in the X-Men had rubbed off more than he'd known.

It wouldn't be long now, however, and they had to be more careful than ever. This kind of caution was time consuming, but Bobby had already said he didn't think they had more than ten or fifteen blocks to go, and there was no way to tell what kind of safeguards Magneto might have in place. No, this way was best.

Together, Wolverine and Bishop clung to the shadows on the east side of Seventh Avenue. It was going to be difficult the further they got into Times Square, with the glare of neon stripping away most of the shadows they might have used for cover. But they would do their best. As always.

With Bishop just behind him, Wolverine moved past the entrance to a strip club. From inside came the scent of stale beer and . . . people. Mutants. Familiar scents that raised the hackles on his neck. Emotions roiled within him that were so powerful he could not keep his adamantium claws from sliding out and snapping into place with a *snikt*. His nostrils flared, eyes narrowing with hatred and he reached a hand behind him to stop Bishop.

The future X-Man's only question was in his eyes. He was a good enough soldier to know when not to speak. Wolverine pointed into the strip club, then at himself, then held up a hand to let Bishop know he wanted to go in alone. There was a score to settle.

Still, he was no fool. If he'd been alone, he would have tried to settle the score alone. But he was with the X-Men, he was one of them. And what he owed the Marauders, they also owed. It was time to square a debt longstanding, but they would all be handicapped by the lack of room inside the club. Wolverine planned to draw them out into the street.

Maybe it would be like the OK Corral after all.

* * *

The Beast and Iceman moved together down Broadway. While they had seen only humans, mainly looters and hard looking teens, they didn't want to take any chances. As he scanned the streets and the buildings above for any sign of mutant activity, Hank McCoy silently wished for backup. It was a big city, quickly filling up with enemies, as if they hadn't had enough already. In his years with the X-Men, he had become known for his optimism.

Not today.

"Attention X-Men," Bishop's voice crackled from the comm-badge on his belt. "Wolverine has apparently registered the presence of some threat. He has entered an establishment here at 46th and Seventh. I expect we'll need backup."

"Then you shall have it," Storm's voice replied, and the Beast could hear the wind whipping past her, even though the volume on his comm-badge was quite low.

"Beast, you and I will backup Bishop and Wolverine," Storm continued. "Iceman, continue tracking with that remote unit, but proceed with utmost caution. We will contact you to ascertain your location as soon as we have cleared up this situation."

"Storm," the Beast asked, touching a small button on his comm-badge, "is that wise, to allow Bobby to continue alone?"

"Perhaps not, Hank," Storm's voice crackled. "But our mission must take priority. And as we don't yet know what threat Logan has discovered, we also need to provide him with as much backup as we can."

"I'll be okay, Hank," Iceman said beside him. "You can't babysit me forever."

The Beast looked up, a little taken aback by his friend's attitude, but then he saw that Bobby was merely joking, as usual. Iceman knew that of all people, the Beast was not going to underestimate his abilities. Just as Hank did not underestimate the dangers they faced.

"Watch your back," the Beast said, and Iceman only nodded before moving on.

* * *

Wolverine crouched low as he inched his way into the strip club. There was a five foot barrier between him and the bar, which kept passersby from being able to see the dancers from the street. But there were no dancers inside. Only five killers. And Wolverine made six. Thing was, compared to him, the others were amateurs.

Each of their scents was indelibly etched upon his sensory memory, and on his soul. Together, they had perpetrated one of the most horrific acts Wolverine had been witness to in all of his long life, the so-called mutant massacre. They had mercilessly slaughtered un-armed mutants, with or without powers and regardless of their political affiliation. The tunnels under New York where the mutant outcasts known as Morlocks lived had run red with innocent blood.

All the work of the Marauders. And Wolverine had waited a long time to pay them back.

"Well, well," he snarled, slipping out from behind the partition. "Ain't this a touchin' little reunion."

The Marauders responded instantly. Arclight and Blockbuster stood on alert, waiting for the signal to move from whomever was giving orders. Riptide began to spin, in a blur, but did not attack, apparently also awaiting instructions. That left Harpoon and Scalphunter, and Wolverine figured Harpoon was too quiet to be the leader. A moment later, he was proven correct.

"You just made the biggest mistake of your life, Ca-nuck," Scalphunter said, a slow smile creeping across his face. "Coming in here and getting up in our faces, all by your lonesome. Did you forget what happened a few years back? We trashed the X-Men but good, Wol-verine. All of 'em. And here you are, solo."

"Wait, Scalphunter," Harpoon said, and Wolverine was stunned to hear him talk at all, never mind that he was taking up for one of the X-Men.

"We came here for sanctuary, not for battle," Har-poon continued. "Magneto wants this to be a haven for all mutants, does he not? If we expect him to offer it to us, we cannot do this."

There was a lull in the room, as if, in that moment, nobody knew what to do. Except perhaps for Wolverine.

"I got three things to tell you murderers. First off, there's no sanctuary to be had here," he said, gnashing his teeth with every word. "Magneto's little experiment is temporary, and nobody is going to recognize him as sovereign of anything. Second, and this one goes real specific for you, Harpoon, if you're worried about whether or not you should throw down with me right here and now, well . . ."

Something happened to Wolverine's face in that momentary pause. It was not quite a smile, though it did bring a sparkle to his eye and reveal his sharp, gleaming teeth.

"Who ever said it was up to you?"

With a vengeful roar, Wolverine launched himself across the bar at Scalphunter, completely unmindful of any danger from the others. He slammed the claws on his left hand into the man's right shoulder and sparks flew as they penetrated armor and flesh and sank up to his fist. He used that hand to pin Scalphunter in place and, in the space of a heartbeat, brought his right-hand claws down toward the Marauder's heart.

Arclight grabbed his wrist before he could fulfill his murderous intentions, and as she swung him away he felt his adamantium laced bones grind. His equilibrium was momentarily shot as he sailed across the room and slammed into the wall with a thud that brought jagged shards of broken mirror crashing down behind the bar.

Wolverine was up so quickly the entire thing might have appeared to be one, fluid, intentional movement. His skeleton was laced with adamantium, otherwise his wrist would have been crushed to a pulp rather than merely bruised. One of the gifts of the x-factor in his genetic structure, part of what made him a mutant, was the extraordinary speed of his healing process. By the time he faced the Marauders again, there wasn't a cut or bruise on him.

"You're faster than you look, lady," he growled low. "I won't make that mistake again."

Scalphunter was having trouble standing, and Blockbuster went quickly to his side, helping him remain upright despite his obvious pain. Blood poured down the gleaming front of Scalphunter's armor, staining it crimson, and Wolverine smiled broadly.

"It's not as sweet when it's your own blood, is it babykiller?" he snarled.

"Kill him," Scalphunter snapped.

Harpoon let loose with an energy-charged Slayspear, and Wolverine sidestepped it. There was no way he could avoid a joint attack, however. Even as he dodged, Riptide began to spin even more rapidly, disappearing in a tornado blur out of which projectiles exploded at blinding speed. There were small knives, Japanese throwing stars called *shuriken*, and metal burrs like a child's jacks with razor sharp points.

Wolverine's claws flashed as he moved sideways in a fluidly graceful motion that, to an untrained observer, might have looked like dancing. In truth, he had been trained intensively in Japan for many years, and was a master martial artist, equally at home fighting in a bar brawl or a formal ninja honor duel. He protected himself from more than half of Riptide's weapons, despite their speed, then dove behind the partition again for cover.

"Oh, Wolverine, please," Scalphunter said, and Wolverine could hear the pain in his voice. "Why drag this thing out. Can't we just get it over with?"

"Come and get me, bub," Wolverine said, his voice low, taunting, despite his pain. His body was in overdrive, mending the wounds he'd received from Riptide, but it would take several minutes for him to fully heal. It didn't matter to him. It wouldn't be the first time he had bled on a battlefield, and it would likely be far from the last.

Even as two *shuriken* popped from his skin, driven out by his rapidly healing flesh, and plinked to the ground, he began to get impatient. Scalphunter might actually be correct. He might not be able to take them all. Not a pleasant thought, but something he had to keep in mind. Not that it meant he would have backed off under any circumstances. Just a possibility to be registered. On the other hand, he hadn't had any intention of taking the Marauders on by himself.

But time was wasting. Their mission was of primary importance, and these losers had taken up way too much time as it was.

"Come on you bunch of cowards," he snapped. "Come get me!"

"Die!" Blockbuster shouted as he charged through the wooden partition.

"There you go!" Wolverine responded, even as he crashed backward, out of the strip club and onto neon-lit Seventh Avenue. "That's the spirit."

Blockbuster was the stereotypical musclehead, all brawn, no brains. Nothing like Arclight, who was not quite as strong but a lot more dangerous. The huge mutant's fists pummeled Wolverine's gut and chest until Logan held up his left hand and simply popped his claws into Blockbuster's descending arm. The foot long adamantium blades sliced cleanly through Blockbuster's bicep, but the momentum of the punch pulled down on the claws, ripping through meat and bone.

With an agonized howl, Blockbuster fell back away from Wolverine and curled up on the ground cradling his thrashed arm. Blood ran freely from his wounds onto the pavement. Wolverine remembered the blood that had splattered the walls of the Morlock tunnels after the mutant massacre, and he felt good as he rose to his feet.

Scalphunter emerged from the club, a long, silver plasma rifle pointed at Wolverine's head. Harpoon rushed out beside him and held a Slayspear at the ready. Riptide spun onto the street like the Tasmanian Devil, tossing old beer cans and empty paper bags into a dervish around him, cackling madly. Arclight went to crouch by Blockbuster, to comfort him, and glared at Wolverine.

"You're dead," she said.

"Arc, get away from him," Scalphunter said. "No more weakness, no more individual attacks. All together, now, and we'll dance on the little runt's corpse."

"Sorry, bub, it'll take more than your lot to kill me," Wolverine said. "And you don't pay attention too good anyway. I said there were three things I had to tell you. The third was, I didn't come alone."

Scalphunter's eyes widened in alarm, and Wolverine snorted derisively.

Lightning flashed and Wolverine squinted against the sudden brightness. The air sizzled with energy between himself and Scalphunter as lightning struck the ground, leaving cracked and melted pavement in its wake. Above them, Storm hovered on the winds at her command, imperious as always. Wolverine loved that about Ororo. Proud yet quiet on the ground, once in her element, she took control of any situation with ease.

"The Marauders!" Storm observed. "Now, Wolverine, I see why you diverted from your course. We should not take the time for battle here, but the need for vengeance is undeniable. Also, if there is any chance at all that Magneto is unaware of our approach, we cannot allow these mass murderers to go free.''

''While you talk, Storm, you die!'' Scalphunter shouted, and lifted his plasma rifle to aim at the spot where Storm floated aloft.

Wolverine was about to dive forward, to slice Scalphunter's weapons, and perhaps the man himself. He had barely turned away when he heard Arclight moving in behind him. He spun and slashed, and caught her a glancing blow that scored the mesh alloy metal armor she wore. He had noted her speed earlier, and vowed not to let her surprise him with it again. She had tried and failed, but her real goal had been to distract him from saving Storm. In that, she had succeeded.

When Wolverine turned back toward Scalphunter, the leader of the Marauders was already pulling the trigger.

Suddenly, a blast of energy slammed into Scalphunter's chest. His shot went wild, completely missing Storm, and he was knocked to the ground. Two more energy blasts ripped into him, and Scalphunter shook and jittered with some kind of seizure as blue light rippled back and forth across his body. Wolverine looked up and saw Bishop taking aim at the other Marauders, and his nostrils flared with a low growl that built into a great roar.

The biggest threat, without question, was Riptide. He began whirling ever faster, and razor sharp projectiles flew from the dervish he had become. But before they could reach their intended targets, they were whipped up into an even greater storm, a minor tornado that seemed to suck both the weapons and Riptide into itself. As he blocked a Slayspear that Harpoon had hurled at his chest, Wolverine noticed that the tornado Storm had created was spinning counter to Riptide's own turns. It effectively cancelled out his powers, for no matter how he tried to turn, Storm kept the wind moving in the other direction. In essence, he was hung in midair, completely immobile in the center of a tornado.

With one shot, Bishop took Riptide down.

Harpoon aimed a Slayspear at Bishop, and Wolverine shouted to warn him of the danger. Bishop turned and ran directly at Harpoon, screaming like a madman. Harpoon hurled a Slayspear and Bishop incinerated it in mid-air with his blaster. Wolverine moved in on Harpoon as well, and in a moment, the two X-Men had the Marauder trapped between them.

"Your move, Harpoon," Wolverine growled.

With fantastic speed, Harpoon drew another Slayspear from behind him and hurled it at Bishop, who brought up his weapon as protection. The spear struck the gun, discharging its deadly energy, and the gun exploded, knocking Bishop back several paces.

"You still stand?" Harpoon said in astonishment.

Wolverine hung back on purpose, knowing what was to come. Bishop had not been with the X-Men at the time of the mutant massacre. To the Marauders, he was an unknown quantity. Bishop's mutant power allowed him to absorb any form of energy directed at him and release it with destructive force from his bare hands. Harpoon had no idea what to expect, but he pulled another Slayspear from his quarrel and hauled back his arm to hurl it at Bishop.

Bishop didn't give him the chance. He had absorbed

the energy from his weapon's explosion and Harpoon's Slayspear, and now he rechanneled it, turning it back upon the Marauder who, even now, was attempting to kill him. A blast of crackling green power burst from Bishop's fists and buffeted Harpoon's body like hurricane winds, tossing him backward through the blacked out plate glass window of the strip club.

Harpoon did not come out, and Wolverine scanned the street for more opposition.

"This fracas is gettin' downright boring!" Wolverine shouted. "Maybe you killers just don't know when you're beat."

"You want a fight, Wolverine?" Arclight asked as she closed in on him. "Then stop moving out of the way."

"I can take whatever you got, lady, and then some," Wolverine growled, sliding the claws of his left hand against those of his right, creating a chilling sound like six knives being sharpened.

"Come now, Wolverine, you must allow your adorable hirsuite amigo the opportunity for some merriment as well," the Beast said as he leaped between Logan and Arclight.

"After all," Hank added, "I was there in the Morlock tunnels as well. I have some demons of remembrance to excise."

There was a look of smoldering fury on Hank McCoy's blue-furred face that filled Wolverine with uncommon wonder. The Beast was the ever rational core of the X-Men, a good-hearted man who functioned on a practical, intellectual level most of the time. But not, apparently, all of the time.

Quickly, the memory of his run in with Arclight mere

moments ago came back to Wolverine, and it hit him that the Beast did not have his unbreakable adamantium bones. If she got a hand on him, Hank could be in serious trouble. And she was fast.

"Hank, maybe you'd better . . ." Wolverine began, but too late.

Arclight lunged for the Beast, the way a wrestler would, but Hank simply stepped aside and slapped her on the side of the head, knocking her down.

"Come on, then, hit me," the Beast said, tauntingly. "As politically incorrect as it may seem—brand me a sexist if you wish—I would never ordinarily pummel a woman. But when it comes to someone who slaughters innocent people, innocent children, I'll make an exception."

"Aren't I lucky," Arclight sneered with sarcasm and contempt, then swung a large fist at the Beast's face.

Hank caught Arclight's fist in his own.

"Decidedly not," he answered, and slugged her hard in the face.

Arclight's legs collapsed beneath her. If the Beast had not been holding on to her hand, she would have crumbled to the ground. Arclight was a big woman, and with her armor on must have weighed close to two fifty. Hank picked her up, and without any visible effort, hurled her across the street where her body knocked a hole in the outer wall of an electronics store. She lay, unmoving, half in and half out of the hole.

When the Beast turned to face Wolverine, he was not smiling.

"I've heard revenge is sweet," he said quietly. "That was a lie, wasn't it?"

"Revenge doesn't help anyone, Hank," Wolverine

answered. "It's just something that needs doin'."

Storm and Bishop approached slowly, on guard for any other members of the Marauders team.

"You can relax," Wolverine said. "It was just the five of them."

"Then let us secure these miscreants and move on," Storm decided. "We're wasting time."

"And we must catch up with Iceman," Beast reminded her. "The Marauders are not likely to be the only old enemies of the X-Men roaming around Manhattan tonight. I'm beginning to think letting him go on alone was a mistake."

CHAPTER 8

LEONARDI & austin

The conference room was vast and ornate. The door and window frames, and the twenty-foot mahogany table were hand carved with elaborate floral designs. The high-backed chairs were upholstered with burgundy leather. There was a portrait on the wall of a man none of them recognized, but it was clear he was responsible for the splendor around them. The other wall was covered floor to ceiling with shelf after shelf of legal texts.

This, Amelia Voght thought, *is the world that might have been mine had I not been born a mutant.* She had rejected the pursuit of wealth and privilege as measured by human standards, and had instead decided to fight for acceptance on an individual level, for who and what she was. When acceptance was not forthcoming, she realized that obedience might be easier to obtain. To achieve that, she become one of Magneto's Acolytes.

They sat around the conference room, and Amelia thought that almost all of them looked as uncomfortable in that opulence as she felt. Perhaps only Senyaka, whose background was a mystery to her, seemed at home there. The only ones missing were Javitz, who was still injured and whom Amelia sorely missed, and Scanner and Milan, both of whom Magneto had constant use for in the rapid construction of his new empire. Scanner was needed for communication and to pinpoint mutant bio-signatures as they approached Magneto's new headquarters. Milan, of course, was online and had become the nerve center of the empire, as well as the monitor for media and other transmissions.

That left Cargil, Senyaka, the Kleinstock brothers, and Unuscione. There were a dozen empty seats around the table, but Unuscione had taken the one with the tallest

back, at the head of the table. As field leader, Amelia
Voght had every right to that chair, and she knew without a doubt that Unuscione had taken it with every intention of rubbing it in her face.

Amelia ignored her, choosing instead to stand at the
opposite end of the table. Their conflict, as they silently
confronted one another across that expanse of wood, had
never seemed more clear.

"Okay, let's get down to business," Voght said.
"Dawn isn't far off, and Magneto has asked that we
forget about policing the city for the rest of the night.
Things have calmed down some for now anyway. People
are likely waiting to see who ends up on top."

"Aren't we all," Unuscione commented drily, and it
was clear to Voght that the woman wasn't talking about
the Empire Agenda at all.

"There were plenty of mutants in the city already, and
more are coming in by the hour," Amelia continued.
"The Sentinels have logged and identified most of them,
and it's only a matter of time before they show up here.
Magneto also believes that we'll see an even larger wave
in the morning."

"So do we finally get some sleep, then?" Harlan
Kleinstock asked gruffly.

Amelia shot him a withering look and shook her head.

"Sadly, no," she answered. "We've got a few more
important things to deal with just at the moment.
Namely, the X-Men."

"Those buffoons," Unuscione scoffed. "I was wondering when they'd show their faces. Don't worry,
Harlan, you'll be sleeping like a baby come dawn."

"I wouldn't be so quick to laugh them off, Unuscione," Amelia said, unable to stop herself. "You were,

if I recall, defeated by Iceman, were you not? And isn't he supposed to be the weak link in that team?''

"Don't start with me you bitch!'' Unuscione shrieked, leaping up from her chair and starting along the table toward Amelia.

Senyaka and Cargil were up immediately, holding her back. More accurately, she allowed them to hold her back, as her psionic exoskeleton could have tossed them both aside like rag dolls if she so chose.

"You cross me one more time—'' Unuscione continued, but Amelia cut her off.

"Do *not* presume to threaten me, girl,'' Amelia said, loading each word with menace. "Magneto has made me field leader of the Acolytes and until such time as he chooses to revoke that title, you will follow my commands as you would his.''

"And if I do not?'' Unuscione asked defiantly.

"If you do not, then Magneto will never have the opportunity to correct you, for I will have disciplined you myself,'' Amelia said curtly. "It is not something you would enjoy.''

"For all your talk, Voght, you have ever been the softest of us,'' Unuscione said smugly as she sat back down. "Do not think your laughable new rank changes that a bit.''

"For the last time, keep silent,'' Voght said.

This time, Unuscione acquiesced.

"The Sentinels have recorded the entrance into New York of five members of the X-Men aboard the same *Blackbird* jet they used as transport to Colorado,'' she began. "While the Sentinels could not be spared to confront, or even trail, the X-Men, we have independent confirmation that the *Blackbird* landed in Central Park and was abandoned there.''

"How the hell do they think they'll find us?'' Cargil asked. "Unless they brought Professor Xavier with them.''

"Xavier is not in Manhattan,'' Voght responded. "These are the same five we dealt with so unsuccessfully in Colorado—''

"Speak for yourself, Voght,'' Senyaka snapped. "We did just fine against the X-Men.''

"We outnumbered them, Senyaka, but they handed us our heads,'' Amelia corrected. "If not for Magneto, we'd be in federal custody right now, heading for the Vault. Of course, the situation is a little different now. We've got Magneto *and* the Sentinels on our side, not to mention all the new recruits that are pouring in even as we speak.''

"What I want to know,'' said Sven Kleinstock, "is where are the rest of the X-Men? I mean, there's at least ten of them, not even counting the various other mutants that are part of their little clique. Do you think this could be a setup?''

"Maybe it is,'' Amelia admitted. "Magneto supposed just that. But even if they do have reserves on hand, they aren't in Manhattan already or we'd know about it.''

"Unless there's some new recruits that you don't know are part of the X-Men,'' Cargil suggested. "That'd be just the kind of thing they'd pull.''

"Enough chit-chat,'' Amelia said finally. "We've got our marching orders. The X-Men have got to be on their way here. Lightning was just spotted in Times Square, and it's a clear night otherwise. That's got to be Storm.

Unuscione, you and Cargil will take Magneto's first recruits out to find the X-Men, while the rest of us remain behind and cover the building's lobby.''

"You've gotta be kidding," Unuscione spat. "The two of us and a couple of rookies up against the X-Men?''

"If you miss them, or they defeat you, the rest of us will be here to capture them when they reach the building," Amelia explained, then allowed a small smile to turn up the corners of her mouth. "Unless, of course," she teased, "you don't think you can handle it?"

"You bitch!" Unuscione screamed. "You're setting me up for a fall."

Amelia sniffed dismissively. "That's what I thought you'd say."

"What the hell is that supposed to mean?" Unuscione demanded.

"You're a smart girl," Amelia said. "You'll figure it out."

"That's it!" Unuscione screamed, and used her high leather chair to stomp onto the mahogany table. With a loud, almost melodic hum, her psionic exoskeleton seemed to burst from her body in a three dimensional spray of green light. It enveloped her in a square-edged armor of energy that changed its shape to fulfill her every whim.

"It's time you were taught a lesson about how you speak to your betters!" Unuscione declared, and began to stomp toward Amelia with murder in her eyes.

"All right, you little brat," Amelia spat, "you've been living off your Daddy's reputation for way too long. And he wasn't much to speak of in the end, was he?"

SANCTUARY

"You're gonna die, Voght!" Unuscione roared, and her psionic exoskeleton lifted huge glowing arms and brought them down to crush Amelia with their power.

But Amelia wasn't there. At the last instant, she teleported out of the way, and appeared behind Unuscione. To one side, the Kleinstocks, infantile as they were, began to snicker, giving her away. A battering ram of psionic energy shot out from Unuscione's back and slammed Amelia hard against the wall. Her breath was knocked out of her, but she teleported again. When she reappeared, she stood next to Unuscione, just beyond the electric green shell that protected the other Acolyte.

"You idiot!" Unuscione cried with delight. "Do you want to die?"

Unuscione reached out and huge psionic energy hands wrapped themselves around Amelia's throat, and began to squeeze. Stars exploded in Amelia's head as she instinctively fought for air. But this was what she wanted, to have Unuscione so close. The other woman was merciless and would pound an enemy to gory pulp without blinking an eye. But this close, Amelia had wagered that Unuscione would not be able to resist a more intimate attack, and she had been correct.

That was all Amelia needed, to get her hands on Unuscione's exoskeleton.

Struggling to keep from suffocating, even as Unuscione gloated and, more than likely, prepared to break her neck, Amelia slapped her hands over the monstrous psionic energy fingers that choked her.

Then she teleported.

As she reappeared, Unuscione was screaming, her psionic exoskeleton being drawn back into her in tattered ribbons. On top of the mahogany table, Unuscione doubled over in pain, holding her hands tight against her chest.

"What have you done?" she screamed.

"I've hurt you," Amelia said softly, as she stepped toward Unuscione, still on top of the table. Around her, the other Acolytes stared at her in astonishment, as if she had suddenly become a total stranger to them. And in a way she had. None of them had ever really thought of her as a powerful or dangerous woman. Just transportation. That was about to change.

"I've hurt you bad, I hope," Amelia whispered as she crouched by Unuscione, who knelt now, still holding her hands to her stomach. "I took hold of your exoskeleton and I teleported part of it away."

"You what?" Unuscione asked, her face red with pain and fury. She began to get unsteadily back to her feet.

"I stole a piece of you," Amelia said coldly. "I might just as easily have taken your head and teleported away with that. But Magneto would not have been pleased. I hope it hurt. A part of you is gone forever, though I don't suppose it will prevent you from using your powers.

"Now," Amelia continued, leaning in to speak through clenched teeth, even as Unuscione finally stood straight and tall once more, "you will not question my orders again. Is that clear?"

"Crystal!" Unuscione said, and slammed her fist into Amelia's face with such force that Amelia fell back and rolled off the table. Cargil sidestepped to get out of the way, even as Unuscione dove at her.

"I don't need my power to defeat you!" Unuscione screamed. "I'll kill you with my bare hands!"

SANCTUARY

Amelia stood quickly and moved into a fighting stance. Unuscione came for her and Amelia ducked her blow, brought up her left leg and kicked the other woman three times in quick succession, twice in the face and once in the chest, sending Unuscione stumbling backward.

"Care to try that again?" Amelia asked, and was astounded when it appeared Unuscione was going to take her up on it. For the first time, she began to worry that she would have to kill the other woman to defeat her. Magneto would be sorely displeased, but she knew that if that was what it took, if she had no other choice, then she would do just that.

Unuscione charged at her, roaring. Amelia readied for the assault, just as Magneto entered the room.

"Enough!" Magneto commanded. He lifted his hands and Amelia felt herself plucked from the ground by his magnetic power, as if she were nothing more substantial than a child's doll. Unuscione also was lifted from her feet, and the two women glowered at one another as Magneto slowly lowered them back to the floor on opposite sides of the table.

"I trust, Voght, that this is the 'conversation' that you had planned to have with Unuscione, and that it is now over," Magneto said evenly as he looked first at Amelia, and then Unuscione. "However, in the unlikely event that there are any among us here who still do not understand, let me make something completely and ultimately clear.

"Regarding field excursions, or any battle situation where I am not present and specifically in command, Amelia Voght's orders will be noted and obeyed by each and every one of my Acolytes," Magneto said, meeting their eyes one by one and finally letting his admonishing gaze rest on Unuscione. "Should I learn otherwise, should any one of you balk at these instructions, you will be severely chastised. If that is not completely clear, speak up now, and I will try to say it more plainly."

No one spoke. Though Amelia was tempted to smile, she fought the urge. Though there was satisfaction in her victory over Unuscione and Magneto's rebuke, the Empire Agenda took precedence over all individual concerns. Magneto seemed to think Amelia above such petty things as vengeance, and she did not want to give him reason to think otherwise. Not that it would matter. She had no doubt that her conflict with Unuscione was far from over. The woman had been humiliated in front of her comrades. No matter what Magneto said, Unuscione was stubborn and ignorant enough to seek revenge.

Frankly, Amelia was glad. If she didn't kill Unuscione first, Magneto would get around to it eventually. Unuscione would leave him no choice.

"Now that I have your attention," Magneto said, some of the tension leaving his face, "I would like to introduce you to three new Acolytes, the first to be recruited from the growing mutant population of Manhattan. Two of them have fought at my side before, and were, in fact, well acquainted with your father, Unuscione. While we have had our differences in the past, I am pleased to welcome them, and their ally, to their new home."

Magneto stepped aside, lifting his hand with a dramatic flair that Amelia was surprised to discover in him.

"Mortimer Toynbee, alias, the Toad," Magneto said, by way of introduction. The man who entered the room then was familiar to Amelia only by way of his reputation. The Toad was perhaps five and a half feet tall, though it was difficult to tell for certain from the way he crouched. His posture and his face both reminded Amelia of Quasimodo, for Toynbee was far from handsome. Though his super-powerful legs allowed him to leap great heights and distances, they were also perfectly suited for murder.

Once an object of ridicule, the Toad had developed a new reputation of late, that of a merciless criminal who loved nothing more than to bring pain to his enemies. Amelia was surprised, to say the very least. She knew for certain that Exodus, the guardian of space station Avalon, had rejected the Toad from the list of candidates for citizenship on Avalon for various reasons including his deviousness and doubts about his potential loyalty.

That Magneto would take him in now only served to further illustrate two things that Amelia had come to understand only recently. The first was that Exodus did not necessarily know Magneto's every whim. The second was that Magneto's plans for his mutant empire on Earth were far more vast than his original concept for Avalon.

And if the Toad were here, Amelia could guess who was next in line. For Toynbee rarely went anywhere in recent years without . . .

"Frederick J. Dukes, alias the Blob," Magneto announced.

Just as Amelia had suspected, and yet, having never actually met Dukes, she was stunned by the size of the man. To get inside the room, the Blob was forced to duck his head and lean the top of his body through the door, then turn sideways and shuffle the rest of his bulk to squeeze through the frame. Dukes must have been nearly eight feet tall and Amelia judged by his sheer girth that he might weigh as much as nine hundred or one thousand pounds. He was incredibly strong, and according to his modern myth, immovable. If the Blob was in your way, you weren't going anywhere.

Immediately upon entering the room, the Blob set his gaze upon Unuscione, who seemed to shudder visibly at his attention.

"You're her, ain't'cha?" the Blob asked. "I can tell just by lookin' at ya. You're Carmela Unuscione. I knew yer father, chippie. Me an' him was buddies. He was a hell of a guy. Just thought you'd like to know that."

"I, uh," Unuscione began, stumbling for a response as she looked around at the questioning glances of her comrades. Amelia Voght knew that she herself was staring, watching for some sign of a heart and soul in a woman she believed had none.

"Thanks," was all Unuscione said, but the Blob, Dukes, merely nodded in response.

Amelia was fascinated. It seemed Unuscione had a heart after all, or at least had had one until her father's death. As far as Amelia could see, the only thing the other woman cherished was the memory of Angelo Unuscione, the man who had become known as Unus the Untouchable.

"Finally," Magneto continued, "their long-time partner, a man not very familiar to me, but whom I am certain will come to be a great asset to our cause, St. John Allerdyce. More commonly known as Pyro."

Amelia had seen Pyro on television, back when he and the Blob were both members of Freedom Force. Of the three new arrivals, she believed he would be the most effective within the Acolytes' already-established battle etiquette. The man's curly blond hair flowed over the top of his mask, as bright in the dark room as the nearly gaudy yellow and red costume he wore. He was relatively tall, nearly six feet, but rail thin, almost sickly looking. Still, he didn't have to fight with his mastery of fire. Pyro had a reputation for flash and braggadacio, but Amelia had an idea he could back it up.

"Right, then, 'ello there all," Pyro said, his Australian accent obvious but not overpowering.

Cargil stepped forward.

"It's a pleasure to meet you, Mr. Allerdyce," Cargil said, with more warmth than Amelia had ever seen her exhibit or, in truth, ever believed she might possess. "My name's Joanna Cargil, and I've read all your novels. I really enjoyed them, but I wish you hadn't stopped writing."

"Me, too, love," Pyro said, his charm nearly tangible. "But, y'know, things 'ave been a bit busy lately."

Cargil and Pyro laughed together, and Amelia shook her head in amazement. She thought about all the other mutants who were swarming in and around Manhattan at that moment, about the potential for power that existed if they were all to actually join together under Magneto's banner. Finally, it struck her.

Magneto was not merely attempting to create a mutant empire.

In effect, he already had.

• • •

The Beast had been gone only a few moments when Bobby Drake decided he didn't want to walk anymore. What was the point of being Iceman if he didn't take advantage of the few perks his powers offered? At least, that's the way Bobby figured it.

With barely a conscious thought, an ice platform grew beneath his feet, and Bobby stopped walking. He drew in the moisture from the air around him and froze it beneath that platform. By constantly replenishing it, he propelled himself along. Bobby called this mode of travel his "ice slide," but in truth, he wasn't sliding at all, merely standing still and letting his powers do their job. His speed depended upon his level of concentration and effort, and he had yet to test its upper limits. For now, he was in no rush. The other X-Men were supposed to catch up with him, and he did not feel any overwhelming desire to face Magneto on his own.

Bobby's eyes flicked back and forth from the horizon to the mini-Cerebro tracking unit he held in his icy fingers. He was the runt of the litter as it was; the last thing he needed was to slam himself into some building because he wasn't paying attention. Yet he found it difficult not to stare at the digitized face of the tracking unit. Mutant energy signatures were recognized by Cerebro and signified on the tracker as blinking green dots. Since they had landed in Central Park, the number of green dots on the screen had increased dramatically.

But what drew Bobby's attention so powerfully was the red tinge that glowed at the top of the screen. While the original Cerebro unit, back at the Xavier Institute, had the energy signature of every known mutant programmed into it, the mini-tracker had space only for one target signature at any given time. They had, of course, programmed it to track Magneto in particular, and mutants in general. The red glow told Bobby what direction to go in order to locate Magneto. At least, until they got within a certain range. Then . . .

The tracker emitted a low, quick beep. Bobby ducked to avoid getting clotheslined by a flagpole that jutted from the granite face of an aging hotel, then looked down at the tracker. The red tinge was gone. Instead, near the center of the top of the screen, a single dot blinked a glowing red in a sea of green dots.

"Magneto," Bobby whispered, slowing his progress and finally coming to a halt. He stood on a beam of ice twenty feet above the pavement, staring at the screen of the tracker.

"What now?" he asked himself, aloud. The answer was quick in coming: not a damn thing. He was going to contact the other X-Men on his comm-badge and then sit and wait for them to join him before he moved another foot. Bobby Drake may have acted the fool at times, but he assured himself at that moment that he was not fool enough to dare Magneto's defenses on his own.

Bobby sighed and looked around for a relatively inconspicuous place to wait. There was a sudden electric crackle, like mosquitoes frying in one of those backyard bug zappers his parents always had back home. But it was the sound of something else, too, something it took him a moment to recognize.

"Unuscione!" he called, making her name a curse.

Iceman dove from his ice slide even as the vicious Acolyte slammed an extension of her psionic exoskeleton down on the spot where he'd stood a moment earlier. The ice shattered into a thousand glittering shards and rained down with him as he fell. Utilizing his years of training with the X-Men, in the Danger Room and in real battle as well, Bobby tucked his legs beneath him and spun around in midair. When he thrust his legs out again, he had already created another ice slide beneath them.

This time, it carried him away at a great clip. He had blown the X-Men's presence in Manhattan by allowing Unuscione to get the jump on him. He had . . .

"Whoa, camel," Bobby muttered to himself as his escape slowed.

Unuscione had attacked him alone. He'd beaten her in Colorado the previous evening, and he could do it again if she was by herself. And if he could catch up with her before she reported back to Magneto, they might still make a surprise attack.

Already, he had made a U-turn and was speeding back to the spot where Unuscione had attacked him, glancing warily from side to side.

"You've come back?" Unuscione asked in astonishment, and shook her head with amusement. She stood in the center of the street, as if it were high noon in an old Western town. "You've got more guts than I would have given you credit for, Drake."

"Not at all," Iceman said as he slid down to the pavement to stand opposite her, fulfilling the western shootout image he had concocted. "In fact, considering how badly I whupped your ass about twelve hours ago, I'd say you were the one showing surprising courage."

"Arrogant fool," she sneered, and then Bobby heard that frying insect noise again and tendrils of green energy shot from Unuscione's body, quickly forming a force field of armor around her. "You're going to die here, and you're making jokes?"

"Why are people always trying to kill me?" Bobby asked whimsically. "I'm such a nice guy."

"Nice guys finish last, Drake," another female voice said, off to his left.

Bobby turned to see who had spoken and Unuscione chose that moment of distraction to attack. He leaped out of the way of her blow just in time, but looked up only to see the Acolyte called Cargil, an attractive, muscular black woman with a killer right hook, racing toward him.

"Oh, please," Bobby said.

His confidence was growing. Bobby had defeated Cargil before as well. If he could keep the two of them distracted for a couple moments, he thought he might actually be able to beat both of them simultaneously. Iceman froze the ground in Cargil's path, and the woman's feet slipped out from under her. Her weight and momentum sent her sliding out of control, and Bobby whipped up an ice shield that acted as a curved ramp, turning and lifting Cargil until she was flying through the air, directly at Unuscione.

Unuscione wasn't playing games, however. With her psionic exoskeleton, she batted Cargil out of the air. Her fellow Acolyte was sent sprawling several yards away, where she landed hard.

"Oh, Drake, I do so wish I was behind you right now," Unuscione said, and snickered in a way Bobby found extremely unattractive.

"Right here? In front of everyone?" he laughed.

"Not at all," she sneered. "You're not my type. I'd just love to see your face when you turn around."

I'm not going to fall for it, he vowed. I'm not going to . . .

"Oh, hell," he said, and chanced a quick glance behind him.

He couldn't even get an ice shield up in time to block the Toad's attack. The little man, whom Bobby had always despised, leaped toward him and slammed his feet into Bobby's chest. Something cracked in there, and Bobby hoped it was only ice as he sailed backward across the street. He slammed through a picture window, and was immediately on his feet, despite the pain in his chest.

With one instant of concentration, he melted and refroze whatever had snapped within him. One of the benefits of being made out of ice. He hesitated to think what might happen if he was ever really shattered, but he couldn't help entertaining the thought at the moment. For the Toad wasn't alone. As Bobby stepped back into the street, he faced five opponents.

He might have been able to beat Unuscione and Frenzy. He might have been able to beat the Toad as well. But the Blob and Pyro too? Not a chance in hell.

Miraculously, he had held on to the tracking unit and he quickly thumbed the comm-link button from his badge, which he had affixed to the tracker rather than to his icy self.

"Iceman to X-Men," he said swiftly. "We've got a problem."

"Ah, ah, ah," Pyro said, his cockiness and his Australian accent grating on Bobby's nerves as always. "We'll have none o' that."

The mini-Cerebro unit melted in his hands from a burst of Pyro's flame. Bobby whipped up an ice shield to protect himself, and then thought better of it. He let the shield drop, then poured on a barrage of icy projectiles. Pyro had no problem melting them, but it at least would keep the man busy while Bobby thought of something else.

Then he had it! If he could just freeze the flame thrower units on Pyro's back, there wouldn't be any fire for the madman to control.

Which would have been fine, he realized, if he were only fighting Pyro.

Unuscione's psionic exoskeleton expanded, lifting a huge electric green arm to crush him where he stood. Bobby could have stopped her, could have frozen the air inside her exoskeleton again, but that would have left him open to attack from Pyro. He leaped clear, but when he looked up, the Toad was already there. The troll-like mutant kicked him in the face, and Bobby stumbled backward, a ringing in his head.

Cargil and Unuscione were behind him, Pyro and the Toad in front. He tried to slide out from between them, and ran directly into the blubbery belly of the Blob. Fred Dukes grabbed Iceman by the arms and lifted him off the ground. Dukes was huge; Bobby had forgotten exactly how huge. There was no way to move him.

"Let go!" Bobby shouted, and froze the moisture over the Blob's eyes.

Fred Dukes screamed, and dropped Iceman to the pavement. Even as he turned to face the others, Bobby knew he'd lost. Cargil's fist connected with his face, and Bobby Drake hit the pavement with a crack.

For a moment, the Iceman stared up at his enemies, and then the night melted away into a deeper darkness. After that, there was nothing.

Chapter 9

The moon shone brightly over Jackson Square, in the French Quarter of New Orleans. Cathedral bells rang and the smell of chicory coffee wafted out over the cobblestone street. It all seemed to hit Jean Grey at once, as if waking up from a dream, or entering one. An old sax man on the corner played Dave Brubeck's "Take Five." The clip-clop of hooves drew her attention to the horse-drawn carriages nearby.

Jean couldn't see yet just what it was, but something was missing. Something was disturbingly not right about the scene around her. Still, she could not afford to delay. She had one goal in coming here, and that was to discover whether Gambit had suffered any permanent neurological damage from his electrocution, or from Archangel's paralyzing wing-knives.

As she walked down Decatur Street, Jean peered into narrow alleyways, scanning the darkness, searching for Gambit. She heard the slap of her own boots on the pavement, smelled spicy Cajun cooking from a nearby restaurant, and was momentarily startled when a street-corner brass band launched into "When the Saints Go Marchin' In."

A radio blared the Neville Brothers "Fiyo on the Bayou" from a small barber shop, perhaps to counter-program against the brass band, who were rather sloppy, truth be told. On the sidewalk in front of the barber, a wizened old black man sat on a rocking chair. His eyes met Jean's and, though he didn't wave or nod or even smile, there was a twinkle of a greeting there that made her feel a little more solid, a little less surreal.

Other than the barber, for Jean assumed it was he, there were very few people on the street. A handful of folks going about their business, though it was relatively early in the evening. Then it hit her, what had been missing before, what had bothered her. She took a close look at a couple walking by, hand in hand, swaying drunkenly but determined to remain linked together. A bespectacled old woman with an ugly hat and patched canvas bag rode by on a bicycle. Up ahead, a pair of slim dangerous-looking men conversed at the mouth of an alley.

They were all locals. There were no tourists here, though New Orleans was a city that thrived on tourism.

One of the dangerous men up ahead turned slightly to one side, and in the darkness Jean could see the glint of red in his eyes, like flaming coals burned in their sockets. It was Gambit, but not Gambit. He was not in costume, did not even have the long brown duster that she had come to associate with him. No, this was not Gambit but Remy LeBeau, the man inside her comrade in the X-Men. This was Remy LeBeau of the New Orleans Thieves Guild, whose reputation preceded him into every back room in New Orleans Parish. Thief, rogue, troubleshooter, troublemaker.

Remy noticed her, finally. Quickly, he grabbed the elbow of the man he was speaking with, a man who seemed familiar to Jean though she could not see his face. The two of them disappeared into the darkened alley, and Jean quickened her steps to catch up with them.

She turned the corner into the alley, never slowing. There was movement ahead, in the darkness, and she followed. She had nothing to lose now. He knew she was here.

"Remy," she said, finally speaking, "I need to talk to you."

Then the darkness swallowed her, an inky blackness that seemed to wash over the alley, making brick walls and trash dumpsters disappear into an ebony void.

"Remy?" she asked the dark. "Why are you doing this?"

Receiving no answer, Jean knew that her only hope of finding Gambit was finding the light again. She turned back the way she had come and began to run, paying no mind to the trash cans and other refuse she knew would be underfoot. She heard something behind her, and stopped short.

"Jean," she heard Remy say, directly over her shoulder.

She turned, and enough light had come back so she could see again. Remy stood there, in costume now, fully suited up in the garb he had worn from the day Storm first brought him to the X-Men. He held his bo-stick in front of him casually, but she knew how quick he was with the weapon.

That knowledge didn't save her. Gambit lunged quickly, bringing the stick up in a diagonal blow that struck her across the forehead with a solid thud. Jean fell.

* * *

Jean Grey's eyes snapped open and her head rocked back as if the blow had been real. And in a sense, it had been. A blow struck on the astral plane, even by one who was not an adept in such areas, could often be as painful as a flesh and blood attack.

She looked down at Gambit's prone form in surprise.

Almost as if on cue, his eyelids began to flutter. For the first time since he had been electrocuted on the planet Hala, Remy LeBeau was truly awake.

"Well done, Jeannie," Archangel said behind her. "He's out of it."

"Jean . . ." Gambit croaked, his voice low and gruff from unuse.

Jean bent closer to hear what he had to say, her ear only inches from his lips.

"What is it, Remy?" she asked tenderly.

"Keep outta my head, *chere*," he rasped. "Girl could get hurt in dere."

Then his eyes closed again. This time, however, Jean knew that Gambit was merely sleeping. He would recover completely, would in all likelihood have no more physical problems than a little stiffness when he awoke again. His mind was fine as well, as healthy as ever. But there was clearly something, or any number of things, he desired to keep private, even on a subconscious level.

Jean felt a little guilty, though she had acted only out of the most benevolent motivations. She felt like she had been prying. At the same time, she could not help but be curious about the secrets that Gambit kept hidden from them all. She considered these things for a moment, or two. Then Corsair interrupted her thoughts, and their dire situation erased any thought of Gambit. His secrets were his to keep once again.

"Jean," he said, and she turned to face him, noting as she always did the similar features Chris and Scott Summers shared, a similarity only she had noticed the first time they had all met.

"What is it, Corsair?" she asked. "How is Hepzibah?"

"Recovering nicely, thanks," he answered. "In fact, she'll be up in a short while. Raza's another story, though. His arm's out of commission for a while. And you, how's your head?"

"It hurts, but I'm fine," she assured him. "What's happening outside?"

Corsair sighed, his lips pressing together to form a slim line of regret.

"It's not good, Jean," he said finally. "Ch'od and I have been talking to Scott over the comm-link, and we all agree that there's only one way we're going to get out of here."

"We're not going to like this, are we Corsair?" Archangel asked grimly, standing by Jean and placing a firm hand on her shoulder. Jean was glad Warren was there. The nearness of friends always added strength.

"No more than I do, Warren," Corsair answered. "The warp drive is completely trashed. We're not going to get it going again. If the sun doesn't fry us in this big tin can before then, our life support systems are going to run out eventually, and we'll all suffocate on our own breath in here. I've done some tinkering in the back, and despite the fire before, the hyperburners seem to be functional . . ."

"That's great!" Archangel said, obviously elated. "So what's the problem?"

"The computer is fried is the first problem," Corsair explained.

"Isn't there a way to repair that connection outside?" Jean asked, still not understanding what the problem was.

"That's what we've been trying to do, that's what Raza and the others were doing when we had that misfire,'' Corsair explained. "It's a no go. And now that additional damage has been done, we can't even jump-start the hyperburn engines from the outside.''

"So, in essence what you're telling us is that the engines are working fine, we just can't get them to start,'' Jean said, shaking her head in disbelief at their predicament.

"Well,'' Corsair said, obviously uncomfortable with whatever more he had to tell them.

"We don't have time for discomfort, Corsair,'' Jean said irritably. "What is it? What do you want us to do?''

"Ch'od and I believe that the hyperburners can be directly ignited,'' Corsair said finally.

"Oh, that's marvelous,'' Archangel said. "What do we do, crawl up inside the propulsion system and light a match?''

"Close,'' Corsair said. "We think that Scott's optic blasts at full bore can do it.''

Jean was speechless.

"I know you're not thrilled with this idea, Jean,'' Corsair said quickly. "I don't blame you. But we've talked it over, and it's our only hope. With you protecting him from the hyperburners themselves, dragging him outside the *Starjammer* until our momentum has relaxed enough that Rogue can bring him inside, well . . . it's all we've got.''

"Corsair,'' she said softly, shaking her head, "Chris . . . you're his father.''

"Don't you think this thing is tearing me apart?'' Corsair suddenly shouted. "Don't you think I'd go out there and do it myself if I could, that I'd do anything I had to not to have to heave my boy out into space *again*? Come on, Jean, give me a goddamn break! Scott and

Alex are all I have, being their father is the one great thing I've done in my life!

"I know what I'm asking!" he shouted, poking at his own chest hard enough that Jean could hear the hollow echo inside his rib cage. "But it's all we've got, dammit. Otherwise we're *all* going to die out here."

Jean stared at Corsair a moment, unable to think of the words to express her regret, her fear, her doubt that she could hold her lover's life in her hands again without crumbling. Her eyes met his, and she saw all of those things in him as well.

"Chris, I . . ." she began, but then Corsair took her in his arms and held her in a suffocating embrace, and Jean could say no more.

After a long moment, Jean broke the embrace and looked around the main cabin at the sleeping forms of Raza, Hepzibah, and Gambit. She looked at Warren, who bit his lip and nodded slowly. She barely noticed at that moment that his skin was blue. To her, with that look of concern and grim acceptance, with the intelligence and caring she saw in his eyes, he was Warren Worthington as she had always known him. They were friends. They were a team. They were X-Men. That meant more than Jean could ever put into words.

"Tell me precisely what we need to do," Jean said as she turned back to Corsair.

* * *

"I must be out of my mind," Scott Summers said, shaking his head in nervous anticipation. "What kind of fool sticks his head into the engine of a starship?"

"You must really have the jitters, Slim," Archangel said, again calling Scott by his teenage nickname in a transparent attempt to lighten the mood. "In the field, you never let on that you're nervous."

"That's different, Warren," Scott said. "When I'm leading the team, I've got to keep morale up or we won't be at our peak."

"But now, since it's just you, the hell with morale, right?" Archangel said, grinning.

"If I could pacify myself with a little pep talk, Warren, I'd gladly do it," Scott said, somewhat harshly, then began to grin as well. The grin turned to a laugh and he rolled his eyes heavenward. "God, maybe you should just burn me up now, save me the trouble of going out there again."

Archangel stopped smiling, and a moment later, Scott did as well. It wasn't funny at all, he realized. Particularly comments about burning up. It was nearing one hundred and twenty five degrees inside the ship, and the temperature was rising rapidly even with life support systems trying to compensate for their nearness to the sun. If his effort failed, they were unlikely to come up with another plan in time.

But there was more to it than that. Even if he could get the hyperburners to fire up again, and the *Starjammer* and her crew were able to return to Earth, there was no guarantee that he would be on board when it landed. Or even if he would be alive.

"How do we get ourselves into these things, Scott?" Warren asked soberly.

"We do what we have to, old friend," Scott responded gravely. "Which I guess answers my question about what kind of fool I am. The kind that does what needs to be done, just like all the X-Men, and maybe a lot of civilians as well."

"Not enough civilians, Scott," Archangel said. "Most people know what needs to be done, but they wouldn't dare attempt to do it themselves. I've got to hand it to you, Scott, because there are a lot of courageous people who wouldn't even attempt what you're about to do."

"Thank you, Warren, that makes me feel so much better," Scott said, trying for levity again, but failing miserably.

"What I'm trying to say, Scotty, is that, well, I know we've given each other some grief over the years, but you've always set the example for me. I've always had great ambitions, things I wanted to do or learn to better myself. Most of what I've aspired to are things I've observed in Professor Xavier, and in you, Scott," Archangel said sincerely. "I just thought you should know that."

"Thanks Warren," Scott said, with some discomfort. "That means a lot."

Several seconds of silence ticked by, then Archangel put out his hand.

"Good luck," he offered.

Scott shook his old friend's hand, and considered once again the utter insanity of the job before him. It wasn't the space walk that bothered him, or the fact that he would be alone outside the *Starjammer*. In many ways, it wasn't even the fact that he would be forced to jump-start the hyperburners with his optic blasts, risking having his head and shoulders incinerated in an instant.

It was what came after. Sure, Jean would have a hold on him with her telekinetic power, but the *Starjammer* would be moving at extraordinary speed. The odds were stacked up so high against Jean being able to hold onto him that they might as well be zero. And even if she could, Rogue still had to leave the ship during its hyperburn and try to bring him in. After all, the pressure would be tremendous and it was highly unlikely that he would remain conscious.

In some ways, that was good. Scott wasn't sure he wanted to be conscious in that moment when the destiny of everyone aboard the *Starjammer* was decided.

You're thinking too much, Scott, Jean's mental voice whispered in his mind. *As much as I wish I could, we both know there isn't any way I or anyone else is going to talk you out of doing this crazy thing. Perhaps that's for the best, otherwise we die here. My real fear is that, if you fail, then we won't even be able to die together.*

Are you trying to cheer me up? Scott asked in his mind, and he could sense Jean's amusement on the psychic rapport that they shared.

"Jean's here," Scott said aloud, and he and Warren both turned to see Rogue and Jean entering from the gangway.

"Y'all ready for this kamikaze mission?" Rogue asked, with a sarcasm her Southern upbringing would have called sass.

Despite her tone, however, Scott could see she was unnerved by the prospect of their plan. Still, it was not as if any of them had a choice. If any of them, Scott, Rogue, or Jean, had been killed on Hala, or disabled somehow, or had Rogue or Jean not chosen to come along on this trip, then they would not even have had a chance of survival. The people aboard the *Starjammer* would have had to simply sit and wait to die.

But there was a chance. And Scott Summers would be damned if he didn't make good on it.

Scott was suited up for the space walk just as the others were suited up in case there were a sudden loss of life support systems. He said nothing as Jean approached and leaned her helmet against his own. Through layers of fluid force shield and ruby quartz, their eyes met briefly. Jean's face reflected the resolution he had sensed in her mind.

I love you, she said in the intimacy of their psi-link. *Always have, always will.*

Always is an awfully long time, Scott thought, and he saw Jean smile.

It better be, Jean answered.

"Time to go," Scott said, and the moment of tension that had frozen the four X-Men in place collapsed, leaving only action in its wake.

Scott entered the airlock and turned to face the small window as it sealed him out of the main body of the ship. Through the tiny portal, he could see Archangel heading away, back toward the cockpit, where he and Ch'od would share piloting duties while Corsair watched over the injured. Jean and Rogue stood close together, both attempting to smile, both failing.

The airlock was sealed, and Scott attached his lifeline to the clamp at the edge of the outer door then latched it to the belt of his suit. The oxygen in the airlock was cycled out into space, depressurizing the compartment. Otherwise, when the outer door was opened, he would have been blown out at a velocity so great it might have snapped his line. The door slid open, finally, and Scott drifted out into space, using his fingers to find hand holds on the door frame and then the hull of the ship. He scrabbled over the outer hull of the *Starjammer*, and headed for the engines.

Are we sure this makes sense, Jean? he asked in his head. *I mean, we spun out of control when only one engine fired before. Aren't we just going to have the same problem? I know that was the warp drive, but they use the same ignition sequence.*

Ch'od doesn't think so, she answered through their psi-link. *With the small repairs he already made outside, and what he's been able to do in the cockpit, igniting one of the hyperburn engines should immediately ignite the other. The propulsion system was offline before, so that didn't happen.*

And it's online now, right? Scott asked, and sensed a hesitation in Jean that was far from heartening. *Jean?*

It's online at the moment, Scott, but Corsair says it's liable to cut in and out, depending on the way the emergency systems reroute power. They're doing all they can.

That's all I can ask, he thought, and moved on.

As he crawled out to the starboard leg of the ship, toward the engine well, Scott kept Jean apprised of his progress. The sun was on the opposite side of the ship, but its glare glinted off the *Starjammer*, bright enough to distract him even through the face shield and ruby quartz visor he wore. He was alone, the vacuum of space around him, no one and nothing for infinite miles of space other than his family inside the ship. Jean's voice, even her presence, in his mind was the only comfort he had.

Even that was disappearing, however, as Scott began to develop an agonizing headache. A red mist of energy seemed to spill from his eyes and out into space through his face shield. They were so close to the sun that he had passed his potential to store energy, yet he didn't dare let off an ounce even to relax the pressure in his head. He would need every bit of power to ignite the hyperburners.

He thought once again of the people within the *Starjammer*, of how they represented his entire life. His father, lost to him as a child and rediscovered as an adult. Jean and Warren, members of the first X-Men team, which became his family when he was only a teenager. Gambit and Rogue, brash young reminders of how difficult it was to make love stay in a world that hated and feared mutants so explosively—not to mention, in Rogue's case, what a barrier those mutant powers could be to interpersonal relationships. They were more recent additions to the team, especially Gambit, and perhaps Scott saw a bit of his future as he looked at them.

If he had a future. But with or without him—even if none of them survived—the X-Men and everything they stood for would continue. When he realized that, an inner calm seemed to grow within Scott. Any trace of nervousness disappeared as he finally reached the engine well. He would do what was required of him, the only thing he could do, in an attempt to save his father, his comrades, his lover. He would do his best. Beyond that, there was nothing. The silence of space was no longer intimidating, but rather, it had become serene in its power, sublime in its apathetic immensity.

Do or die, Scott thought, to himself this time, and if Jean heard him she made no reply.

He felt nothing, no trace of her influence, but Scott had absolute confidence that Jean's telekinesis would both protect him from the infernal blast that would burst from the engine well, and catch him and drag him behind the ship as it got under way. He placed his life in her hands more completely than he had ever done before, and he did not give it a second thought.

Scott lay along the outside of the engine well and took a last look around. The stars seemed as distant from him here as they ever had from Earth. Still admiring the cold points of distant light, he grasped the edge of the engine well with both hands and pulled himself around, letting his legs drift out and away from the ship.

He looked up slowly, narrowing his eyes to peer within the engine well. Scott did not know what he had expected to see, but he was disappointed when his eyes found only darkness within the long metal alloy cylinder. Rotating his head to stretch his muscles, he heard a series of soft pops and crackling sounds from within his own body. He tried to pinpoint the exact center of the darkness ahead.

Then his eyes exploded in a burst of energy that would have decimated the ship had that been his intention. Never had Scott stored so much energy. Never had he cut loose with such total abandon.

There was a bright flare in the engine well as the engine converted the kinetic energy of his optic blasts and ignited, and a split second where the flame seemed to go sideways as it in turn ignited its twin. Scott had a moment to realize the flame was erupting toward him, and despite his confidence in Jean, he began to duck his head out of the way.

Propelled by the power that Cyclops had brought to bear on its engines, the *Starjammer* shot forward into space. Scott lost his grip in an instant and went limp just before his tether snapped taut, and suddenly the ship was towing him—for a moment. Then the tether snapped and there was a moment when the ship seemed to be leaving him behind. Suddenly, he was caught up in invisible hands, pulled far behind the ship by Jean's telekinesis, at a distance which gave Scott cause for great concern.

His eyes hurt, so finally he closed them. His mind ached and he felt empty inside, drained as if he had been fasting for weeks. When he began to lose consciousness, he was dimly aware of having grown much closer to the ship, and of the sensation of motion.

When he felt Rogue's arms embrace him, his eyes fluttered open for a moment, and through his pain and exhaustion, Cyclops felt a small smile fighting to be born on his lips.

Jean? he asked, floating on a sea of semi-conscious delirium. *Jean, are we all right? Did we do it?*

For a moment there was no answer, and even in his disoriented state, Cyclops began to be overwhelmed with panic. Then her voice appeared in his mind.

You did it, Scott. You did, she said. *We're going to be all right now. We're going to make it.*

The words were a jumble to Scott, but he got the general impression. Comforted, he allowed himself to slip down into unconsciousness once more. There was something nagging at him, a voice in his head warning him that it wasn't over until they were back on Earth, but he pushed the annoying pessimist away and settled into Rogue's strong arms.

His job was done.

Chapter 10

Exchange Place was awash with frantic humanity, from the media to the military to those who had fled the mutant empire. An almost palpable haze of desperation-derived energy surged in Jersey City, connecting person to person in a massive network of tension. Perhaps the single most powerful concentration of that tense energy was the stretch of pavement in front of the PATH station that served to separate the two sets of trailers and tents that had become the military and media camps—the former on Washington Street, half-out of sight, the latter in the plaza overlooking lower Manhattan.

The only thing occupying that lunatic focal point was the temporary trailer headquarters of Valerie Cooper. Gyrich had set his trailer up with the military personnel, but Val had been unwilling to commit to either side. Still, despite the bedlam around her, Val was calm. It was always safest at the eye of the storm.

"Ms. Cooper, are you insinuating that Mr. Gyrich has been attempting to obstruct you in the execution of your duties?" the Secretary asked over the scrambled vid-comm link he and Val had set up.

"I'm insinuating nothing, sir," she said firmly. "I'm just telling you what happened exactly the way it played out. How you choose to read it is your business. However, we both know that Gyrich would be only too happy to obstruct me in the execution of my duties if he found an opportunity to do so."

The Secretary frowned, and Val knew she had crossed the line again. It was damn hard not to, though, what with the parameters of propriety changing with every passing moment.

"Ms. Cooper," the Secretary chided, "I will ask you,

for the final time, to please remain objective during this operation. It is of the utmost importance that you and Mr. Gyrich put aside your mutual animosity and work to resolve this situation.''

Val lost her patience.

"Sir, with all due respect, I'd be more than happy to do my job and put aside my animosity toward Mr. Gyrich if he would simply hand over the Sentinel over-ride codes, as he was instructed to do by the President himself,'' she fumed, her tone edging into sarcasm.

The Secretary was not a forgiving man.

"Listen, Cooper," he snapped, "I've had just about enough from both you and Gyrich. Maybe you're missing this, what with your own little crises and all, but my ass is on the line here with every second this fiasco holds the nation's, and the President's, attention.

"You know as well as I do that Gyrich was ordered to cooperate with your mission, not specifically to turn the codes over to you. If you have the X-Men, and your mission is being held up by Gyrich, then he would be disobeying direct orders from the Commander-in-Chief. But you don't have the X-Men, do you?''

Val did not respond.

"Do you?" the Secretary asked again, insistent.

"No, sir, not at this time," she answered, reluctantly.

"Well, if you can produce them, and Gyrich doesn't give you the codes, get back to me," he said, exasperated. "Until then, I'm waiting for the President to decide upon a course of action independent of your earlier recommendations. That will probably be Gyrich's play, and you'll be out of it. You want a part in this, Cooper? You'd better get some mutants in your court, so we can have a go at the Sentinels. Otherwise, stop wasting my time!''

Val sat in stunned silence inside her trailer as her vid-comm unit flashed a blue screen, indicating no source of input. She was out of it. The only way to convince the Secretary otherwise was to explain that they could contact the X-Men telepathically and provide them with the codes. But that would mean allowing the X-Men control of the Sentinels without herself or another government official monitoring them, and the Secretary wasn't likely to go for that. It would also mean letting the government know that Professor Charles Xavier was himself a mutant. And *Xavier* wasn't likely to go for that.

Sure, there were other mutants. But Magneto's vision was alluring, and she could not trust that any of them would be unmoved by it. She did not even trust the X-Men completely. Just the most. Other than her X-Factor team, of course. But they were out of the—

What they were, Valerie suddenly realized, was her only hope.

She typed in a command code on the vid-comm controls, then an override code, and finally an eyes-only destination code. The blue screen turned to white noise, hypnotic static, and there was a high trilling sound that she knew came from the other end of the connection. Suddenly, a face snapped into view amidst hissing static. The picture was distorted, but the identity of the man was unmistakable. It was the leader of X-Factor, Alex Summers, also known as Havok.

''You picked a hell of a time to call, Val!'' Havok shouted to be heard over the sounds of explosions and gunfire in the background. "We're in the middle of a firefight. I hope it's important."

"It's important, Alex," Val said firmly.

Alex Summers was a brash young man, and Val had never really gotten along with him. However, like his brother Scott, better known as Cyclops of the X-Men, Alex was a born leader. Not only did he have the raw instinct, but there was a certain charisma about him that demanded loyalty. While Havok had not ever really attempted to hone his skills in the way that Cyclops had, nor had he ever become as grave as Scott often was, he was a firm believer in Xavier's dream.

And X-Factor was definitely a part of that dream. With the anti-mutant sentiment at an all time high, it was important for the public to see that the federal government was willing to work with mutants. X-Factor's job was to capture outlaw mutants for the government. It was equally important, however, that they simply exist as a government-sanctioned operation. Part of Havok's value was that he understood both parts of the job.

"We've got a major situation here, Alex," Val said. "Like nothing else we've encountered. Have you heard anything about it?"

"Val, gimme a break, will ya?" he said gruffly. "We're in the middle of the latest outbreak in a seemingly endless civil war. X-Factor is about the only thing keeping the two sides from slaughtering each other during peace negotiations. I've been fighting for days! I'm not exactly near a TV set, y'know!"

"Okay, relax," she said. "Look, all I want to know is, how soon could you get out of Genosha if you had to?"

"You mean, if we decided to let it all go, to let chaos

tear Genosha apart? Just up and left?'' he said, astonished.

"If that's what it takes, yeah,'' she responded. "How long?''

"Three to six hours, depending on Lorna's wounds and how badly our transport was damaged,'' Havok said grimly. "But I mean it, Val. Tomorrow, maybe they won't need us this bad. Right now, though, with the UN dragging their heels, we're the only thing holding Genosha together.''

"Plus, it would take another ten hours for you to get here,'' she said, thinking aloud. "Damn.''

"What's that, Val? I couldn't hear you. What's our next move?'' Havok asked.

"Stay put, Alex,'' she said finally. "But as soon as your presence isn't absolutely vital, get back here. And be prepared to withdraw immediately on my command if it gets too hot here.''

"What is it, Val?'' Havok said. "What's going on back there?''

She considered telling him, but thought better of it. Knowing Alex Summers, it was completely possible he'd say the hell with Genosha and evac immediately. Which, despite the country's crisis, would have been fine with Val if she thought it would make a difference. But sixteen, even thirteen hours, would very likely get them there too late to make a difference.

"Just stay put, Havok,'' Val said curtly. "Let me worry about it.''

Valerie Cooper stood, ran a hand over her blonde hair where it was tied back in a tight ponytail, and stepped to the door of her trailer. When she stepped outside, she noticed a glow in the eastern sky and realized that dawn was not far off. She wasn't sure if that would make things easier or more difficult for what was to come.

The first order of business, however, was to acquire the Sentinel override codes. Val was certain that her original plan was the only one with a prayer of succeeding without massive loss of life and property damage. Perhaps the only one with any hope of succeeding at all. Otherwise, Magneto might very well achieve his dreams of empire. No, she had to get those codes.

One way, or another.

* * *

For many years, Charles Xavier had been repulsed by the manner in which the media vultures feasted on the helpless, dying form of America. As the night wore on toward morning, Xavier's throat had become parched and sore from incessant talking. Just as swiftly, his sense of moral justice had become, if not dulled, then most certainly numbed by the overwhelming cynicism of the media. It wasn't just repulsive anymore, it was damned depressing.

Only Annelise Dwyer, of all the gathered journalists, had not lowered herself to pander to the fears and prejudices of the nation. Though, admittedly, given the atmosphere created by the agitated military presence, much might be forgiven of those tempted toward confrontation. Xavier had always had a respect for the military—indeed, had willingly served in the Army in his younger days—tempered by knowledge and common sense. He only hoped that there were people in charge who did not share the blind fervor of zealots like Henry Peter Gyrich.

As he wheeled his chair away from his latest

interview—with E! Entertainment Television of all things—the psi-web that emanated from him at all times picked up angry thoughts with himself as their focus. Xavier nonchalantly turned his wheelchair, as though recalling something he needed to do, toward the source of those thoughts.

Val Cooper stalked toward him, filled with righteous anger and a visible sense of plan or purpose.

"Professor Xavier, we need to talk," Ms. Cooper said.

"I am at your service as always, Valerie," Xavier responded. "Shall we go to your trailer?"

Cooper looked at him oddly for a moment, and Xavier caught a hint of amusement in her thoughts. Without prying further, he understood. It had crossed Val's mind that observers, media or military, might believe himself and Valerie to be involved in some kind of affair, that they were sneaking off on a lovers' tryst. Xavier stifled a smile, for he did not want Cooper to think he was reading her thoughts without her consent. And it had been a momentary, whimsical thought.

He didn't have to read her mind to know Cooper realized that it was more likely they would be suspected of some conspiracy than of any intimacy. She was lithe, blond, and powerful. He was bald and crippled, and no matter how handsome he might or might not have been, gossip was not likely to center around a potential relationship between them. Such were the assumptions of the world. What bothered Charles was the reason for the assumptions, not the assumptions themselves. For it was true, he could never be involved with Valerie. But that was because he was sworn to another, not because of his handicap.

"What is it you want, Valerie?" he asked as they neared her trailer. "I sense great turmoil in you."

"What, you mean our current situation isn't cause for turmoil?" she said with heavy sarcasm.

"It's more than that," Xavier prodded. "What's on your mind?"

"It's what's on Gyrich's mind that concerns me, Charles," Val said, letting out an exasperated sigh.

They reached her trailer, and an awkward expression crossed Val Cooper's face.

"Charles," she said. "I'm sorry, I wasn't thinking—you can't get that chair into my trailer."

"I know," he answered. "I just thought this was the most secluded spot for us to have our conversation. Please continue, you were saying something about Gyrich."

"Well, you know our plan can't go ahead without the X-Men, and Gyrich loves that," she said. "It's going to give him a chance to get back in the good graces of the President and the Director of Wideawake. You see, there has been no attack order, but I don't think Gyrich is waiting for the order. I think he's planning to send a small squad in on his own. That was his original plan."

"Even if he does that," Xavier reasoned, "it is very possible that he has been given an unofficial order to do so. Such things are very popular amongst politicians who have ardent supporters but do not want to take responsibility for the actions of those supporters. It's become par for the course in American politics, I'm afraid."

"My point exactly," Val countered. "I'm afraid. And I don't think there is anything I can do to stop him."

"Even if we get the codes from him, we cannot

communicate them to the X-Men without Gyrich coming too close to the truth,'' Xavier said, speaking what he knew were Valerie's greatest concerns.

"That's what I've been dealing with," she acknowledged. "But I want to go ahead and do it anyway. We'll get the codes, get them to the X-Men, and hope they can wrap this whole thing up before Gyrich starts a bloody civil war with his fascist tactics."

Xavier was perplexed.

"I'm sorry, Valerie," he said. "Perhaps I misunderstood. How is it that you plan to get these codes?"

"I'm not going to, Charles. You're going to have to get them."

Immediately, Xavier understood.

"You want me to infiltrate Gyrich's mind, find the codes and pluck them out, is that it?" he asked.

"That is precisely it," she admitted. "It's the only way."

"Then there is no way," Xavier said coldly. "As you should know from the many years we have been acquainted, Valerie, I simply do not do things like that. I will not enter someone's mind without their consent unless I am required to do so for purposes of self defense."

"Don't you see, Charles," she pleaded. "This *is* self defense! If Magneto wins, you are sure to be hunted down eventually."

"That's not the way it works, Val," he snapped. "It is against everything I stand for. I simply will not do it, and you should know better than to even ask."

Cooper fell silent, but Xavier could see from the determination smoldering in her eyes that though the conversation was at an end, the topic would most definitely come up again. He did not relish the thought. There was a line he had set up for himself as a young man, when he had first discovered his abilities. He had crossed the line several times in his life, each with disastrous results.

The most painful had come when his blossoming relationship with Amelia Voght had come to a sudden end. Agonizing over her planned departure, he had psionically commanded her to stay. It had lasted only a moment, but that betrayal of Amelia, of himself and of his ethics had ended any chance they might have had at reconciliation.

Now Amelia Voght was one of Magneto's most trusted Acolytes. Charles Xavier knew that many of his students, and myriad other people he had come into contact with over the years, considered him nearly perfect, infallible. If only that were true, he thought. To them, he was Professor X, more than human, above pain and error and all the petty things that make up a human being.

He was both pleased and saddened to know that it was not true. He made mistakes, as he had with Amelia. He felt pain when he remembered those mistakes. And he was filled with regret and self-recrimination as he wondered if that breach of the love and trust between them had been the thing to drive her, in time, to become one of Magneto's followers. If that were true, he hoped that he never discovered it. Xavier suspected it might be too much for him to bear.

As the world's most powerful psi, a telepath to whom every mind was laid bare, the absolute truth regarding any subject was available to Xavier, awaiting only his whim to reveal itself. More than any other being on the Earth, he knew the power of truth. An extraordinary weapon, it could be used to free people of burdens, to frighten them into submission, or to cause extraordinary and intimate pain.

Simply put, there were times when it was better not to know.

"Look at it this way, Charles," Cooper persisted. "If we can't get the codes from Gyrich, then the ball is in his court. He's going to go into Manhattan like a bulldozer and all hell is going to break loose. We can stop it before it gets that far."

Xavier knew she was right, but he would not compromise himself under any circumstances.

"What of X-Factor?" he asked.

"I tried," Cooper snapped. "They're unavailable."

A tense silence emerged between them. They shared a long history as allies, but they had never really been friends. Xavier began to see why the relationship had remained so strictly professional. For Val Cooper, the ends most definitely justified the means. The very thought was anathema to Charles Xavier.

"I will consider your recommendations, Ms. Cooper," he said, then turned and wheeled his chair away from her, heart heavy with thoughts of consequence.

* * *

As he descended into the PATH station for the second time that day, Henry Peter Gyrich entertained several moments of unusual self-reflection. Normally, he was so caught up with his job that he never had time to consider his work, his future, his goals, no time for hollow shouts of victory or the tears of self-recrimination. But this was a rare, quiet moment before the start of what might be his greatest victory.

Gyrich was more self aware than most people gave

him credit for. He knew why he was almost universally disliked, knew why Val Cooper hated him so thoroughly. He represented the ugly truth that mutants, regardless of their initial intentions, spelled doom for the rest of humanity. They claimed to be the next step in human evolution, but Gyrich knew better. Mutants were a genetic aberration, as unfortunate and undesirable as Down's Syndrome, but far more dangerous. If they were allowed to proliferate, to assemble, to present themselves as some minority group deserving of special consideration . . . well, by the time people woke up to reality, it would be too late.

Gyrich genuinely felt bad for most mutants. It was not their fault they were born with that genetic x-factor, not their fault they had become part of the problem. It was also not their fault that, just as there were human madmen, lunatics like Magneto had come to represent the image of the mutant in popular consciousness. The sanctity of the American lifestyle had to be protected from the rise of mutants, but that didn't mean that individual mutants were bad.

Cursed, perhaps, but not bad.

Not until they crossed the line. As far as Gyrich was concerned, that was inevitable. Along with their mutant gifts, he believed they received some kind of genetic trait which gave them a propensity toward violence and hostility toward authority. They believed their special powers gave them the right to do whatever they liked.

That was the greatest evil of the mutant race. They were not human, and acted as though human laws did not bind them. That was the reason the Sentinels and Operation: Wideawake were so important. That was the reason Gyrich had pushed aside much of his other work for the CIA, NSA, and other agencies in order to put emphasis on the mutant problem.

In no way did he want to see the nation torn apart by the issue. But such mutant uprisings had to be dealt with immediately and with extreme prejudice, before others began to get ideas. Already the government had brought mutants into the fold with X-Factor, which Gyrich thought was a major error. Due to their feelings of superiority, by their very nature mutants were not to be trusted.

And for the President to countenance any contact by his people with the outlaws called X-Men, why that was simply outrageous!

Mutants were a human problem, for humans to solve. Bringing in more mutants was not a solution. Some kind of electronic tracking and power-restraining implant, that would allow the government to keep track of mutants while rendering them no more dangerous to humanity than humanity itself, that was what was necessary. In any case, the world needed to see that humanity could handle the problem on its own. If they relied on mutants to rescue Manhattan from Magneto, they would be starting down a dark path to their own extinction.

More dedicated than ever to his chosen course of action, Gyrich reached the guarded door to the parallel access tunnel that would allow Surgical Ops Unit One to travel into Manhattan unnoticed by the Sentinels. Or at least, that was what he hoped would happen. If they were discovered and eliminated by the Sentinels, Gyrich would have to work on a backup plan. And that backup might be full-scale assault, if he could arrange it.

He hoped SOU1, and Operation: Carthage, would be successful.

SANCTUARY

As Gyrich entered the tunnel, Major Skolnick snapped to attention.

"Sir, Surgical Ops Unit One prepared for deployment, sir. Locked and loaded, sir. Operation: Carthage is waiting for your word." Skolnick barked, each word enunciated with military precision.

"Excellent, Major," Gyrich said, and nodded with pleasure. "Gather your men."

Skolnick disappeared into the tunnel, shouting commands with the confidence of one who is always obeyed. The tunnel was poorly lit, and there was a lot of rustling in the shadows, along with the clanging of weapons and equipment being hefted. In less than one minute, SOU1 had scrambled and presented themselves for attention in front of Gyrich as if he were the Commander-in-Chief himself.

He liked that. It fit right in with his image of the future, of what he might obtain and attain once this mission had ended successfully. He reminded himself once again of Graydon Creed's suitability as a Presidential candidate. The phrase "power behind the President" had always intrigued him. There was a definite allure to it.

"SOU1, all present and accounted for, sir," Major Skolnick barked, and the men and women of the team all snapped to attention right along with their commanding officer.

Gyrich knew that he was expected to tell them to be at ease at that point. He didn't. For one thing, he didn't want the team getting comfortable with him, seeing him as just one of them, another soldier. He was hardly that. And for another, he didn't want them at ease. He wanted them angry, furious, mean. That was how the day would be won. It had always worked for Gyrich.

"As you all know," he began, lingering with the words, allowing the rigidity of their attention to weigh on them, "you are about to embark upon the most important mission of your lives. I don't want anyone underestimating what has to be done here today."

He scanned each face for any sign of debate, discomfort, annoyance, and found none.

"Full-scale attack is not an option at this time, at least not one the President is yet willing to entertain. And if you fail, he may have to. That means death and destruction, boys and girls. Let's not make any mistake about that. You can avoid that. That, in fact, is your job here today. That is the purpose of Operation: Carthage. To restore the public faith, both in the American government, and in humanity itself. The people of this country have got to know that when it comes to the mutant menace, we can take care of ourselves! We clear on that?"

"Yes, sir!" they responded in unison, with enthusiasm that Gyrich felt was not merely trained into them, but genuine.

"And what is the primary objective of Operation: Carthage?" Gyrich asked.

"Terminate Magneto, sir!" they answered.

"Excellent," he said proudly. "You may begin."

"SOU1 deployed, sir!" Major Skolnick barked. "Operation: Carthage is under way."

The team hustled up their gear and disappeared back into the tunnel. In seconds, they were gone. Before they were out of range, Gyrich heard one of the grunts bragging to the others.

"I'm gonna tear out that mutie freak's terrorist heart and feed it to 'im for breakfast!" the man announced.

SANCTUARY

"Nobody holds a city hostage in America. We just don't go for that crap here!"

As he made his way back up to the surface, where dawn was already beginning to lighten the sky, Henry Peter Gyrich began to smile.

It was going to be a beautiful day.

Chapter 11

For Storm, the coming of the dawn had a glory unequalled anywhere else in nature. As a child, she had watched the sun rise over the desert sands of Egypt. As a young woman, she had witnessed dawn breaking over the African plains. It was the triumph of light over shadow, the renewal of the spirit, the radiant hope of the future. The sun rose with power enough to send the shadows scurrying underground until it had passed over and night approached once again.

In Manhattan, the arrival of dawn was an altogether different thing, the victory of the light hesitant and uncertain. It was inevitable that the sun would rise, that the shadows would be beaten back. But in the darkened canyons created by row upon row of towering structures, there was a moment each morning when the outcome seemed questionable.

That moment had come. As Storm glided upon the winds at her command, sunlight crept over the tops of buildings, shone down on entire blocks where few walked alone. Guerrilla warfare ensued between light and dark, and finally, the dawn's light flowed like liquid gold through the streets of the city.

Another day was won, another in an endless series of tiny, meaningless battles. But night was not far off, and that would bring another battle, another chance to lose.

Storm marveled, as she always did, about the wonders of nature. She prized the dawn as it charged the city with gold light and blue sky, with bird song even in this polluted environment. And yet, the eternal balance was always in place. Without the night, there would be no day to cherish, without the day, no shadows to fear. It meant everything, and nothing. The two gave each other meaning, but the cycle was so equally balanced that each became almost meaningless.

Were they a part of a similar cycle? she wondered. With the Professor as the day and Magneto as the night, were they fighting an uncertain battle that was merely a tiny part of a ceaseless struggle? Did it matter, in the end, who won the day, when the struggle would go on?

Inhaling deeply, Storm ran her slender fingers through her long silvery white mane of hair, felt the warmth against her face despite the wind. Dawn had always been a moment of freedom for her, as well. Freedom from the special terror the night held for her personally. Though she might be in open air, no walls in sight, she could not avoid a small tinge of her radical claustrophia when it was dark. She might not be enclosed in any small space, but the darkness felt confining, restrictive, and that was enough.

And if the day surrendered, determined that the fight was useless and withdrew from battle? Why then, the night would win. There would be no day. She would be forever cloaked by darkness, and Storm did not think she could retain her sanity in such a forever night.

In a sense, the struggle was nearly as important as victory.

"Any sign o' Drake, Ororo?" a gruff voice asked over the comm-badge she wore on her clavicle.

"None," she responded, touching the badge to transmit her voice. "I think we'd better discuss this."

At her mental instruction, the wind whipped around her, turning Storm and propelling her back the way she had come. Two blocks ahead, she saw her teammates awaiting her in the shadow of a newsstand. Wolverine and the Beast remained close to the small structure, attempting to be inconspicuous. Though he had more formal training than any of the X-Men, except perhaps Wolverine, Bishop did not make any effort to conceal himself. He stood rigid with tension, his backup weapon ready in his hands to eliminate any sudden threat.

Storm had to wonder whether Bishop was going to be able to handle the mission. Though he had been able to maintain his control when it counted, he had already shown himself prone to frenzied overreaction. It was understandable, given the part the Sentinels played in his upbringing. But it could also be dangerous. Storm had to make sure that didn't happen. She could not allow Bishop's fears of the future to cost one, or all of them, their lives.

Storm had created an updraft beneath her, and now she slowly lessened its intensity until her feet touched the ground. Wolverine moved silently to where she stood, their time together as teammates and as partners on the road having long since eliminated the need for useless chatter and ponderance. Bishop was silent as well, and so flush with nervous energy that Storm could nearly see it emanating from his skin. He was more on edge than she had ever seen him, and with Bishop, that was saying something.

The Beast, on the other hand, was rarely without an opinion.

"Not a solitary indication regarding Robert's fate or present position," the Beast said, his tone betraying obvious concern for Iceman's welfare. "I ought never to have deserted him. If any ill has befallen him, I—"

"Drake can take care of himself, Hank," Wolverine grumbled. "You know that even better than I do."

"Don't be so sure," Bishop added without venom,

but Storm saw the way Hank and Logan looked at him.

"Yeah, I know Logan," the Beast said, for once lapsing into more colloquial language. "But if anything happened to my little buddy, mother McCoy's bouncing boy would still feel responsible."

"We'll find him, Hank," Storm said, and offered a smile in appreciation for Hank's attempt at levity.

"We have another problem none of you seems willing to address," Bishop said, his tone harsher than ever. "If we cannot find Drake, that means we have no way of effectively tracking Magneto. This is a very big city, if you hadn't noticed."

"You're playin' this one wrong, Bishop," Wolverine said, a trace of menace appearing in his voice.

"Indeed, Bishop," Storm agreed. "I understand the kind of stress you must be under, but—"

"You have no idea what's in my mind, Storm!" Bishop snapped. "There is no possible way for you to understand the dread that has frozen my heart since we left Colorado! You have not lived death on the scale I lived it, felt fear with every breath! You could not even conceive of the consequences of your actions today, and you stand here and worry about the X-Men's 'class clown' because he has lost his way! We have a job to do!"

Storm had heard enough.

"That will do, Bishop," she said curtly. "Do not presume to tell me my job. You claim to have been such a model soldier. Good—see if you can follow orders. I am your superior in the hierarchy of this little army called the X-Men. When I issue a command, you snap to it. If I say we look for Iceman, then we look for Iceman. I don't know how you did things in the future, but you're an X-Man now, and we take care of our own.''

"Conversely, Ororo," the Beast interrupted, "it would not do to linger a moment longer than necessary. While we are in motion, there is less risk of being discovered. Without any means to track Bobby, we probably should move on. Once Professor Xavier contacts us again, we can request that he do a psi-search for Magneto in the area wherein Bobby originally noted his presence.''

"But we can't go too far," Storm protested, all the while astounded that the Beast would voice any agreement with Bishop after the future X-Man's behavior.

"I vote we get movin', ten blocks south, then find an out o' the way place to sit an' wait for Charlie's next contact," Wolverine said. "I'll take point, see if I can't pick up the scent o' Magneto or one o' his lapdogs. It's the best we're gonna do, right about now, 'roro.''

"Agreed," Storm said, and nodded slowly.

"One last thing," Bishop said, and Storm could hear the hesitation in his voice. "I recommend that you remain with us. With daylight upon us, you would be a very clear target in the air.''

Storm shared Bishop's hesitation, then released the anger she felt toward him. It would work against them when the time for battle came. She smiled at him, and he returned the favor. Storm touched his elbow and moved him along beside her.

"Let's go," Storm said. "Time's wasting.''

They had not taken twenty paces when Wolverine came to a dead halt in front of them.

"Logan," Storm said worriedly. "What is it?''

Wolverine turned slowly, an amused smile spread

across his features. He shook his head incredulously, then he issued a small chuckle.

"We got company," he said in a low growl. "An' you guys ain't gonna believe who it—"

Before Wolverine could finish his sentence, chaos erupted out of the hot glare of the morning sun. The Acolytes were attacking, but they were not alone.

* * *

The Beast was astonished. He was one of the first generation of X-Men, and had seen members of the team come and go over the years since he had first joined, including himself; indeed, he was the first X-Man to leave the fold, not returning to the team for many years. The opposing side had also gone through an evolution. Early on, Magneto had gathered around him a small group of who gave themselves the unlikely name of "the Brotherhood of Evil Mutants." That was the means to his hoped-for end, at least early in his career. Later, those mutants had gone their own, separate ways, and it had been Hank McCoy's understanding that there was no small amount of animosity between them.

But here were the Toad and the Blob, two of Magneto's original allies, and their teammate in a more recent incarnation of the Brotherhood, Pyro, working alongside Magneto's present Acolytes Unuscione and Cargil.

He knew he shouldn't be surprised. Not really. After all, this was what Magneto had promised, mutants who had nothing in common but their genetic x-factor banding together to conquer humanity. But looking at these five most unlikely teammates, for the first time, the Beast truly believed that Magneto could fulfill that promise if left unchecked.

That was where the X-Men came in.

"Destroy them, Acolytes!" Unuscione shrieked madly half a block away, even as she tried to crush Bishop beneath her exoskeleton. "Death to the X-Men!"

Bishop dove to escape Unuscione's blow, and his gun clattered to the pavement, out of reach.

"So much for Magneto's open door policy," the Beast mumbled, and tensed to spring to Bishop's aid.

A powerful hand clamped on his shoulder.

"Not so fast, McCoy," a female voice said, and Hank tried to dodge the blow he knew was coming. He caught a glancing blow to the back of the head, and tumbled forward. The momentum and temporary disorientation threatened to leave him sprawled on the ground, a perfect target. But he had not trained for so many years to end up in such an ignominious position. Hank used the momentum to tumble into a somersault. As his feet came around to the ground, he sprang away, putting space between himself and his attacker. He spun in the air, and when he landed a dozen yards away, he was facing her.

Joanna Cargil, once known to the X-Men as Frenzy. She was a muscular black woman whose strength was multiplied exponentially by her mutation. And she was faster than the Beast had remembered.

"Joanna," Hank sighed. "Once again you disappoint me."

Cargil strode toward him, on guard but without fear.

"Once, that kind of thing would have hurt me, McCoy," Cargil said. "I was so inexperienced, insecure, when we first met. That's changed now. I know my duty, my destiny. I don't care if you're disappointed. The unenlightened often are."

"Ah," the Beast said with a purposely patronizing smirk, "a zealot. I shall look forward to thrashing you, then."

"Why you pompous, overbearing . . ." Cargil began, and rushed at him, ready to deliver a blow capable of shattering his skull.

Hank had no intention of letting her connect. Once again, his good nature and his reputation had somehow caused an opponent to forget just how strong he was. The Beast felt it was time his enemies were reminded. Cargil moved fast, yes, but he was infinitely faster. He could have leaped from her path, escaped any number of ways, worn her down until she might have been subdued in less violent fashion.

But there wasn't time for niceties.

Cargil swung at him, crouched low in boxing fashion to avoid a counterpunch to the body. But the Beast was out of patience. He put his left arm up to knock Cargil's blow away, steeled himself for the pain that even that tangential impact was certain to bring, and struck. His massive fist curled into a ball of blue fur that looked as though it should be soft, but was like solid stone beneath the downy pile.

It was a testament to Cargil's hardy constitution that she did not simply drop in her tracks when the Beast's fist slammed into her cheek and nose. Her head snapped back at whiplash speed and blood burst from her left nostril. Eyes filled with rage, Cargil began to raise her fists again. A smile spread across her face, and she seemed about to say something, seemed confident that the Beast would give her the time to recover, time to taunt him, time to fight it out the way they had once before. Confident that, if he did, she would win.

The unwritten rules of a fair fight allowed time for your opponent to recover. But Hank McCoy had neither the time nor the inclination for a fair fight.

Before Cargil could speak, Hank hit her with a left, then a right to the gut, and a left again to the face. When she fell to the ground in front of him, nearly unconscious, several things occurred to the Beast simultaneously. He had stooped to a method of fighting he had always tried to avoid—two people standing toe to toe and pummeling one another. He had badly beaten a woman whose major crime had always been ignorance. And he was sickened by it. Sickened and ashamed, and wishing he was home, curled up with Shakespeare and cocoa. Anywhere but here.

He turned to walk away, to offer help to his teammates, who seemed to be at the very least holding their own. Then he heard movement behind him, and spun around to see that Cargil was trying to raise her head. Her eyelids fluttered as she fought unconsciousness. Though it seemed to cause her pain, she sneered.

"Just thought you should . . . know," she said, her words staggered, slurred. "Drake whimpered like . . . a puppy when I . . . took him down."

"What?" the Beast roared. "What did you do to Bobby?"

Cargil's cheek hit the pavement with a wet slap, and she was completely out. He knelt over her, trying to get her to wake up, but it was no use. She and the others had ambushed Iceman, that much was clear. But Hank did not know if his old friend was alive or dead. When he turned back to the battle, it was with the single intention of discovering Iceman's fate.

* * *

Whenever he saw Mortimer Toynbee, the Toad, Wolverine was tempted to underestimate him. After all, the man had always passed himself off as a benchwarmer, as the Peter Lorre character in a film, or Igor to Magneto's Dr. Frankenstein. A loser. A third-rate coward who was little or no threat. But his heart was filled with evil and hatred, and he could do quite a bit of damage with those powerful legs.

So he was no third-rater. Still, he was second-rate at best. In any case, it was hard not to underestimate him at first. Wolverine was going after the Blob, eagerly anticipating the idea of putting Dukes on the adamantium claw diet, when the Toad slammed into him from behind. The impact, with the power in those legs, knocked Wolverine from his feet. He sailed across the street and slammed into a wall hard enough to knock the wind out of him, and loosen several bricks.

When he stood up, Wolverine was furious.

"Once again you ignore the terrible Toad!" Toynbee shouted, his righteous anger a poor mask for his fear. He couldn't hide the fear no matter how brave he tried to sound.

Wolverine could smell it on him.

"You hit a normal guy like that," Wolverine snarled, his claws popping out with a *snikt*, "woulda broken every bone in his body. Guess it's lucky I ain't normal."

The Toad leaped at him again, with astonishing speed. Anyone else might have gotten overconfident, assumed Toynbee's fear would have made him hesitate to attack again. But Wolverine was the best there was. He knew better. To Logan, the attack was telegraphed by the tiniest motion, the smallest change in scent. He ducked. As Toynbee passed above him, Wolverine raked his claws across the diminutive mutant's legs and the Toad let out a piercing wail of agony.

Even as the Toad hit the ground, feeling his legs to check the damage, Wolverine had already moved on. The X-Men were prevailing, but the fight had not been won yet. And, given Magneto's plans, it would hardly be the last battle they fought that day. Unless, of course, they lost.

The Beast was bounding around the dull-witted, quick-tempered Blob, getting a blow in here and there while avoiding the Blob's enormous fists. He was going to need help, but Wolverine banked on Hank's ability to keep dodging a few moments longer. He had to prioritize, and right now, Storm seemed to need him more.

Pyro would normally be no match for Ororo, but before he had gone up against her, the psycho had set fire to an old, boarded-up movie theater. The flames had kindled quickly within the dry wood and dusty curtains, and he had stoked them high. Now the theater was a raging inferno, and Pyro had the flames at his disposal.

He could not create fire, and Wolverine knew they had to be thankful for that. Pyro wore a complicated getup on his back that fueled the dual flamethrowers he held in each hand. His mutant ability was to control the fire once it existed, to direct it, shape it into whatever he wished. The key was, while Storm ought to have been using her weather control abilities to attack Pyro, she was forced to battle the blaze. Giant hands of solid fire shot suddenly from the theater lobby, reaching for Storm where she had suspended herself on the winds.

A gale force wind kept the flaming hands back, even as torrential rain began to fall on the flames. But the fire burned brightly still. Eventually, Pyro might actually be able to wear her down. And if Storm weakened, the hands of fire might be able to reach her. Fortunately, the X-Men were a team.

Wolverine approached Pyro from behind, with a predator's silence. Allerdyce never knew what hit him. With one swipe of his claws, Wolverine severed the tubes supplying fuel for Pyro's flamethrowers, making certain he could not create any new fires. With the second, he punctured the tank on the mutant terrorist's back. The fuel began to spill out onto the sidewalk, and Pyro spun to face him.

"Wolverine!" Pyro said, his Australian accent tainted with false levity. "'Ow are ya, mate? It's a pleasure to see ya as always. Let's be gentlemen about this, eh?"

Logan said nothing. He brandished his claws before him, the sunlight glinting off the adamantium with blinding radiance, except in those spots where the Toad's blood had dried.

"Come on, now, Wolverine," Pyro pleaded, backing up several steps. "What'd I evah do to you, eh?"

Pyro tried to smile, but his smile faltered as he realized Wolverine was backing him toward the burning building, as the highly combustible chemicals he used to fuel his flames were pouring off his back. He began to move, to attempt to go around Wolverine, but Logan darted in and nicked his arm, very lightly, with one claw.

"You're cornered, Allerdyce," Wolverine said grimly. "You'd better hope Storm puts out that blaze before you get a little too close, or a spark jumps our way.''

''You'll be killed as well, you madman!'' Pyro shouted, panicked.

Again, Wolverine did not respond. With his peripheral vision, he watched as Storm lifted her hands and gathered the air itself into her control. Suddenly, a small tornado seemed to spring up from nowhere. The vortex lowered itself out of the sky to encircle the burning theater. It was there for a few seconds, no more, and when it lifted into the air and dissipated, the fire was out. Rain fell on charred wood.

Moments later, Pyro was doing his best to plead for his life without making it sound too much like begging. Wolverine bared his teeth but did not advance upon the mutant. Storm rode the winds at her command until she lightly touched down on the pavement. When Pyro turned to her, prepared to continue his pleas, Ororo lifted a hand, flicked her wrist in a dismissive gesture, and the winds whipped Pyro from his feet and slammed him through the display window of a GapKids across the street.

He did not emerge, and Wolverine had a moment to wonder if he was unconscious, or merely hiding. Logan and Storm did not speak, then, for they did not need to. It reminded Wolverine of the time they had spent on the road together, just the two of them, forming a bond of friendship that could never be broken. It was a pleasant memory amidst a barrage of hellish new events.

* * *

''I'm really beginning to enjoy myself, Bishop,'' Unuscione ranted. ''Thank you for being so cooperative, and giving so freely of yourself . . . and your blood!''

The shimmering green exoskeleton Unuscione's psionic powers generated was completely at her command. She raised an arm encased in a giant block of glowing energy, and swung it down toward Bishop. He barely escaped being crushed by it, but could not save himself completely. Unuscione struck him from behind with her exoskeleton—the third time she had connected—and Bishop stumbled forward and slammed his head against the pavement.

When he stood, blood flowed from his nose and mouth, and from several scrapes on his right cheek.

''You are a madwoman, Unuscione!'' he shouted. ''Perhaps I sound as mad as you with my raving, but you must listen to me. You all must listen. What Magneto has built this day cannot stand. The Sentinels may be temporarily under your control, but that cannot last. They have but one purpose, to keep the human race dominant through the containment and eventually the destruction of mutants.

''I have seen it, don't you understand?'' he cried. ''If Magneto should triumph, all mutants will suffer, millions will die!''

''Magneto is the savior of mutantkind, Bishop, not its destroyer!'' Unuscione retorted, even as she swung at him again. ''It is because of such blasphemy that the X-Men must die!''

Bishop was slowing down, becoming slightly disoriented. It was impossible for him to dodge Unuscione this time, and he was battered down beneath her onslaught. For the space of several seconds, he lay stunned. Unuscione likely believed him beaten, for she appeared about to move on to another foe. Bishop felt a strange tingling all through his body, and his hands felt as though they'd fallen asleep, all pins and needles.

To his great surprise, he found himself charged with energy. With throbbing in his head, he looked up at Unuscione. When he saw her, Bishop realized where he had garnered this power supply. Unuscione's exoskeleton had dimmed noticeably, its glowing green a far lighter hue. In the sunlight, it was gossamer as cobwebs. And the woman, overconfident in her abilities, did not seem to have noticed it as of yet.

Without either of them realizing it, Unuscione had, with each blow, filled Bishop with explosive energy. If he had a few moments to recover, he felt he would be all right. But Unuscione would not allow him those moments if she suspected he was not completely defeated, or even dead. Painfully, Bishop rolled over onto his stomach, facing Unuscione. Immediately, she lashed out again with her exoskeleton. But this time it barely fazed him. It was as if she had dumped a bucket of water on him, for all the harm it did.

And when she withdrew, the green glow had faded even further. Bishop felt it growing inside him, the heat stoked like a furnace.

"For the future," he grunted, and released all the pent up energy he had unwittingly stolen from Unuscione.

Even if her exoskeleton had been at full strength, Bishop was attacking with the same energy, only rechanneled through his own body. His blast passed through her force field as if it were not there. Unuscione screamed and crumbled to the ground.

"For the future," Bishop muttered again, then began to drag himself to his feet in order to help his comrades.

SANCTUARY

* * *

Fred Dukes was a little bit concerned. All four of his companions, including his old buddy Unus's little girl, had been downed by just four X-Men. He wasn't worried that he might lose. No, the thought never even occurred to him. After all, he was stronger than the Beast, Wolverine's claws couldn't penetrate his rubbery hide, Storm could not call up a strong enough wind to move him, and this Bishop guy . . . hell, all he had was a gun, it looked like.

No, the Blob was mainly concerned because he didn't think he could capture them like Magneto had ordered. Sure, maybe he could keep them busy until the other Acolytes came around, that was possible. But just as he didn't think they'd be able to defeat him without Professor X or Jean Grey, who might be able to get into his head, or Cyclops, who had once burned a hole in his body, he didn't think he could do much in return. If he could get his hands on any of them, why, he'd snap them like twigs. But they were all much faster than he was.

Storm's winds buffeted his body, but he did not even have to lean into the wind to stay upright. They started to whip around him like a tornado, and at first he thought she might be trying to lift him off the ground with it. Then it hit him—this was something she had tried in earlier fights. Well, actually, it had worked before. She was trying to cut him off from oxygen so he wouldn't be able to breath and he would just pass out.

Just before all air left him, Dukes inhaled deeply, filling his massive lungs. He'd be able to hold his breath like that for several minutes. That's all the time he had to do something, something that would let him win.

Fred Dukes knew he wasn't the smartest guy in the world. But he also knew a good idea when he had one. Rolling his eyes as if he was about to pass out, Dukes fell to the ground, sending a tremor through the street around them. As soon as Storm let up with her winds, he sank his fingers into the pavement and tore a huge chunk out of the street. Sitting up, he threw it at Storm with all his strength. The pavement broke apart in the air, and one piece did clip her arm, enough to distract her for a moment.

"All right, Beast, Wolverine, come on," the Blob taunted. "I'm ready for ya. I'm gonna take you guys down, then grab that Storm chippie and make like Kong. I'll be the Blob, the Eighth Wonder of the World!"

Suddenly, both the Beast and Wolverine stopped moving toward him. For a moment, Dukes didn't understand. Then he got it.

"Oh, no . . ." he began, but it was too late. The X-Men were laughing at him.

"Why, thank you, Fred," the Beast said. "Without Iceman, we were going to have a decidedly difficult time finding Magneto. If I am not mistaken, and I do not believe that I am, you have just told us precisely where to look."

The Blob was flustered.

"Okay, maybe so, but you rubes still have to get by me, and you know from experience that nothing moves the Blob!" Dukes said, sure he could still pull it off. He'd blown it big, that was for sure, letting it slip where Magneto's headquarters were. But it wasn't over yet. Not by far.

"We don't have to move you, Fred," the Beast said.

"We don't even have to get by ya, bub," Wolverine

added, lighting up a cigar that Dukes hadn't even seen him produce.

"What are you . . ." he began to ask, then saw that the one called Bishop, who the Acolytes had said was from the future, if you could believe it, had slung his plasma rifle over his shoulder. He wasn't even aiming at the Blob anymore.

"Indeed, Mr. Dukes," Storm continued as she walked calmly to where the other X-Men stood. "In the past, you see, we have been forced to fight you to the finish because you were committing some crime, or endangering innocent lives. We were, obviously, after you."

"This time," the Beast continued for her, "you are after us, as it were."

"That's right," Dukes said, still baffled by the X-Men's behavior. "So come on an' mix it up. I'll hand all you jerks your heads this time around."

"It ain't gonna happen, Dukes," Wolverine snarled. "See, we don't have to fight you. All we gotta do is make sure we're all faster than you. An' I seen you runnin', bub. No problem there."

"You gotta be kiddin'!" the Blob shouted, understanding suddenly what they were saying. "You've gotta stay an' fight me. I'm dangerous."

"True," Storm said. "But Magneto is our priority today."

The X-Men turned and started off in the direction of the Empire State Building, moving at a good clip. Though he knew he had no hope of keeping up with them if they started to really run, and he was resigned to the idea of failure yet again, Fred Dukes started to move after the X-Men as fast as he was able.

Which wasn't very fast at all. When he had gone half

a block, they had gone two. He was so wound up in the chase, and in his disappointment, that he stopped paying attention to where he walked. His right foot landed on one of the eight by eight sewer gratings that ran along above the subway lines throughout Manhattan.

The grates were sturdy steel, but no match for eight hundred and fifty pounds, in motion and concentrated in the fourteen inches of flesh the Blob called a foot. The grating caved in, and Fred Dukes went with it, tumbling down into a darkened subway tunnel forty-seven feet below.

The only thing hurt was his pride.

The Blob looked up and down the darkened tracks. After a moment's consideration, he headed south, in the general direction of Magneto's headquarters, and hoped he'd find a subway station—and steps to the surface— before too long.

CHAPTER 12

The open-air observation deck that circumscribed the top of the Empire State Building had been closed to the public for years. Too many children, and immature adults, had dropped things off the building from there. A nickel or quarter dropped from that height might kill a human being. Too risky, the authorities had apparently believed.

Magneto had opened the observation deck, made it the seat from which he would survey his domain. And it was a glorious view, without a doubt. Everything below was tiny, insignificant, which Magneto felt was appropriate given the gravity of the decisions that would be made from this, his new aerie. Decisions that were already being made.

It had begun to come together quite nicely. Mutant recruits were pouring in by the dozen, both from within the city and from around the country. Soon, he expected to receive the first foreign immigrants, and he would welcome them with open arms. Their international citizenship would be an example for the rest of the world, an example of how to live in peace. But the humans would not have time even to learn from it, since Magneto planned to rule the rest of the world before long.

When the sun had risen, Magneto's pulse had quickened with the spreading of the light. Office buildings gleamed in the distance, light glinted off the surface of the Hudson River. The sky was perfectly clear and blue, the kind of summer day from which memories were made. Magneto could see much of the city from his perch, could see several of the Sentinels he had positioned to keep watch over the mutant sanctuary, their deep purple armor shining.

SANCTUARY

Though his dream had always been to improve the world for his fellow mutants, as selfless a goal as any man had pursued, still he felt the swell of pride in his chest. It was not completed yet. There was still so much to do, so many obstacles to overcome, but it had begun. It occurred to him that he would need a name for the place. Manhattan would most definitely not do. His space station was Avalon. Camelot or Shangri-La would be laughably trite. Still, something simple, direct, would be best.

Haven. He could think of nothing more apropos.

Below, the many citizens of Haven were beginning to gather. The word was going out to the odd groupings that had sprung up around the city that there was to be an address by Magneto. By the emperor. He had wondered what kind of resistance there might be to his leadership. But, according to the Acolytes, other than some humans and, of course, the X-Men, there had been no open opposition. After all, there would be no Haven without Magneto.

Ah, but the X-Men. One of the obstacles he had been considering a moment earlier. Xavier's students were vast in number, and yet only a handful had appeared to oppose the foundation of Haven. Magneto was both puzzled and somewhat alarmed by this. What might Xavier have planned, he wondered. It was possible the small group sent in advance was merely a diversion, to mask a greater, more ingenious attack.

It did not seem likely, given how far Magneto had already progressed with his plans. Xavier would normally have made his move already. But then, Charles had been changing of late, becoming somewhat unpredictable. It made him a more dangerous opponent. Not that Magneto was concerned. Merely curious.

Still, though there were only a handful of X-Men on hand, Magneto had long since learned that even a single follower of Xavier's dream was enough to create serious problems. That was why they needed to be captured and made an example of as expediently as possible. The citizens of Haven needed to have their faith in Magneto bolstered by the realization that Xavier's chosen path could only lead to failure.

First, though, he needed to capture the X-Men.

Magneto breathed deeply of the air, despite the pollution that clogged it. Wind whipped his white hair across his eyes and he felt a bit of a chill, though it promised to be a very warm day. There was much to be done. But he did not feel as though he could move forward until the nuisance of the X-Men was eliminated.

The wind carried a sound to him, then, a chittering noise as though a swarm of locusts was about to descend. It lasted only a moment. Then the gossamer, three-dimensional image of Scanner flickered into existence directly in front of him, suspended in the air many hundreds of feet above the street.

"My lord," Scanner's projected image addressed him, performing a proper reverance with her hands to her forehead, then her lips, and finally her heart.

"Yes, Scanner, what news?" he asked.

"Mixed, I am afraid, lord," she answered. "The team you sent out eliminated Iceman, who appears to be dead. They then confronted the other four X-Men, but were soundly defeated. Inadvertently, the Blob revealed our location. The X-Men are on their way here, and will arrive within minutes. They are, of course, attempting to be inconspicuous in their approach, but we have little time before their attack.''

''Excellent,'' Magneto said happily.

''My lord?'' Scanner asked, and the puzzled expression on her face amused Magneto greatly.

''It is almost over, Scanner,'' he said. ''Very soon, we will consolidate our gains, and move forward. And there won't be anybody to stop us.''

''I am honored to play whatever small part I may in your grand design, lord,'' Scanner said proudly.

''Scanner, please ask Voght to gather up Unuscione and the others,'' he said. ''Have those who are badly injured seek immediate attention, and assemble the others in the lobby. The X-Men will have a surprise waiting for them.''

Scanner shimmered and disappeared, even as a smile of real pleasure spread across Magneto's features.

''I only wish I could see Xavier's face,'' he said. Then, for the first time in a long time, Magneto laughed.

* * *

''What the hell are we doing here, Kevin?'' Trish Tilby asked, somewhat rhetorically.

Trish had worked with Kevin O'Leary a dozen times, maybe more. He'd always been a pro, no matter what kind of crisis they were trying to cover for the network. But this was another story entirely.

''Well, I don't know, Trish,'' Kevin said, a caustic tone to his voice. ''You tell me. Are we doing our jobs, or just trying to stay alive?''

A little of both, was how Trish wanted to respond. But she figured Kevin was too on edge to be anything less than argumentative, perhaps even hostile, so she kept her thoughts to herself. They were, indeed, doing their jobs. In fact, there was no question that this was the biggest story either of them had ever covered, probably ever would cover. And from the inside, no less.

But that was also part of the problem. Though Trish had always been on the side of the angels where mutants were concerned, as liberal as they came, she had recently begun to wonder if there were not some truth to the argument that mutants, as a race, were dangerous to humanity. Now, with Magneto's latest triumph, she was certain of it.

Certainly mutants were the next step in human evolution, and therefore by their very existence threatened the human race. But it was more than that. In the here and now, mutants were hazardous to the world's health.

It shamed her that she would even consider punishing all mutants for the actions of a few, but the potential for death and destruction was just too high. If Magneto could be defeated, and the world recovered from this incident, there would be a host of politicians calling for mutant work camps, which Trish would find abhorrent. But there would also be calls for the forcible registration and tracking of all mutants, an idea that had been made law and repealed once before. She wasn't sure where she would stand on that issue.

Her uncertainty bothered her deeply. The X-Men, the Beast in particular, had trusted her. Though she and Hank were no longer involved romantically, the change in her philosophy that Magneto's actions had brought about made her feel as though she had betrayed them. Betrayed him. She had been their ally. Trish knew the X-Men were virtuous and necessary, and admired all that they stood for.

But they were constantly protecting humans from other mutants, essentially saving the world from themselves. Which only proved the danger they posed to humanity.

On the other hand, Trish wondered if her feelings, and the feelings of those so afraid of mutants, weren't really based on the fear that humanity was going to die out soon. If humanity was making its next evolutionary step, what did that mean for their comfortable little lives and lifestyles?

"God, I feel so guilty!" Trish said aloud.

Not only did it seem to her as though she had betrayed Hank and the X-Men in her heart, but she and Kevin had become Magneto's propaganda machine. Already they had sent half a dozen videotapes by mutant messenger to the network studio in Manhattan, where two producers and an anchor had apparently stayed on through the crisis.

Censored by Magneto, the material really was propaganda. They wouldn't be able to tell the real story until they were allowed to leave his presence. They had no choice. At least, that's what Trish tried to tell herself. In truth, she did have a choice. She could simply have said no.

"Hey, Trish, listen," Kevin said, trying to assuage her anguish over the events of the past few hours. "We're doing all we can to serve ourselves, our beliefs, and the public here. I know you're worried about your buddy McCoy, but he and the X-Men have been through worse than this. They'll be fine. And he would definitely understand . . ."

The air buzzed with energy and the holographic image

of the Acolyte called Scanner appeared in the middle of the office space they had appropriated.

"Lord Magneto has commanded that you appear on the street in one hour, prepared to document his victory over the X-Men, and his first state of the nation address to the citizens of Haven," Scanner said.

Then she was gone.

"Haven?" Kevin asked.

"Obviously where we live now," Trish answered.

But that wasn't the part that had piqued her attention, the part that had made her wince with painful regret. "Victory over the X-Men," Scanner had said.

"Hank," Trish whispered to herself. "Oh, God. It wasn't supposed to be like this."

* * *

Operation: Carthage was well under way. Surgical Ops Unit One made its way in stealth through the maintenance tunnel that ran parallel to the PATH train tracks. Several minutes had passed since they had moved directly under the invisible barrier set up around Manhattan island by the fleet of Sentinels at Magneto's command. Major Ivan Skolnick felt like he'd been holding his breath for an hour.

Skolnick held up a hand, halting SOU1's progress. They stood completely still, each of them listening for the mechanical whine that would signal a Sentinel's approach, the crumbling of pavement and tons of soil that would give way under its attack.

One hundred and twenty seconds ticked by without incident. For good measure, Skolnick waited twice that time before signalling the team to move forward again. Not long after that, they were hustling into the World

SANCTUARY

Trade Center PATH station, up two sets of escalators, and then out to the street.

By the time they emerged from the World Trade Center building, the sun had risen. It was strange to Skolnick. Most covert operations took place under cover of night. This was different, however. The freedom of the world was at stake. The future of Major Ivan Skolnick, his children, and their children hung in the balance. He would do whatever was necessary to safeguard that future.

"Major," Sergeant Greenberg, the point-man, stepped up to report. "Firefight up ahead."

"It's time, then," Major Skolnick said, and sighed, steeling himself for what was to come. "Let's do it."

* * *

The Blob was considerably out of breath when he took the last step out of the subway station into the sunlight. It was warm on his face and neck, and he was already sweating. There was a light breeze, but it didn't help. He hated the summer.

There was a sudden flash in front of him, accompanied by a brief burst of sound that reminded him of one time when Pyro had torched an old wooden footbridge, just for fun. He lifted an arm to shield his eyes, but it was over as soon as it had begun. Where the flash had been, Amelia Voght now stood.

"Time to go, Mr. Dukes," Voght said. "I hope you're in the mood for a rematch."

Dukes grimaced.

"Am I in trouble?" he asked, knowing from experience just how much of a drag it could be to have Magneto pissed at him.

"In trouble?" Voght repeated, as if she had not understood the question. "Certainly not, Mr. Dukes. This is your country now, and it is your duty to defend it. You would only be in trouble if you did not do that. In any case, you are about to get another opportunity to beat the X-Men."

"Yeah," Dukes said, and nodded. "Yeah, I'm ready."

Before he realized it, the Blob was disappearing. Every inch of him.

* * *

"Y'know, this might just amount to the craziest thing we've ever done," Wolverine said grimly. "But I don't see as how we have much of a choice."

He looked around at his teammates and saw that each of them wore the same expression: one of fierce determination and somewhat reckless abandon. Bishop was fidgety, could barely keep his fingers from his weapon. Storm's brow was creased, her voice firm, resolute.

"Whatever the odds," Storm said sternly, "we may well be the world's only hope against Magneto and the Sentinels. The job has fallen to us, as we have always known it would."

"Let us be off!" the Beast said, attempting to lighten the mood by quoting one of his favorite bad movies, *The Sword and the Sorcerer*, which Wolverine had seen with him half a dozen times. "There's a battle in the offing! We've got kingdoms to save and women to love!"

"Speak for yourself," Storm said, and her harsh countenance crumbled in favor of a small grin.

They moved fast, rounding a corner a block away

from the Empire State Building and hugging close to shop windows as they ran for the glass doors of the lobby. Wolverine felt the wind kick up around him, and didn't have to turn around to know that Storm had taken to the air. He had point, with Beast and Bishop flanking him a few steps back and Storm above.

They expected opposition, and immediately. Like the Blob, most of that opposition would assume the X-Men were there for a fight. But they were there to take down Magneto, or remove him from Manhattan, and so draw the Sentinels away as well. Wolverine knew that the Beast and Storm would both hesitate to kill Magneto if the opportunity arose. Under any other circumstance, Bishop might have been undecided as well, but if it meant preventing the future holocaust, he would kill Magneto in a heartbeat.

And Wolverine? Hell, he'd been waiting for the opportunity to pop a claw through Magneto's skull for years. But they weren't there quite yet.

"Suddenly, I think of Dante," he heard the Beast mumble behind him as they hit the pavement and rushed toward the glass doors.

"You got it, bub," Wolverine growled. "Abandon hope, all ye who enter here."

"Shouldn't we have hit resistance already?" Bishop asked.

Nobody responded, but it was a thought Wolverine had already had. He imagined the others had as well. If this was indeed Magneto's headquarters, Scanner, or some electronic surveillance, would surely have picked them up by now.

"It's a trap," he said, completely certain.

"Indeed," the Beast concurred.

They did not slow down.

"Bishop, the doors," Storm ordered from above.

In mid-stride, Bishop slung his weapon around front and let off a stream of concussive plasma bolts that shattered the long row of floor to ceiling windows and the revolving doors in a deafening crash that lingered like an infinite echo on the ear.

"There they are," Bishop snapped, and Wolverine scanned the lobby again, eyes fighting to adjust to the differential between daylight and the interior shadow of the building.

The enemy had been spotted, all right. And sure enough they had spotted them as well. Inside the lobby stood the Kleinstocks and Senyaka, along with half a dozen unarmed combatants who were unfamiliar to Wolverine. New recruits, no doubt. That meant mutants.

"This could be a problem," he snarled. "They got a bunch o' rookies over there. We're runnin' into this blind. We got no idea what we're up against."

"It won't be the first time," Bishop said.

"We shall merely have to hope it will not be the last," the Beast added.

Then they were inside, in the thick of it. Wolverine ducked a plasma blast from one of the Kleinstocks and dove at the man. Senyaka's whip snagged his ankle, and Wolverine fell short of his aim, claws tearing a ragged gash in Harlan Kleinstock's chest instead of ripping him open.

Logan lashed out, hacking through Senyaka's psionic whip and making the mutant cry out in pain. A young boy of not more than fourteen was tossing Bishop around off to one side, while a feral teenage girl with a mouth full of hundreds of needle-thin fangs faced off against the Beast.

Without warning, Storm drove a huge blast of cold air, damp with rain, into the lobby and knocked all of the combatants from their feet. Wolverine tried not to become disoriented as he was borne aloft and slammed into a marble column. A moment later, the wind died down and Wolverine leaped to his feet once more. Bishop and the Beast were pulling themselves free from the rookie mutants, and Wolverine knew they had to make quick work of the group or they would never reach Magneto.

"Enough o' this penny-ante crap," he snarled. "Let's move!"

Wolverine went for the stairwell, knowing the elevators would not be safe for them. Sven Kleinstock blocked his way, side by side with a muscle-bound guy who seemed to be sweating acid that ate into the marble floor wherever it dripped from his body.

"You hurt my brother," Sven Kleinstock said angrily. "You're gonna pay for that, wild-boy."

Wolverine lashed out at Sven Kleinstock before the Acolyte could even begin to formulate an attack out of the threats he had made. Rather than skewer the man, as he wished, he slashed Kleinstock's chest just as he had done to the man's brother.

"You guys are twins," Wolverine said, his voice a cynical drawl. "Figure you oughta have a matched set o' scars, too. Don't want to make it too easy for people to tell you apart."

"You've made a mistake, X-Man," the acid-dripping brute said, his voice confident and menacing. "Magneto's will is law. I am called Acid, and you cannot touch me. The chemicals in my skin will instantly eat away your flesh if you try to harm me. Surrender, or I will be forced to attack.''

Wolverine looked at the rookie in astonishment for a moment. The guy was either ignorant or stupid.

''Should'a made your move when you had a shot, bub,'' he said, and grabbed Acid's throat with his left hand even as he buried the claws of his right into the chest of the novice Acolyte. He didn't kill the guy, just perforated him a bit. With the neophytes, there was always a chance they'd come around to ol' Charlie Xavier's way of thinking.

''What are you . . . aarrgh!'' Acid shouted. ''But you can't touch me! The acid . . .''

Wolverine let go and Acid toppled to the marble floor. His adamantium claws were not even scratched or pitted from contact with Acid's skin, but the palm of his left glove had been eaten away, along with much of the flesh beneath. The knuckles of his right hand had suffered the same fate. They were already healing, and Wolverine steeled himself against the pain. There were times when the healing hurt more than the injury itself, and this was one of them.

Off to Wolverine's left, Senyaka attacked Bishop, which was foolish of the Acolyte if he knew anything of Bishop's powers. The force of his psionic whip was absorbed by the future X-Man, and Bishop shocked Senyaka with a blast of his own power. The Beast leaped above the needle-fanged girl and caused her to slam into the wall, where she howled in agony.

Harlan and Sven Kleinstock were concentrating their efforts on taking Storm down. She stood in a scatter of shattered glass where the revolving doors used to be. When they went for her, Storm raised her hands and out of nowhere came a massive bolt of lightning. The Klein-stock brothers were frozen in place as the electricity of the lightning coursed through their bodies, and then they slumped to the ground.

"Now, let's take Magneto!" Storm yelled, and they headed for the stairs. Already Wolverine could feel the wind swelling behind them, a wind Storm might be able to use to shoot them up toward the top of the stairwell. In other circumstances, moving all four of them would be difficult, but the stairwell was enclosed, and Storm would be able to focus her power.

They raced for the stairs, were about to pass the elevators when their doors exploded outward in a shriek of metal. Wolverine had only a moment to notice Magneto floating, in all his imperial grandeur, out of the elevator shaft. Then he and his teammates were thrown back by a wave of magnetic power. While he might move the other three X-Men by the iron in their blood, Magneto could simply grab mental hold of Wolverine's adamantium skeleton and push. He did.

The four X-Men tumbled to the ground in front of the shattered face of the Empire State Building. The Beast was first to his feet, but the rest quickly followed. Wolverine's claws had retracted during Magneto's attack, but they slid out once again, gleaming in the sunshine.

"You can bring on as many toy soldiers as you like, Magneto," Wolverine snarled. "But at the end of the day, it's us against you. And like always, you're gonna lose!"

"Surrender, Magneto," Storm urged. "Do not push this insanity any further."

"You X-Men are either brave or very stupid," a female voice said, and Wolverine spun to see Amelia Voght, and a few unwelcome friends.

Voght stood at the center of the street, with the Blob, Pyro, Cargil, Unuscione, Scanner, and a whole bunch of other mutants that Wolverine would have called losers any other day. He recognized Hairbag and Slab, a couple of super-strong stooges who once worked for Mr. Sinister. There were other faces he recognized as well, and none of them friendly.

Emerging from the Empire State Building were Magneto, Senyaka, half a dozen rookies and a pair of angry, bleeding Kleinstocks.

"You are hopelessly outmatched, X-Men," Magneto said calmly. "I don't think I will even need to call any Sentinels in to subdue you. In fact, I believe I can say with confidence that you are as good as defeated already."

"The X-Men can never be defeated, Magnus," the Beast said. "You know that. Take down one or two, or four of us, but there will always be more X-Men to pursue Xavier's dream."

"Charles Xavier is a fool," Magneto snapped, and Wolverine took satisfaction in that. The Beast knew how to push the mutant terrorist's buttons, that was for sure.

"I didn't hear nobody yellin' forfeit, Magneto," Wolverine growled. "Come on, slick. Just you an' me."

"I'm tempted to kill you, you know," he said. "Particularly you, Wolverine. Your boastful ranting has become most tiresome. But I believe I will allow you to bear witness to my great triumph, the victory of mutants over humanity. Perhaps I bear some small foolish hope that you will begin to see the wisdom of my actions and join with me.''

"You madman!" Bishop shouted suddenly. "You've doomed all mutants with your actions!"

Bishop fired off several plasma rounds, but Magneto easily deflected them.

"That will do," he said. "Take them, Acolytes. Now."

A sea of mutant warriors charged the X-Men from all sides. With the Beast and Bishop at his back, Wolverine began to fight. Still, he knew it was useless. Magneto could probably beat the four of them singlehandedly, and he was simply hanging back and allowing his Acolytes to make a go of it. They didn't have a chance in hell of winning. Not without reinforcements. And reinforcements were not forthcoming.

"Now, Magneto, it is time to face your destiny!" Storm cried as she rose into the air and began whipping her hands around to command the winds and the storm, to call lightning down on Magneto.

"Ah, Ororo, perhaps the most powerful of the X-Men in your way," Magneto called to her. "But with a fatal flaw."

Wolverine saw what he was going to do, but Storm, unfortunately, did not. Before Logan could warn her, Magneto had used his powers to tear off the trunk of a Toyota parked nearby. The huge metal square flew through the air behind Storm. She didn't even see it coming, and then Magneto had wrapped it around her as though it were nothing more than tissue paper. The noise it made as it hit the ground, with Storm inside, was terrible to hear.

His mind reeling, heart sick and gut on fire, Wolverine

resisted the urge to tear Magneto's throat out. The man knew Storm was a severe claustrophobe, and had played on that fact for amusement. Still, by himself, even with his comrades, Logan knew he could not win. There was only one thing to do.

With a roar of fury, he charged toward Magneto, who looked up in surprise, then narrowed his eyes with displeasure.

"Oh, please, Wolverine," Magneto said. "You of all people . . ."

With a flick of his wrist, using the magnetic power at his mental command, Magneto picked Wolverine up by his adamantium skeleton and threw him a block and a half.

* * *

"Enough!" Magneto shouted. "It's over!"

The fighting had finished, and his Acolytes were just taunting the X-Men now. Beast and Bishop were restrained, barely conscious, and Storm was still confined within the car trunk. Magneto could hear her screaming. At some point, he would have to release her from that metal shroud. The sooner he was able to get the restraints on them that would prevent their minds from accessing their powers, the more comfortable Magneto would be. As confident as he was now, any living X-Man was dangerous.

Why, then, was he letting them live?

It was simple. For the moment, at least, it was the next best thing to being able to rub his victory in Charles Xavier's face personally. His philosophy had triumphed, but it would do no good if his opponents did not witness it, and concede defeat. It was even possible that, before long, he might be able to force Xavier to concede defeat. In person.

That moment was a long time coming. It would be wonderful.

Yet, something was amiss. Something . . .

"Where is Wolverine?" he asked, realizing immediately what had gone wrong.

A moment later, Amelia Voght confirmed it for him.

"I am sorry, Lord Magneto," she said, uncharacteristically using the proper deference. "It appears that Wolverine has escaped."

Magneto breathed deeply, wondering whether he should simply allow Wolverine to run. It was not as if he could do much harm to the mutant empire, now that it had begun. Yet, his Acolytes would expect him to give chase, and it would not do to allow them room for wonder or conjecture. Now that he had truly assumed the mantle of emperor of mutants, his plans demanded complete obedience in the ranks.

"Amelia, take Senyaka, the Kleinstocks, and Needle, and go after Wolverine. Do not return without him," Magneto instructed.

Amelia nodded and began to withdraw.

"Attention, followers of Magneto!" a voice boomed over a bullhorn. "This is Major Ivan Skolnick of the U.S. Army. Surrender yourselves immediately, or you will be terminated!"

Stunned, Magneto turned to see a dozen soldiers, armed with weapons even he was unfamiliar with.

"Scanner, how did they . . ." he began, but already he could see that Scanner was shaking her head in anticipation of his question. She did not know how they had gotten past the Sentinels.

Then it hit him. "Followers of Magneto," Major Skolnick had said. But what of Magneto himself? It was all too obvious. He was to be slaughtered, eliminated. They were taking no chances. And Magneto had no idea what their weapons were or what they could do. With his magnetic ability he reached out for those weapons, prepared to shatter them. He was hardly surprised when he realized the weapons had no metal parts, none at all. After all, they had been made to kill him.

"On my mark!" Skolnick shouted.

Too late to attack, Magneto braced to defend himself.

CHAPTER 13

Magneto instantly erected a magnetic force shield around himself that he hoped would protect him from their assault. And after the initial barrage, he would destroy them.

That, at least, was his intention. What happened next astonished him, as well as the rest of the mutants gathered in the street. But it was clear that no one was more astonished than the soldiers under Major Skolnick's command.

"Abort mission!" Major Skolnick shouted.

Silence reigned supreme for the space of several heartbeats. All eyes were on Major Skolnick. Magneto stared at the man as though he had spoken in some ancient, forgotten language. So did his subordinates. Magneto's gathered followers, the new citizens of Manhattan, of Haven, began to close in on the soldiers.

"No!" Magneto said, his deep voice rumbling through the air, breaking the silence. None of the mutants moved again.

"Major?" one of the soldiers shouted across the street to Skolnick. "What the hell . . . ?"

Major Skolnick hung his head, lowered his weapon, then dropped it to the pavement.

"He must be under the mutie's control somehow," a female soldier shouted. "Take them down!"

"No!" Skolnick commanded.

Weaponless, he lifted his hands and gestured toward the members of his squad. Magneto watched in fascination as the air in front of Skolnick's hands seemed to bend and warp. Then there was a resounding boom as a blast of directed sonic energy burst from Skolnick and slammed the rest of the soldiers to the ground, covering their ears. None of them moved to get up. In truth, none of them moved.

"Are they dead?" Magneto asked as he moved slowly, warily toward Skolnick. It had occurred to him that this could still all be part of some plot to capture him. There was a more likely scenario however.

"God, no," Skolnick said, self-loathing tainting his response. "I could never do that to my own people."

"*We* are your people, Major," Magneto said, testing his hypothesis.

Skolnick looked up at him, perhaps preparing a sharp retort, but then the man seemed to collapse with relief.

"Promise you won't hurt them," he said. "They're good people, just doing their jobs."

"If only they had known that which they despised the most was also the leader they looked up to and admired," Magneto said, truly saddened by the state of the world. "Don't worry, Major, we will deposit them at the border unharmed. In the meantime, welcome to Haven, my friend. With your obviously substantial mutant power, you will be a great asset to the community, I am certain."

"I joined the army to fight for freedom, for people's right to be free," Skolnick said. "Now, I want to make sure that I stay free, that what children I may one day have will remain free, even if they're mutants like their father."

Magneto looked closely at the man, and decided to accept him at face value. His emotions were so powerful, so raw, that they had to be genuine.

"Then you share my dreams, Major," Magneto said. "Come with me, now. I need someone to organize my many new recruits, and I believe you're the man for the job."

Skolnick seemed to brighten somewhat at the prospect of responsibility, to stand a little straighter with the knowledge that he would still be part of the hierarchy, commanding a fighting force.

"I don't relish the idea of fighting against my former comrades," he said, not quite saluting but speaking in tones reserved for a commander.

"If they will allow us our freedom, you will not have to," Magneto said. "I know you may feel as if I forced your hand, forced a decision upon you by my actions. Indeed, that was my intention. To force a decision upon many hundreds of thousands of mutants around the world. My message to those mutants is simple: stand with us, or stand aside."

"I stand with you," Skolnick said.

"Excellent," Magneto responded. "In twenty minutes, I will address the citizens of Haven. I would be honored if you would stand with me on the platform."

"Yes, sir!" Major Ivan Skolnick snapped. And this time, he actually did salute.

Magneto liked that. Quite a bit, actually.

* * *

When Magneto had bent and twisted the car trunk around her like a metal shroud, Storm had begun to scream. Thirty seconds passed before she was even capable of rational thought. She had forced herself to stop crying out in panic, then fought to slow her fast, heavy breathing to avoid hyperventilation. It was an exercise she had been through before, each time she had needed to fight against her claustrophobia. It had not become any easier.

Childhood trauma had given her an obsessive, uncontrollable fear of confinement in small spaces. Magneto had known that, and taken advantage of the fact. Unlike so many other enemies they had faced over the years, Magneto did not consider himself one of the bad guys. Indeed, for a time, he had affiliated himself with the X-Men, attempted Xavier's dream, tried to live within the parameters of the life the X-Men led.

The attempt failed rather spectacularly. But that had not stopped Magneto from learning about them. Who they were. What made them tick. Their strengths and, unfortunately, their weaknesses. They had never completely trusted him, never really thought of him as a friend, or even as a teammate, but he had gotten in close. Magneto knew them better than any warrior should ever know his enemy. Many times, it had worked to their disadvantage.

But to Storm's thinking, never so horribly as now.

Storm was sweating, but her arms were trapped at her sides making her unable to wipe the beads of moisture from her face. She blinked to clear them from her eyes and fought against the urge to grind her teeth, or, conversely, to open her mouth and scream again.

''Goddess, no,'' she whispered.

It took all of her concentration, every good memory she could summon into her mind, every scent of air that snuck into her iron coffin, but she held the scream inside, held back the tide of panic. She could not defeat the fear, however. The fear was there, monolithic in its stature, completely insurmountable. It washed over her in waves with the ache of her body, bruised and battered by the fall to Earth. She didn't think anything was broken. She hoped not, anyway.

She had tried to close her eyes, but that did not help. Better to stare at the darkness, stare at the tiny cracks of light that seeped into the seam Magneto had left. Using mental exercises taught her by Professor Xavier and Jean Grey, Storm began to block out, little by little, her predicament. She removed herself, her mind, from that confined space and delved instead into her memories.

As a child, she had been an orphan thief in Cairo, Egypt. The city was stifling, heat and humanity pressing in from all sides. Though the sky was blue above, she had never felt comfortable there. As a young woman, she had come into her mutant abilities and ventured out over the verdant African plains. The people of the plains called her Wind-Rider, and when she brought the rain, they began to call her goddess.

Goddess.

Soaring the skies by azure day and sable night, she grew into the role, became protective of her people. From a ragged, barely noticed street urchin, she had grown into the focus of an entire people. Yet still she was blind to the world and its problems, fortunate enough to be innocent. Until Charles Xavier arrived to recruit her. He opened her eyes, then, and try as she might, she had never been able to close them again. When Ororo became Storm, she started on a road that would give her a hard, jaded edge.

But inside she was still the little street thief. Inside she was still the Wind-Rider. Inside she was still the goddess of the plain. Still innocent. That was where she retreated with the flow of memories. Somewhere neither

Magneto nor her claustrophobia could ever hurt her, at least until panic overwhelmed her again.

And just as she had arrived there, at a kind of tenuous peace, the metal sheet wrapped around her began to shriek as it was peeled away from her body. Harsh sunlight rushed in, and Storm lifted her hand—she was able to lift her hand!—to block out the sun. She blinked several times, trying to force her eyes to adjust. Someone was leaning over her, though she could not quite make out who. She didn't have to. She knew his voice well enough.

"I'm so very sorry, Ororo," Magneto said with apparent sincerity. "I know how terrible this must have been for you, but it was all I could think to do in order to expedite matters. I hope you understand."

"You've made a grave error, Magneto," she said, even as he lifted her from her premature tomb. "The world will not allow you to go on unchallenged. If you'd picked some deserted island, a frozen tundra or desert wasteland, perhaps they would not have bothered with you. But there's no way you can simply appropriate one of the largest and most important cities in the world."

"It's just the beginning," Magneto said proudly, and now she could see him clearly, white mane gleaming in the sunshine, looking as regal as he hoped to be.

"Restrain her," he said.

After the time she'd spent confined, Storm was still somewhat disoriented and unable to focus quickly enough to defend herself. Before she even realized what was being done, metal alloy clamps had been placed over her hands and wrists, and a similar collar around her neck. The restraints not only held her body in check, but cut off access to her mutant ability. It was not the first time Magneto had used such technology on the X-Men, but Storm silently vowed that it would be the last.

"What are we now, Magneto, pets to keep you company?" she asked, and though her voice seethed with sarcasm, a part of her was sincere.

"Nothing of the kind," he replied, feigning shock. "No, Ororo, though I hope one day you will be converts, for now you are witnesses to the creation of Haven, the mutant empire. And, of course, you will also serve as excellent teaching tools, examples to show that Magneto cannot be defeated. A kind of ornamentation if you will."

"You are as vile as Wolverine has always insisted," she spat.

"You'll never know how sorry I am that you feel that way," Magneto said gravely. "I hope one day you will see that I have offered you what Xavier never could, freedom. I offer you brotherhood, a homeland where you are loved and embraced instead of hated and feared. Today I am a terrible villain in your eyes. But mark my words, Ororo, there will come a day when you and all the X-Men will hail me as a hero."

Storm breathed deeply, truly feeling her freedom from confinement for the first time, shaking off the terrors of her claustrophobia. She looked away from Magneto a moment, considering his words not for their value but for their delusion. It was a beautiful day, and Storm felt as if something had been stolen from her because she could not enjoy it.

"I want what you offer, Magneto," she said honestly, looking once more at his face, into his steel grey eyes. "I want it more than I have ever yearned for anything."

Magneto seemed surprised at first, and then pleased.

Finally, his eyes narrowed. For he knew Storm, knew the X-Men, all too well.

"But the price you ask is far too high," she continued. "I am not willing to sacrifice so much of what I believe. The ethical fight is, in many ways, far more important than the physical one. For the moment, you have won the latter. But the former you lost decades ago. Thus, in effect, you cannot win."

A cloud seemed to pass over Magneto's face. Ororo knew she had angered him with the truth, and it felt good.

"You are mistaken, Wind-Rider," Magneto said, his animosity revealing itself. "Look around you, Storm. *I have already won.* It is over. Xavier's dream has been defeated forevermore."

Magneto spread his arms wide, and Storm turned fully around for the first time. She was astounded and appalled by what she saw. They stood on a thrown together platform, as if at a political rally, at the center of Times Square. Filling the street for blocks in every direction, packed tight shoulder to shoulder, were people. Magneto's people. Mutants.

Storm saw many she recognized, but far more she did not.

"Goddess," she whispered to herself. "Where have they all come from?"

"From fear, from hiding," Magneto answered from behind her. "I have drawn them out of their terror, given them freedom, given them life. They have traveled here, are even now traveling here from around the world. They are the citizens of Haven. They are our long-suffering brothers and sisters, now vindicated. They are the hope for the future. Now do you see what I have done?''

Storm scanned the crowd, still stunned. There had to be many hundreds, perhaps a thousand already. And it was only the beginning. If Magneto was correct, there would soon be tens of thousands of mutants in Manhattan. At that point, it might be too late to reverse what the madman had begun.

To her left, Bishop and the Beast stood, trussed as she was, the object of ridicule from many in the audience. Several of the Marauders they had faced the night before were there. The Blob and Pyro were also in the crowd, but the Toad was nowhere in sight, apparently too badly wounded to appear. On stage near the X-Men were several of the Acolytes.

Where were the others? Storm wondered.

Then it hit her. Wolverine was not here. Magneto must have sent them out after him. That was when hope began to bloom in Storm's heart. As long as Logan was free, she knew that victory was still within their grasp. Someway, somehow, they would find a way to stop Magneto's mad dream before it tore the world apart.

* * *

The Beast was despondent. Iceman had been ambushed, might even have been . . . but no, he dared not even think it. In any case, Bobby would be no help to them for the moment. Wolverine had escaped, but was likely to be heading out of Manhattan. Even if he made it, and found help, Hank wondered if Logan could make it back in time.

And after all, what help was there? The military would be of little or no assistance. Unless Scott and the others had returned from Hala, or X-Factor had made it back from Genosha in time, they were on their own. That was how he'd have to play it. He would have to assume they were on their own, that they could not expect help from any quarter.

The gears of his mind began to click, turning their predicament over, trying to find a way not only to escape, but to take Magneto out of play simultaneously. Hank did not expect to find an answer, but it was not in his nature to surrender. He was considered among the most brilliant minds the United States had produced in the twentieth century. He wasn't going to give up just because some fascist mutants had tied his hands.

Searching for inspiration, he scanned the crowd, the street, the buildings around him. Inevitably, he thought of King Kong, who had scaled the building just to find some private time with the woman he loved, and died for his trouble. Stupid ape. Granted, that was fiction, but unless you could fly, up was never an option for escape.

On the platform behind him, Storm and Magneto argued heatedly. Hank barely paid attention. To his right, Bishop stared out at the gathered mutants, his eyes glassed over with horror. He didn't move, or speak a word. Bishop wasn't going to be much help.

Hank looked to his left, checking to see which Acolytes were still there, what the odds were if he managed to get his restraints off. There seemed to be more of them every time he looked. With them were a man with a TV camera, and a slender woman with dark hair and . . .

"Trish?" he mumbled to himself in wonder.

Trish Tilby had been his girlfriend for a while, before it got to be too much for her. He wasn't sure if it had been his constant disappearing act when he ran off with the X-Men, or if she just couldn't handle going out with a mutant, but she had ended it. She claimed she still wanted to be friends, but Hank had heard that before.

Still, the Beast could not help it. He knew they had no future together, but he cared for Trish Tilby deeply. Probably always would.

The woman turned slightly, and Hank saw her in profile for the first time, the glare of the sun not obscuring her features. It was her! Trish. Immediately he assumed that Magneto had taken her captive, that she must have been covering the story and been discovered, along with her cameraman. Now Hank really needed to wrack his brain for a plan. Not only did the X-Men have to escape, and take down Magneto, but they had to get Trish and her friend out as well.

Magneto turned from Storm and stalked across the platform, directly toward Trish. The Beast tensed, planning to at least make a try for Magneto if he did anything to harm Trish. Instead, as soon as Magneto neared them, the cameraman focused his lens on the mutant terrorist and Trish began to ask Magneto questions. She was doing an interview, of all things!

It was almost impossible for Hank to believe. She was not a prisoner of Magneto's, after all. She had the air of total professionalism about her, just a woman doing her job. It sickened him to even consider that she might be that callous.

Suddenly, Trish looked his way, as if Magneto had made mention of her and indicated that she should do so. She did not try to break loose of the guards, did not rail against Magneto or curse him. Just a pro, doing her job.

"Hank!" she finally saw him. "Hank, it's me, Trish. Are you okay?"

Their eyes met across the platform, and Magneto turned slightly to observe the exchange. She seemed about to approach, to speak with him, to explain, but Magneto said something to her and she merely looked away. Then the Beast looked away as well. His mind continued to work on the question of victory, but part of him seemed to wander far away for a moment.

"No," he said, softly enough that Trish could not possibly hear him. "No, I am most definitely not okay."

That was when Bishop went ballistic.

* * *

During the battle with Magneto and his growing number of Acolytes, Bishop had lost consciousness. When he came to, he discovered that his enemies had used the intervening time wisely. He and the Beast were captive, each of them stretched out in a sort of pseudo-crucifixion on large steel struts, set up at cross angles to form, ironically, a huge "X."

He found that his hands were bound with some kind of metal alloy restraints, and there was a metal collar around his neck that matched. There seemed to be an energy emanating from the restraints, but he could not seem to use his mutant power to absorb it. It finally occurred to him that this might be the hidden secondary, and more valuable, purpose of the restraints. Bishop could almost feel his power draining away.

They had lost.

A crowd of mutants had gathered to listen to Magneto speak. Bishop could see the fervor in their expressions, could feel the excitement in the air. Many of them, he knew, were noncombatant, nonviolent individuals who likely spent their lives trying to hide their genetic mutations. To them, Bishop realized, Magneto must have seemed like some kind of savior, a mutant messiah come down to free them from the hatred and humiliation, the fear and frustration of their lives.

Bishop understood, perhaps far better than the other X-Men. Though he came from a future where the X-Men were legends, where the ideals espoused by Charles Xavier had been perpetuated until they were almost religious doctrine. But like religious doctrine, they were seen by most average people as unattainable and unrealistic. In a world of violence, where self-preservation was the first order of business, harmony seemed as distant as judgment day.

It had been quite a shock for Bishop to be thrust back in time, to meet the X-Men and realize that Xavier's dream had once seemed so very possible. Violence was part of their lives as well, but their cause was far greater than self-preservation. They had a different code of honor, different dreams, different attitudes. Bishop had adopted these as best he could. But he could never completely abandon the world he had grown up in.

Xavier's dream meant hope, and the X-Men believed wholeheartedly in that dream. But Bishop came from a time of hopelessness. As he glanced at individual faces among the crowd, he knew he was seeing people who were experiencing the same epiphany he had upon traveling back in time. From a world of hopelessness, they had been given hope.

Though the X-Men were sworn to protect humanity, despite humanity's obvious fear and hatred of mutants, these poor souls had no such noble goals. Magneto had offered them a home, a better life, a place where they might raise children to be proud of themselves and their heritage. If the cost of all that included war, included conquering humanity, well that was okay. What had humans ever done except ridicule them, hound them until they had to hide from the world?

Without question, there were many in the crowd, some he recognized and some he did not, whose motives were not so benevolent. Many mutants who now followed Magneto had been using their gifts for anarchy, power, and personal gain all along. This was just the latest step in their careers, as the X-Men had already seen with the Marauders.

But the others, those whose hearts were numbed by the world, whose minds had come alive at Magneto's promise of sanctuary, Bishop could understand them. He could not blame them even a little for anything they did from that point on. But it was also those people that he knew he must appeal to. For despite his intentions, Magneto had likely put mutantkind on the road to armageddon. Bishop had lived in the shadow of that armageddon, and it was his duty to do all he could to prevent it.

"Listen, all of you!" he shouted, vying for their attention with whatever else was happening on the stage. "You must listen. I know that you have been greatly wronged, as have we all. But this is not the way to right those wrongs! By using the Sentinels to achieve his goals, Magneto may have doomed us all!"

Several dozen people, among the hundreds gathered, glanced toward him, then looked away just as quickly. They were ignoring him, unaware of the insight he had to offer, or simply uncaring. Which meant that Magneto had already won. The future that Bishop had vowed to prevent seemed, all at once, to be inevitable. It was not merely going to happen, it was happening. The Sentinels were already in use, and as soon as the government got them back under control, they would be turned on mutants the way their creator intended.

It was over.

"Noooooo!" Bishop screamed in despair. "Listen, I said! You all must listen to me! I have seen the future, I have lived it! Magneto cannot succeed! The Sentinels will be used to destroy him, to destroy the X-Men, to destroy you all! Don't you understand what he's done, what you're doing? I know you only want freedom, but you are bringing about your own terrible destiny! You must fight him, you must show the world that mutants do not have to be feared! And then the Sentinels must be destroyed!"

There was silence for several moments. Somewhere, Bishop heard a bird singing. Overhead, cottony wisps were all that marred the perfect blue summer sky. It was warm enough already that he had begun to sweat in his heavy XSE uniform. His heart beat loudly in his ears as he sent a prayer up to a god he was not even sure existed, a hope, a dream, that these people would listen.

Someone in the crowd began to snicker, and one by one, the gathered mutants erupted in a deafening roar of laughter.

All the energy left Bishop. He went slack in his restraints, hanging from the clamps that held his hands. Desperately, he searched for some shred of hope to cling to, and found none.

For the first time, it occurred to him that the only hope of avoiding the catastrophic future might lie with the X-Men's greatest enemy. If Magneto were to triumph, were truly to conquer the world for mutants, Bishop's future would never be.

Yet, who was to say if that future would be any brighter?

$$\bullet \quad \bullet \quad \bullet$$

Surgical Ops Unit One had not reported in at the assigned time. Operation: Carthage was a failure. Gyrich had no idea what happened to his team, but it didn't matter. They had been expendable from the beginning, but he had hoped they would be able to achieve their goal before they were decimated by the mutants gathered in New York.

Gyrich sighed. He did not relish the idea of a full-scale attack on Manhattan any more than the next guy; despite Val Cooper's claims, he was no warmonger. Yet he was, above all, a realist. He was willing to make the tough decisions. He only wished they were his to make. Instead, he would have to begin in earnest his attempts to convince the Secretary and the President that there was no other way.

Every second that passed further jeopardized their chances of success.

There was a knock at his trailer door.

"Who is it?"

"Colonel Tomko, sir."

Tomko. The same idiot soldier who'd screwed up the Colorado operation. If he'd done his job, none of this would have been happening. But the President did not see it that way. In fact, Gyrich thought the President might have assigned Tomko as some kind of reprimand directed at him, personally. Granted, the man had more experience with mutants than most officers. But . . .

In any case, he was stuck with the colonel. He would have to make the best of it.

He took two steps down and opened the trailer door. As Tomko moved to enter, Gyrich blocked his way and stepped outside instead. He closed the door, and checked to see if Tomko looked offended. He saw no sign of such a reaction, but knew it had to be there. Gyrich didn't care. His trailer was off limits to everyone but himself, the Secretary, and the President. To hell with anyone else.

"You called for me, Mr. Gyrich?" Colonel Tomko asked.

"Indeed I did, Colonel," Gyrich responded. "This is not my operation, as you know. You are not under my command. I will not be giving any orders here."

Gyrich thought he caught a slight smirk of pleasure on Tomko's face, but then wondered if he wasn't just being paranoid.

"Still," Gyrich continued, "I wanted to make you aware that I am urging the President to immediate action. There is no time to waste. I thought you should be aware of that, and prepare accordingly."

Colonel Tomko did not respond immediately. He looked past Gyrich, and seemed to be contemplating what had been said.

"You have a problem with that, Colonel?" Gyrich asked, hostile, ready for an argument.

"Not at all," Tomko answered. "I was just wondering, if the President does order us to attack, do you think we've got anything in the arsenal that is even going to be a nuisance to one of those?"

Tomko pointed east, and Gyrich turned and looked out over the Hudson River. A Sentinel stood there, certainly aware but completely unconcerned about the massive military buildup across the river. The sun gleamed on its metal body. It did not seem quite so sinister, quite so dangerous, in the daylight. But Gyrich had seen the schematics on the massive robots. He knew what they were made of, what they were capable of, and he had to admit he had no answer for the colonel.

If he were able to convince the President to attack, he could not be absolutely certain that they would win.

Chapter 14

The first things Scott Summers became aware of were the motion of the *Starjammer* as it sliced through space, and the hum of the hyperburners that traveled through the entire vessel as tiny vibrations. In fact, he could feel the vibrations against his cheek, which lay on cool metal. There were voices, but his brain hadn't woken up enough for him to focus on any one in particular, so he had no idea what they were saying.

His eyelids opened a crack, almost of their own volition, and light flooded in. Annoyed by the sudden light, he closed his eyes tight, then began to open them more slowly.

Scott? He heard Jean's telepathic voice, felt her probing to see if he was awake. Then he heard her true voice, speaking to him, and of him.

"Scott?" she asked aloud. "Corsair, I think he's finally coming around."

Scott opened his eyes fully, and was immediately reminded, as he was every time he awoke, of the limitations of his vision. Through a red veil, he saw Jean's face above him. He opened his eyes as wide as they could go, scrunched them shut, and opened them wide again, trying to fight off the urge to sleep once more.

"I'm awake," he said in confirmation. "I'm still here, I guess."

Jean smiled, and Corsair stepped up next to her.

"We're all still here thanks to you and Rogue," Corsair said happily. "I'm proud of you, son. How do you feel?"

"Like I've been running with the bulls, Dad," Scott answered, and pulled himself up to a sitting position. He stretched out his arms, testing his muscles and back, then rolled his head around to work the kinks out of his neck.

"I'm a little bruised, and I've got a bit of a headache, but nothing compared with the migraine I was expecting," he said. "More importantly, how are *we*, really? What's our status?"

"We're doing okay, Scott," Jean began. "We—"

"Listen, I've got to check on Ch'od and Warren, then see about waking Hepzibah up for re-entry," Corsair interrupted. "I'll give you two some privacy."

He moved off into the cabin, and Scott looked around for the first time. Raza and Hepzibah were still on the medislabs in the cabin, with digital lifesign readouts displayed above their heads, now that the ship had much of its power back. On the other side of the cabin, Rogue spoke quietly with Gambit, who seemed to have made a complete recovery.

That was when Scott realized that he had not noticed a major change on board. None of them were wearing their space suits. Even his had been removed sometime while he was unconscious. He remarked on this to Jean.

"I guess we're doing okay," he added.

"We're not out of the woods, yet," Jean answered. "There are a number of variables that have come up."

"Well?" Scott urged.

"For starters," Jean began, "and the real complicating factor, is that, now that we've got the hyperburners engaged, we can't afford to slow down until we're well within Earth's atmosphere. The engines could cut out at any time, and we'd either be back where we started, floating in space, or we'd be making an unguided descent through the atmosphere, which has all sorts of problems of its own."

"That's not good news," Scott agreed. "An unguided descent would more than likely mean crashing the ship. Of course, if we can't slow down, that's going to put a huge strain on the heat shields. We might melt into slag before we ever shut down the engines."

Jean nodded solemnly, then took in a long breath.

"That was my next point," she admitted. "Add to that the fact that, though we can't slow down, we also can't be sure the navigational system is working correctly."

"So we could hit the atmosphere at the wrong angle, slice right through and be back in space," Scott said in realization. "Which might not leave us enough power to turn around."

"Actually," Jean said, "it might force the engines to cut out again, which would leave us stranded one more time. I don't know about you, but I don't relish trying that jumpstart stunt again any time soon."

"No," Scott agreed. "It's not first on my list of things to do. But Corsair said Ch'od and Warren were piloting. What's going on?"

Jean cocked her head slightly to one side and her face was transformed into a look that Scott had become familiar with over the years. He was missing something, something obvious. He looked around the cabin again, anywhere but at Jean. Then he saw Hepzibah, lying prone on the medi-slab. Alone.

"I thought she was going to be okay?" he said, realizing immediately that Corsair would stay by his Mephisitoid lover's side until she had recovered.

"She is," Jean answered. "In fact, we're all a little surprised she hasn't come around already. We had thought to keep her sedated, in case there are any injuries we're unaware of. But Corsair said he didn't want to be a burden to anyone, that if anything went wrong, we had to be able to move as fast as possible. That means Hepzibah's got to be up and around.''

''I understand his concern, his needing to be with her,'' Scott said. ''I know how I'd feel if it were you on that medi-slab. But Warren, good as he is, isn't half the pilot my father is. Isn't that more of a risk than anything else?''

''Ch'od's piloting,'' Jean answered. ''Warren's co-piloting. If anything happens, if they really need him, Corsair will be there as always. You know that.''

''You're right,'' Scott said, nodding slowly. ''I just wish we had a little more going for us on this one.''

Look at it this way, sweetheart, Jean's mental voice said in his head. *It's amazing we've lived this long. I can't believe the powers that be would get us this far if we weren't meant to go all the way.*

''Faith,'' Scott said. ''I thought we'd used up our supply on this trip.''

''Not quite yet,'' Jean answered.

''Good,'' Scott said, and smiled. ''We'll need it.''

* * *

''I guess I missed a whole lot, eh *chere*?'' Gambit said, and smiled.

''Y'ain't exactly been the life of the party, sugar,'' Rogue replied. ''But don't worry none, Remy. As long as you ain't glowin' after that shock you got, I'd say you're doin' pretty good.''

They shared a knowing look, a slightly forced chuckle, and slowly, their hands crept across their laps to meet in the middle and intertwine. Gambit was greatly disturbed that he had been unconscious for so long, that he had been so useless to his teammates. Not that he was any expert on space travel or repairing starships.

He was also more than a little embarrassed by his attack on Archangel, and the way he had snapped at Jean earlier. Something had been shaken loose in his head when Warstar electrocuted him. It had sent him into dreamland, yes, but it had also brought him great hostility and anxiety. Something told him it would be best not to share his concerns with the X-Men, even with Rogue, but it would be on his mind every moment. He would have to watch himself for odd behavior.

Still, he felt fine, so maybe it was all over. On the other hand, fine was a relative term. Every single muscle ached, as if he'd been bent over hauling nets of crawfish into his Uncle Louis' fishing boats all day. But he was really okay, he knew it. And just seeing the sweet relief in Rogue's eyes, knowing that she had been worried about him, well that was worth what little pain he had left.

"I feel like I missed a lot, Rogue," he said. "I can't believe dat Cyclops stuck his face in de engine. I might butt heads wit' 'im now and again, but dere's a man wit' more guts den I ever seen before. I don' know if I could have done dat."

Rogue looked at him with scolding eyes.

"Don't sell yourself short, Remy," she chided. "Scott Summers is a brave man, sure. And maybe you're a little rougher around the edges, but you're cut from the same cloth. When there's trouble, y'come through for the people y'care for, the people who care for you."

Gambit said nothing. He valued Rogue's good perception of him too much to argue, but her words rankled within him. He was a good man, a courageous one as well, given the chance and no time for second thoughts. But he had not always been there when he was needed, not for his family, nor his ex-wife, Belle. He had reasons for everything he had done, had never had a choice. But still he was haunted by the times he had let other people down. Silently, he vowed that would never happen with Rogue. He would always be there when she needed him. Remy only wished he could do something to help her now. To help them all.

Corsair appeared from the cockpit, checked on Hepzibah briefly, then turned to address the X-Men.

"We're getting close, folks," he said. "We'll be scratching the atmosphere in just under four minutes. Time to get strapped in."

Gambit looked at Rogue, saw anxiety and regret in her eyes and realized that, with all her power, she must be feeling as helpless as he was. Probably more so. He squeezed her gloved hands between his own and realized, finally, that there really wasn't anything either of them could do except hold on tight to one another.

Just hold on.

* * *

Once he was certain that Scott, Jean, Gambit, and Rogue were strapped in, Corsair returned to the medi-slab where Hepzibah lay. He stood over her prone form and looked, for just a moment, at her peacefully unconscious face. For a moment, he wished his lover could find such peace in her waking times. More often than not, she could barely rein in her ferocity, her hostility.

Corsair had been fascinated with Hepzibah the first

time he had seen her, when they had been slave-prisoners of the Shi'ar Empire together. She had already formed an unbreakable bond with Raza and Ch'od, and when Corsair met the three of them, despite their differences, it felt as though the last pieces of a puzzle had been put in place. And a big part of that feeling had to do with Hepzibah.

Not that he did not have his misgivings. In truth, Christopher Summers had always worried that Hepzibah had returned his affections because it was convenient, because they were a team. He believed that she loved him, but he could never quite understand why. Beyond that, however, was something more. Something perhaps more troubling.

Corsair had led them to become the Starjammers, interstellar pirates, out of need. Certainly they needed to survive in a system still ruled by the Shi'ar emperor D'Ken, who had murdered Corsair's wife. There was that need. But it was more than that. He had fancied himself some kind of galactic Robin Hood, a rogue hero. It felt good. Necessary.

For Hepzibah, however, Corsair had come to suspect more and more over the years that the fight itself was the thing. She seemed to thrive on combat, to hold eternal grudges. There were times when he believed she incited battle where it had not been necessary. It was all far from the way he wanted to live his life, from the philosophy to which he had attempted to remain faithful.

There were things about this woman that Christopher Summers did not like very much at all. But when he heard her soft, trilling laugh or her intimate purr, when he saw those blue feline eyes sparking, when they surged into battle side by side, he knew beyond any doubt that he loved her. It was a conundrum, but such was the nature of love, he believed.

Corsair ran his fingers over the light fur on Hepzibah's face, just as he felt the first rumble of atmospheric turbulence beneath his feet. The ride was about to get very rough, and he cursed himself for delaying so long. Quickly he turned his attention to the medical readouts on the display above Hepzibah's chest. He entered a series of commands that would introduce adrenaline into Hepzibah's system, eliminating the sedative.

The *Starjammer* shimmied slightly.

"Corsair," his son warned from the other side of the cabin. "Get strapped in, now. You don't have time for anything else."

"I just need a moment," he responded.

The adrenaline kicked in, and Hepzibah opened her eyes with a feline hiss of anger.

"Sorry, m'love," Corsair said gently, even as Hepzibah's features softened with affection at the sight of him. "We need you up and around now."

"What's happening?" she asked, obviously confused. "Where are we?"

"Entering the atmosphere of Sol-3," Corsair answered. "Hyperburners only, and they're so fried we can't slow down or they might shut down. Just stay there and hold on tight."

"Set . . . VTOL . . . for landing," she muttered.

Corsair had thought Hepzibah still seemed disoriented, and her nonsense words confirmed it. She seemed to drift away slightly, but did not lose consciousness. That was good enough, he thought. As long as they didn't have to carry her in an emergency. Though, of course, if it came to that Corsair would accept the burden of her weight without a second thought.

The *Starjammer* lurched, as though it had slammed into a barrier and broken through, and Corsair stumbled several steps toward the cockpit. Before anything further could happen, he pulled himself along the cabin to his seat, right by the medi-slab, and strapped in.

• • •

Archangel knew he was a hell of a pilot. He'd trained on planes at the age of nine, flown solo at thirteen, and had his own jet when he turned eighteen. All thanks to the Worthington family fortune. Part of his mutant gift, so that he could understand how to use his wings, was an instinctual comprehension of the laws of flight. He had flown the X-Men's *Blackbird* dozens of times, had a higher performance rating on it than anyone else on the team. But this was much different.

Once, in a crisis, he had flown a Starcore space shuttle. But that had been several years earlier, and the *Starjammer* was a much bigger ship. Still, as co-pilot, which meant watching the instruments and backing up the pilot's judgement calls, he seemed to be doing okay. Just as long as Ch'od held it together.

"You're doing great, big guy," Archangel said. "How are you feeling?"

"To be honest, my friend, not so well," Ch'od admitted. "I am afraid the explosion during my spacewalk might have left me with what you would call a concussion."

Warren felt slightly nauseous.

"You can't be serious," he said.

"Of course I can," Ch'od replied, unaware of the

sarcasm in Archangel's voice. "Though I urge you not to worry. I am confident that I will be able to complete this mission without succumbing to disorientation."

"Oh," Warren said, raising his eyebrows, "that makes me feel so much better."

An alarm sounded on the command control readout. A red light began to flash rapidly, then burnt out with a small puff of smoke.

"What the hell was that?" he asked, then proceeded to check the instruments himself. Ch'od was busy trying to keep them on course, and Warren didn't dare interrupt him again.

He scanned the instruments, and was appalled by how fast things had gone from bad to worse. The communication system had never been repaired, but it had been left on. The resulting power drain had gone unnoticed until, with maximum demands placed on the ship, the comm system had shorted out, taking the navigational computer with it. When he informed Ch'od, the reptilian alien only nodded his huge head and kept glancing back and forth from the space-window to the readouts still on his display board.

"More good news," Archangel said. "Heat shields are at 91 percent capacity, but they're already placing a drain on life support."

"Brace yourself," was all Ch'od said by way of an answer.

The *Starjammer* lurched as if it had smashed into the ocean. The seat harness was the only thing that kept Archangel from smashing his face into the command control unit. Momentum threw him forward, whipping his head toward the viewport, then back with a tearing of muscle tissue. Warren felt the pain immediately, and held his neck as straight as possible. After a moment, when the worst of it had subsided, he turned his head from side to side and found that only a little pain remained.

Then he noticed the instruments, flashing lights, warning him of impending danger.

"Ch'od," he said softly.

There was no response. Archangel turned his head gingerly, so as not to exacerbate his injury, and saw that Ch'od was limp in his harness. The pressure, the whip-crack of striking Earth's outer atmosphere at that speed had taken its toll. He was unconscious.

"Oh Lord," Warren said as he switched piloting controls to his own station. He got the ship under his control, at least for a moment, then he sounded the only alarm he had, his own voice.

"Corsair! Get your ass up here!" he shouted. "Ch'od's out and we're in major league trouble here!"

In seconds, Corsair had replaced Ch'od in the pilot's seat. Turbulence was rocking the *Starjammer* hard. The only thing Warren could compare it to was flying a twin engine plane in a massive thunderstorm. Even if the heat shields held, he wasn't at all sure that the *Starjammer* could take much more of the turbulence without shattering into a million pieces.

"Sitrep," Corsair demanded.

"We're in trouble," Archangel said simply. "Hull integrity is in question. Life support's being drained to support the heat shields, which are burning at 117 percent of capacity. They've gotta be melting, Corsair. I don't think we're going to make it."

* * *

SANCTUARY

"We've got a problem," Jean said quietly, her voice trembling with the shuddering of the ship. "I can sense Corsair and Warren's distress even without trying to read it. I don't think we're going to make it, Scott."

Scott Summers was the only man she had ever really loved, the one part of her life she could literally not live without. Jean watched his eyes, hidden behind the ruby quartz lenses of his visor. She was looking for something to hang on to, some hope or idea or solution that would bring them out of this okay.

There was love there, no question. Undying and complete devotion the likes of which she knew most women searched for their entire lives but never found. She was fortunate in that, had always been fortunate. When most women might have gone for the playboy that Warren Worthington was in their first days at Xavier's School, Jean wanted Scott. When most women might have fallen for the danger that seeped from Logan's every pore when the second wave of X-Men came along, Jean wanted Scott.

He was strong, cute, tall, smart, sure enough. But he was never the strongest, the cutest, the tallest, or the smartest. He was quiet, with a fair to middling sense of humor and a total lack of confidence where girls were concerned. But he was, by unanimous unspoken consent, the heart of the X-Men. He was, second only to Professor Xavier, the team's leader and its conscience. And in his eyes, Jean saw that he had silently become as devoted to her as he was to Xavier's dream. She loved him then, at that very moment. For of all of them, in his way, he was the most passionate.

Now she searched those eyes again for a vision of the future. In them she found everything that had always been there, everything they meant to each other. But there was one thing in particular she sought: hope. At first she didn't see it, then Scott squeezed her hands tightly in his own, and she heard his voice, the voice of his heart, speaking in her mind.

Don't be afraid, Jean. We're going to be okay.

There was no lying to a telepath. Jean knew Scott really believed they would be okay, that they would live through this. Silently, she struggled to believe him.

• • •

"Hull integrity is failing, Corsair!" Archangel shouted. "Heat shields at 123 percent capacity and barely holding. We've got about forty-five seconds until life support shuts down."

The vibrations of the ship rattled his teeth in his skull so hard Warren thought he might actually have chipped a couple of them. He looked over at Corsair, whose entire body was locked in combat with the *Starjammer*'s throttle, trying to keep the ship on course without putting her into a nosedive out of which they could never recover.

"Corsair!" Warren shouted. "If we can't slow this ship down we've got less than two minutes to live!"

There it was. He'd said it. And now that the words had come out of his mouth, Archangel realized that they were true and there was not a single thing within his power to change it. He only wished that he was in the cabin now with the others, that he could say goodbye to his friends, that he'd shared a proper goodbye with Bobby and Hank before leaving Earth. Sadly, he knew there were no last wishes when the reaper came to call. The best they could hope for was . . .

"Take the stick!" Corsair shouted. "Warren, take the goddamn stick!"

Suddenly the throttle came alive in his hands and he was piloting the *Starjammer* yet again. He pulled back on it as hard as he could and strained every muscle in his body, feeling once more the pain in his neck, trying to keep it straight on course.

"What in God's name are you doing?" he screamed.

"I think I've figured out how to slow us down," Corsair yelled as he dropped down to the deck and began fiddling with the exposed wiring of the console.

"Whatever you're doing, do it fast," Archangel responded. "We've got about ninety seconds here before we lose life support or the heat shields melt, one or the other."

For a moment, the ship seemed to take on a life of its own, pulling down and away from him like a dog trying to escape its leash. Warren held on tight, then looked back to where sparks were flying as Corsair worked feverishly.

"Well?" he asked. "What exactly are you doing?"

"I thought she was delirious," Corsair called up to him. "But Hepzibah said something about the VTOL, the vertical takeoff and landing program. It was knocked out with the navigational program, but I'm bypassing that right now."

Sparks flew, landing on Corsair's arms. He cursed, but kept working.

"The program the computer goes through includes retro thrusters that reroute energy from the hyperburners to the front of the ship. It's supposed to stop the *Starjammer* in midair so the VTOL can take effect, lowering us to the ground," Corsair explained.

Archangel was stumped.

"I thought we couldn't cut power to slow down or the engines might flare out and drop us to Earth like a stone?" he said, shaking along with the ship as he tried with all his might to keep the ship on course.

"We can't, but this doesn't cut the power," Corsair explained, cursing several more times as sparks landed on his exposed flesh. "The engines are firing at maximum, but a portion of the power is diverted in the opposite direction."

"Can you do it?" Archangel asked.

"Done!" Corsair announced and nearly jumped into the pilot's seat once more. "Now all we have to worry about is whether or not the hull can take the pressure. It's going to be like hitting a brick wall."

"Hey, X-Men!" Warren cried back to the cabin. "Hang on, back there! The ride's about to get a whole lot worse!" Turning back to Corsair, he asked, "Can I give you back the stick now?"

"Nope," Corsair responded, punching up some data on the command control display. "You're going to have to pilot us until we're into blue skies, Warren. The only way we're going to be able to do this is if I turn the VTOL retros on and off and on and off in sequence, timed perfectly, otherwise we'll be torn apart for sure."

Archangel was silent.

"Can I count on you, 'Angel?" Corsair asked. "Come on, now. We're going to die here!"

"Do it," Warren said.

"Hang on," Corsair whispered, and flipped a toggle switch on the console.

Archangel shouted in agony as his head whipped forward once again, this time with much more force. He felt the harness cutting into his flesh and all the air rushed from his body. The hull of the *Starjammer* shrieked with the pressure and for a moment he pictured it simply shattering to pieces and all of its passengers being blown out into space.

Corsair was so far forward in Ch'od's harness that he was nearly pinned to the console. He flipped the toggle switch again and they were slammed back into their seats so hard that Archangel felt his wings embed themselves in the soft leathery material.

"Again!" Corsair shouted, and turned on the retros.

They were all thrown forward once more as the ship fought its own momentum. But this time wasn't quite as traumatic. Half a dozen times Corsair fired the retros, and each time the ship slowed even more.

"Life support systems at 70 percent, heat shields suffering only 46 percent capacity," Archangel happily reported. "Corsair, I think you did it. I think we're going to be okay."

"Huh," Corsair grunted in response. "Hepzibah did it, saved us all, and she doesn't even know it."

"We're all right!" Warren shouted, and he could hear the others cheering in the cabin.

Then the *Starjammer* broke through a layer of clouds into blue sky.

The X-Men were home.

Chapter 15

"What about that deli?" Lamarre asked.

Gabriela rolled her eyes.

"What's the matter with you, Lamarre?" she asked. "Most of the stuff in there is fresh, or already cooked. What's it gonna last, a few days maybe? Let somebody else worry about tonight's dinner, we're looking for non-perishables, long-term stuff. Cans, boxes, frozen foods if we can get that damn cooler working. What we don't need is sushi and Caesar salad!"

"Hey Gabi, just chill okay? We're all doing the best we can under the circumstances," Michael said, and the entire hunting party fell into silence.

Magneto had ordered humans to either bow to the new order or evacuate the city. For Gabriela Frigerio and her brother Michael, neither option had been acceptable. So they had created a third. They had stuffed what they could of their vital belongings and some food from the kitchenette in Michael's apartment, and gone underground. Via the subway, they had descended into a new world where they could set up a resistance to Magneto's rule.

It wasn't long before they realized that they weren't the only humans either brave or foolish enough to flout the will of the new "emperor." A short Puerto Rican man they all called Miguelito had become their de facto leader. He and Lamarre had been two of the first people Gabi and Michael had run into. Though their instincts told them to run, Gabriela had insisted they work together. That was the only way they had a chance of making any real stand against the mutant onslaught.

There were well over one hundred of them now. They'd split up into groups and gone above ground to gather what supplies they could find. Now was the best time, before the new regime was firmly entrenched, before the humans who had stayed had the courage enough to return to their businesses. Gabriela wasn't comfortable with looting, but at least they were looting for a reason, unlike the anarchist idiots they had already seen too much of.

It was a gorgeous day, by Manhattan standards, but its beauty was marred not only by the sudden outbreak of genetic war, but by the smashed shop windows, the burning buildings, and the shattered glass, garbage, abandoned cars, and abandoned lives that littered the streets.

Gabriela's group consisted of herself, her brother Michael, Lamarre, and a recently married couple named Steve and Joyce, who mostly kept to themselves. They'd been sent on a food run, maybe the most important job they'd ever undertake. Gabi wasn't about to let them screw it up.

"Look," she said. "There's a little market a few blocks from here. Let's hit that, then if we get the cooler working, we'll come back topside and hit a steak house or something, take all the frozen meat back. How's that sound?"

Everyone seemed to agree that was a sound plan, even Lamarre, whom Gabriela had taken an instant dislike to when they had first met. He seemed to want to turn everything into a military exercise out of one bad movie or another. The man had obviously watched way too much cable in his life. He had a couch potato body, which was too bad because Gabi thought he had a handsome face. He was no Denzel, but then, who was?

"Hey, Gabi, check this out," Michael said,

overexcited about something, as usual. He was a handsome guy, her brother. Auburn hair and hazel eyes, chiseled features. And he was her twin. Strange thing was, though she was happy to think of him as handsome, she would never allow that she herself was equally attractive. "Poor self image," he'd always tell her. She'd retort that it was easy to see how her esteem had dropped so low when the only man who ever told her she was pretty with any amount of sincerity was her brother.

He never had an answer for that, except "Move out of Manhattan." As if you couldn't have a real life or real relationship in the city. Maybe he'd been right. But it looked like it was going to be too late to find out.

"What is it?" she asked, her attitude tempered by her obvious fondness for her brother.

"It's a guy," Michael said. "Hurt. Maybe dead."

Gabriela picked up her pace, and the others did so as well. They reached the spot where Michael stood, and on the other side of a badly banged up Cutlass, they saw him.

He was young, that's the first thing that Gabriela noticed. Not a kid, but young just the same. Early twenties at most. Maybe younger, maybe younger than she was even. He had brown hair, and through the smear of blood on his cheek and forehead, she thought he might actually be pretty good looking.

And he sure wasn't dead. Gabi had noticed right away that his chest was rising and falling, that he was breathing. It was just like Michael to overdramatize. But then, in their current situation, Gabriela had to wonder if it was possible to be too dramatic.

The guy lay on the ground in a large pool of water. In fact, the whole street seemed dotted with puddles and, in the distance, she thought she could see some kind of ice sculpture. He wore a very tight fitting uniform of light and dark blue, and she couldn't help but notice what good physical condition he was in. Beyond that, she wondered what the uniform meant, if it was some military thing, if he was part of a team sent in to reclaim the island for America.

"What's he wearing?" she asked.

"Some kind of uniform," Joyce said, and she was surprised that the other woman in their group had spoken at all.

"I can see that," Gabi responded, somewhat testily. "But what is it?"

"You're all fools," Lamarre said, pushing past them to stand by the injured man. "You don't recognize that insignia?"

He pointed at the unconscious man's belt, where a black 'X' on a field of red was affixed. Then Lamarre did something that astonished Gabi. He pulled a pistol from a holster under his arm and aimed the gun at the injured man's head.

"Lamarre, what the hell do you think you're doing?" she asked.

Lamarre looked at her, then back at the man on the pavement, and Gabriela thought he was deciding whether to explain himself before shooting the poor man. Finally, Lamarre looked up again.

"He's a mutie," Lamarre sneered. "One of the X-Men. That's what that thing on his belt stands for, X-Men."

Lamarre knelt and touched his hand to the puddle of water around the prone man, and pulled his fingers back quickly.

"It's gotta be near on ninety," Lamarre said, standing up again. "That water's cold still. This has gotta be Iceman."

He smiled at her, and Gabriela felt a chill in her bones.

"We finally bagged one," Lamarre said with perverse glee. "One of Magneto's mutie crew. An' I'd say it's time to ice the Iceman."

He pointed the pistol at Iceman's face. Part of Gabriela wanted to turn away, to hide from the violence, from the reality that had reared up around them. But another part of her knew that the only solution, the only way to survive in that new world, was to act. She stepped forward and batted Lamarre's hand away.

"Girl, what the hell you think you . . ." he started, but she got up in his face, waving a finger at him.

"No killing!" she said. "I mean that, Lamarre. That's not what we're here for. If it's us or them, fine, but this guy needs help more than we do right now. You want to leave him here, fine, but we don't kill him. We've got no way of knowing if he's who you say or not, nothing but your opinion. And I'm not going to be accomplice to some murder just because you've seen *Red Dawn* one too many times."

"You're starting to get on my nerves," Lamarre said in a low, angry voice.

"Good, then we're even," Gabi snapped, unwilling to be frightened off. "Now, let's take a vote on what to do with your Iceman, here. Killing isn't an option. Then do we leave him or bring him back and let Miguelito decide what's to be done."

"Let's bring him back to Miguelito," Lamarre said happily. "He's only going to tell me to kill the mutie anyway."

"I think we should leave him," Steve said. "If he's a mutant, all we'll be doing is bringing them right into our headquarters. It's suicide."

"There are a hundred of us, Steve," Joyce said. "And what if he's really injured? He could die because of us. I don't want to live like that."

"I agree," Michael said. "Let's take him back to the tunnels."

"Do it then," Gabi said. "Who gets to carry him?"

"I'll take him," Michael said. "He doesn't look too heavy."

And, apparently, he was not. Michael, who tipped the scales at more than two hundred twenty pounds and was over six feet tall, lifted the smaller man, mutant, whatever he was, over his shoulder with relative ease.

"Steve, Joyce, you two hit that market and then rendezvous with us," Gabriela said. "We'll see what's to be done about this Iceman character."

"I hope you know what you're doing," Lamarre said disparagingly as she fell into step with her brother.

"Yeah," she agreed. "Me too."

* * *

It was already mid-morning, and despite the psychic barriers he had placed in his own mind, Charles Xavier could not shut out the overwhelming sense of imminent catastrophe that enveloped all of Exchange Place. Whatever was going to happen, the gathered civilians, media, and military all believed it would happen today. There was an all-encompassing feeling of dread, as if the thousands of people crowded into the area were collectively holding their breath.

It might have been calm before the storm, Xavier

thought grimly, but the sky became awfully dark. All of which was little more than metaphor. The sun was beating hot upon the pavement and the people, its heat only slightly diminished by the light breeze off the Hudson River. It should have been a glorious day, but it was devoid of pleasure.

He had been interviewed by news organizations he never knew existed, by everyone and anyone with a camera and a microphone, and he had issued the same call for rational behavior, the same message of peace, each time. Frankly, he was becoming tired of being a spin doctor. And simply tired. It had been too long since Charles Xavier had rested. But his X-Men had not had any more sleep than he. Nor had Valerie Cooper. And so he went on. They all went on.

Xavier sensed Cooper's approach a moment before she reached him, and turned to face her. He could see from the grim set of her jaw and the coldness of her eyes that she brought more bad news.

"What is it now, Val?" he asked, exasperated. "Are we officially at war yet?"

Cooper tilted her head to one side, regarding him with a surprised look.

"You don't sound like yourself, Charles," Val said. "You're ruining the image I have of you as eternal optimist."

Xavier offered a slight smile in appreciation, and nodded his head.

"You know, Val, that's one of the biggest misconceptions about me," he said. "I'm actually a terrible pessimist. I don't believe that humans and mutants are such good souls that they can live in harmony simply because it is the best way to live. That just isn't reality.

I dream of a world where humans and mutants live in harmony, that much is true. But I know that if it happens, it will be because the alternative is so terrifying that we have no other real choice.''

Cooper was visibly stunned. Xavier understood her reaction. He was rarely so verbose without cause, and even more infrequently so bitter. But he found it difficult not to become bitter with the gleaming Sentinel just over his shoulder as an illustration of how close they already were to losing the dream. And maybe he had lied a bit. Maybe a part of him believed in the innate goodness of people, believed that peace could arise for its own sake. Even if that were true, a greater part of him had begun to grow cynical.

He didn't like it one bit.

"What was it you wanted, Val?" Xavier asked, attempting with his demeanor to erase the previous minute. And failing.

"Well, to answer your question, we're not at war yet," Cooper answered, running a nervous hand through her blond hair. "But it's getting close. I don't have all the details, but apparently Gyrich did just as we suspected. He sent a team in."

"And they failed," Xavier observed.

"He just came out of a meeting with Colonel Tomko," she continued. "They were on the line with the President and the Director of Wideawake, but they've cut me out of the loop. That means that they're close, that they're really considering going in full force. If Gyrich has his way, that's just how they'll do it."

Xavier raised an eyebrow.

"I know what you want, Valerie, and I cannot do it. I won't compromise myself like that."

Cooper flushed, seemed about to speak and then bit back her words. After a moment, she turned to leave, then stopped with her back to Xavier.

"No!" she said finally, turning and angrily advancing on the Professor where he sat in his wheelchair. "I never thought I'd say this but I don't think you understand exactly where we are, Professor. And with all you've done in this fight for harmony, with all you've sacrificed, I can't believe I'm saying this, but you're being a very selfish man."

"You forget yourself, Ms. Cooper," Xavier said coldly.

"No, Charles," she snapped. "I'm afraid it is you who forgets himself. Everything you have fought for, your entire life, and everything you believe in, is wrapped up in what you do today, right now, to resolve this crisis. If we can stop this without full-scale military assault, people will still hate mutants more because of what Magneto had done. But there will still be a battle to be fought, still a chance for your dream to come true.

"If we have a civil war here today, you will have lost that dream forever. The people will never forgive. Before you worry about compromising yourself, why don't you think about what you are compromising by not using your every ability in this struggle."

At that, Cooper turned and stormed away without a look back at Xavier. Charles flinched, not merely at the harshness of her tone, but at the ring of truth he suspected lay therein. Her words resonated within him. If they could avoid using military might, avoid Gyrich's method of dealing with the situation, that would save lives. And Val's description of the long-term effects, he was forced to admit, sounded accurate. If they could avoid military conflict, the public would remain split on the mutant question. There was still hope.

Without hope, they would be lost.

That was the deciding factor, then. Suddenly Xavier realized that, argue the issue as vehemently as he might have, he had never really had a choice in the matter.

Instantly, he let down the walls that kept the rest of the world's thoughts from his own mind. Before the torrent of babbled words could flood into him, Xavier focused his psi power into a mental net, which he cast out over the people gathered in Exchange Place. He sifted through them like a prospector sifting for gold, but he sought something much darker: the mind of Henry Peter Gyrich. It took him only a moment to pinpoint it.

Xavier hesitated. What he was about to do was an invasion of privacy of the highest order. It violated every tenet of his belief system. There had been times he had entered the minds of others without their consent, but with few exceptions, it had always been done in the best interest of the violated party. That was not the case here. No, instead, Xavier was about to cast himself in the role of the common thief.

Though his mind was, quite literally, wandering, his eyes were still focused on the here and now, in case anyone should approach him. Slowly, he wheeled his chair around to stare across the river, for perhaps the hundredth time that day, at the Sentinel that stood there symbolizing everything he had fought for, and against.

He hesitated no longer. It was the only way. Xavier reached out to Gyrich's mind with his psi power once again, and this time he entered. He would do his best not to give attention to anything but the information he specifically sought, but it would be difficult not to come away with anything else.

Then he hit a barrier, a psychic shield erected by some mercenary psi employed by the federal government to protect their top agents from precisely the kind of mind-theft Xavier was currently perpetrating. For most tele-paths, it would have been enough. It might even have stopped Jean Grey. But Charles Xavier had the most powerful mind in the world. The mental barrier fell beneath the force of his probe in seconds.

Without desiring to, he began to get a much clearer picture of Gyrich as a person. As he had suspected, the man was not nearly the villain Cooper always painted him as. And yet, he was perhaps even more dangerous because he fought for what he believed to be right. Patriots were always more passionate than mercenaries. The greedy were never martyrs.

Pushing away everything but the information he had entered Gyrich's mind to find, Xavier moved on. Several minutes passed, for the information was buried very deep. Finally, though, he discovered everything Gyrich knew about Operation: Wideawake. Xavier concentrated on the override codes for the Alpha Sentinel. With a last, fleeting, thought of regret, he extracted the codes.

Gyrich would never know they had been stolen.

* * *

"I don't get it, Amelia," Needle asked. "I mean, Wol-verine is, like, this great tracker and stuff. How does Magneto expect us to find him in a city as big as this?"

Amelia Voght kept moving at a good clip, with Nee-dle at her side and the Kleinstock brothers bringing up the rear. Senyaka was on point about twenty-five yards ahead.

Needle was new to the game, Voght realized. Not much more than a kid, really, a young woman whose genetic mutation had destroyed any hope she might have had of a normal life. Unlike Amelia, who could 'pass' for human without any trouble, Needle had changed far too much to ever be considered human again. Her mouth had distended slightly, and was filled with several rows of long, thin, razor sharp teeth like needles. They seemed to extend when she opened her mouth, and retract within the girl's head when her mouth closed.

It was not an attractive mutation. She had been bitter, angry, despondent. Then Magneto had come along and shown her that the world had a place for her, that she was as good, no, better, than the humans who had ridiculed her. As part of her mutation, Needle had become more savage. But as Voght considered it, she wondered if that had been more of an environmental change than a genetic one.

In any case, she was the perfect recruit. In it one hundred percent, with nothing to lose and everything to gain. She also illustrated, for Amelia, one of the prime differences in the conflicting philosophies in the mutant community. Charles Xavier touted harmony between the two races. Magneto spoke of conquest. What Xavier would never understand was that, like abused children, mutants like Needle would never be able to rise completely above the past. They could forgive, if they had the heart for it, but they would never forget.

Harmony, for Needle, was out of the question. And if it was out of reach for some mutants, it was out of reach for them all.

"Amelia?" Needle asked tentatively.

"Sorry, I heard you," Voght responded. "Just thinking for a moment. Back to Wolverine, though. What do you know about him?"

"He's the best there is, and the meanest," Needle said. "That's what I've always heard."

"And it's true," Voght agreed. "Which means that Wolverine isn't afraid of us. Sure, with the five of us against him, he isn't likely to win. But it's possible. He's not afraid of us at all."

"I get it, but I don't get why you're so sure we'll catch him," Needle said. "We're headed straight for the Lincoln Tunnel, as if he'd make a beeline for the closest escape without even trying to cover his tracks."

"I'm betting that's just what he'll do," Voght said. "Magneto was too, otherwise he never would have sent us out after him. That's my point, exactly. He just isn't afraid of us at all. He's running, but not running scared. He'll go for the quickest way out, because he wants to get reinforcements as quickly as possible."

"Oh," Needle said softly. "So he expects us to catch up with him?"

Voght smiled thinly, letting the irony of the hunt, the danger of it, seep through.

"Actually," she said, "I expect he *wants* us to catch up with him. Magneto and the Sentinels are our ace in the hole. Out here, it's just us. If Wolverine can take us down, it improves the odds when he makes it back with the cavalry, if there is a cavalry."

Needle slowed a bit, prompting curses from the Kleinstocks.

"What is it?" Voght asked.

"Nothing, really," Needle said unconvincingly. "It's

just that, all of a sudden, I'm not sure I want to catch up with him.''

''Ah,'' Voght said. ''Now you understand.''

They continued west for three more blocks, until Voght thought they might have gained some ground. The next time Senyaka looked back, she signaled him to stop. He waited for them to catch up, and Voght addressed the others.

''Here's where it gets interesting,'' she said. ''We're hunting one of the world's foremost predators. We'd be safer staying together, but we don't stand much of a chance of catching him that way. We're going to have to split up, spread out . . .''

''You've gotta be kidding me,'' Needle hissed.

Voght smiled.

''Harlan, two streets north, Sven one,'' she ordered. ''I'll stick with this one. Needle one street south, Senyaka two. Move as fast as you can, but stick close to the buildings. Use whatever stealth you can muster, but not so much that you waste time. We're just trying to spook him from the brush now, get him out in the open where we can take our best shot at him. If you see him before he sees you, find your nearest teammate. If you have to engage him, shout an alarm as loud as you're able.

''If we do our job right, what we're doing is herding him toward the tunnel, which is where he's going anyway. We'll narrow the field and take him long before he can get there. One way or another, we'll stop him.''

''Yeah, I know just how to stop him,'' Sven Kleinstock bragged, overflowing with machismo, and Voght was reminded why she felt such strong dislike for the Kleinstock brothers.

"Just follow orders," she insisted. "You try to take Wolverine on by yourself, you're going to find yourself sorely disappointed. In fact, you're likely to find yourself dead. You're no good to Magneto or to Haven with your throat cut. Understood?"

Senyaka and Needle nodded their assent, but the Kleinstocks looked at one another like mischievous schoolboys, then turned back to glare at Voght, eyes dimly unintelligent yet glaring with anger. If it ever came to a power struggle between herself and Unuscione, she knew which side the brothers would be on. She knew to watch her back. Voght counted herself fortunate that their loyalty to Magneto and their thirst for Wovlerine's blood were far more powerful than their opposition to her leadership.

But the Kleinstocks were fortunate as well.

Magneto would be very displeased if she were forced to teleport their heads away from their necks.

Which, now that it had occurred to her, did not sound all that bad.

CHAPTER 16

As many times as Hank McCoy had heard people refer to Times Square as garish, gaudy, or tacky, he had never once believed it himself. Certainly it called up many different images, of hit Broadway shows and darkened pornographic theatres, of Dick Clark on New Year's Eve, and guys selling imitation Rolex watches for fifty dollars.

It was a spectacle, he couldn't deny that. From the place on the platform where he was captive, on display for the gathered mutants, he could see it all. The Coca-Cola sign that had hung for years; the gigantic Sony TV screen; the Viacom building that housed MTV; the little glowing sign for Carmine's, one of his favorite Italian restaurants. A neon nightmare, some might have called it, but Hank McCoy thought of it as the heart of America.

To him it represented the best and worst human society had to offer, built with the blood and sweat of democracy. That it could be so easily taken by a man who, no matter his intentions, was little more than a tyrant repulsed the Beast.

That tyrant stood several feet away in conference with some of his Acolytes as he prepared to address the gathered mutants. Hank could see the fervor in their faces, knew that Magneto would be preaching to the converted, that through his power they had been empowered to conquer and destroy. Perhaps it was hopeless, but he knew he had to try and provide a voice of opposition, of reason and logic, of humanity.

Even as he considered that obligation, he glanced to the edge of the platform, where Trish Tilby stood in front of a TV camera, doing her job. That's what he kept telling himself, she was doing her job. She was free, not shackled in any way, and yet if Magneto wanted to keep her there, Trish would not have been able to escape. Hank tried to convince himself that was it, that Trish was a prisoner but not a captive, that Magneto had forced her to document his triumph. It made a strange sort of sense, knowing Magneto. And knowing Trish, if that were the case, she wouldn't even try to escape. She'd rather stay and get the story.

On the other hand, it was also possible that she'd just waltzed in and asked Magneto for an exclusive. The Beast could easily see where Magneto would have said yes. Neither solution to the riddle of Trish's presence was comforting.

In any case, he no longer had to worry about whether or not he was playing to the cameras. In one sense, he was. But he knew Magneto might very well edit out whatever he might say or do and Hank was determined to do it anyway. Someone had to stand up to Magneto. Someone had to speak the truth.

"Look around you!" he said, as loud as he was able without shouting, and with all the calm he could muster. "Look at the world you have driven to its knees, the society you have brought down. Maybe you're proud of yourselves. Yes? Well, you should be ashamed!"

"What the hell is this?" Unuscione shouted as she, the other Acolytes, and Magneto spun to stare at the Beast in astonishment.

"Gag him!" Unuscione ordered, but Magneto held up a hand.

"I give the orders here, Unuscione, not you."

Magneto walked to where the Beast was restrained.

He tilted his head to one side and looked at Hank curiously, with all the detached interest of a scientist. Hank knew the look well, it was one he had worn often enough. But that was in a laboratory. This was real life.

"Please, Dr. McCoy," Magneto said, a warmth and smoothness in his voice that made him seem almost reasonable. "Do go on."

The Beast's tufted furry eyebrows rose, but he was not about to let the opportunity go to waste.

"I speak to you now because, more than most of my comrades, I know your pain," he told the crowd. "Those of you who are too different to fit in, too different to hide in the throng of humanity. I know what it is to be called a freak. I know how it feels to be hounded, to have your life threatened simply because you were born different, because you look different.

"But we are not the first minority to be treated thus. The sad truth is, we are not likely to be the last. And all along, armed conflict has been a less effective tool than time, tolerance, and reason."

"Ah, shut yer yap, ya furball!" the Blob shouted from the crowd, laughing at his own crassness.

"You should know what I'm talking about more than most, Fred," he said. "You were a carny sideshow freak, a spectacle that so-called normal humans paid money to laugh at. The X-Men offered you a place beside us, a chance to work for peace and understanding between humans and mutants, and you rejected us. Just as you all are rejecting that brightest of all possible futures by standing here today.

"Eric Magnus Lehnsherr, the man you know as Magneto, is not an evil man, and that has ever been the greatest difficulty we have faced in battling him. It is easy to call him a hero or a martyr, because he is willing to sacrifice everything, has already sacrificed much, to offer a safe haven to mutants.''

The Beast paused, allowing his words to sink in. The crowd was astonished at his endorsement of Magneto, very few, perhaps even none of them having previously had any understanding of the nature of the conflict between Magneto and the X-Men. He didn't look at Trish, but he knew that she, too, would be taken aback by his words.

''How can you say that?'' a woman called from the crowd. ''You X-jerks have hounded him from the get-go.''

''Perhaps that is the way it seemed,'' the Beast answered. ''The truth is much more subtle. Magneto is of the philosophy that humans are inherently flawed and cannot be forgiven those flaws, that they must be subjugated in order for mutantkind to be free, even to prosper. What he leaves out of that equation every time is that, regardless of whatever mutations we have received, gifts or curses, we are all essentially human. We are equally flawed.

''Maybe the reason we hate humanity so much, aside from the pain we have felt, is that they constantly remind us of those flaws. They are our mothers, fathers, brothers, sisters, and friends. Like the American civil war, genetic warfare can only lead to the murder of your own loved ones. Are you prepared to do that? Even if your family has turned its back on you, are you prepared to take their lives in return?

''The X-Men have a vision, a dream. We believe that

with time and effort, humans and mutants can learn to peacefully coexist.

"Through the actions Magneto has taken in the past twenty-four hours, he has endangered that dream. Further, he is doomed to failure."

"Sez you!" a burly man in the crowd screamed angrily. "Why the hell should we listen to you? We got our own world now, our own homes! This is just the beginning."

The Beast hung his head. He knew it was hopeless, but just as certainly, he knew he had to try. These people belonged for the first time in so many years, in a lifetime for some. They weren't going to give that up. Humanity had wielded the power of majority over them for so long. Now that they had a taste of power, they would never surrender it.

"Humans are a dangerous animal," the Beast said, not missing the irony of his words. "We—and I include all of us humans gathered here today—we guard what is ours jealously, become violent at the merest hint that it might be taken away. Like all animals, that includes territory. Throughout history there have been examples of humans destroying the land, through scorched earth or salting, that they were about to lose. Out of nothing but spite. If they could not protect it, they would destroy it.

"Don't think that can't happen here! Don't think, even for a moment, that if you become a large enough threat, the world won't turn around and decide to erase your little empire from the face of the Earth. If they decide to do that, Magneto cannot protect you. The Sentinels cannot protect you. You'll be shadows on the wall, like the innocents slaughtered at Hiroshima and Nagasaki.''

Off to one side, Magneto began to applaud.

''Oh, well done, Dr. McCoy, but you're beginning to rave now, so we'll have to put an end to your little show,'' he said. ''I think the people have made up their minds.''

Magneto turned toward the crowd, displaying a showmanship the Beast would never have thought he had the patience for.

''Haven't you?'' Magneto asked them.

The crowd roared.

Defeated, the Beast lowered his gaze.

''My turn,'' Magneto whispered by his ear, then stepped to the front of the platform and raised his arms.

When the crowd roared again, Hank could not help but be reminded of a charismatic little man whose mad vision had led to the murder of millions. It was sickeningly ironic that Magneto was a Jew whose family had fallen victim to the Nazis late in World War II. Just as abused children grow to become abusers, Magneto the victim had become Magneto the tyrant, prepared to sacrifice another race for the supremacy of his own.

''My people, my Acolytes,'' he began, and they roared again. ''I know many of you think we have already won. We have stolen the center of American business out from under humanity's nose. We have stood up for ourselves, carved a home where mutants can not be discriminated against. We have a sanctuary.

''But a sanctuary is only the beginning, a haven is nothing more than a resting place. And we can rest, now, for a day or two, as the humans slowly realize that there is nothing they are able to do, or, if the Beast is to be believed, nothing they are willing to do to stop us. For most certainly, we can repel any but the most apocalyptic of attacks, and they would never sacrifice this entire city just to claim victory. That would be more foolish than even I believe them to be.

"So we allow them two or three days, respite . . ."

Magneto paused then, and there was utter silence. The Beast could feel the excitement in the air, but it was more than that. He was horrified as he found the word he searched for. The way the crowd treated Magneto was more than reverence, it was worship. He glanced quickly at Trish, and saw that she and her cameraman were on the job, recording everything.

"Then we expand our borders!" Magneto cried.

The crowd went wild.

* * *

Bishop listened to Magneto rant, and the madman's words froze his heart. He wanted nothing less than to rule the world, to ride herd over humanity and make them slaves. It was a fruitless endeavor, Bishop knew. It was destined to backfire, to create a world where the opposite was true. While Magneto was trying to free his people to live as equals in society, he was actually dooming them to suffer as slaves. For Bishop, that was reality.

A reality he could not allow to come to pass.

Magneto had created the restraints he wore specifically to hold the X-Men. He knew them all, knew their powers, well enough to calibrate the restrains specifically to prevent each of them from using their powers. But when Magneto had been closest to the X-Men, Bishop had still been living in the future. The two had never held a conversation, never really faced one another in battle. Magneto was aware of Bishop, certainly, and aware of his mutant power. But there had never been an opportunity for him to truly evaluate Bishop's powers.

The restraints were calibrated for him, personally, and for his ability. But the energy field that was intended to block his power had not been calibrated correctly. Magneto knew that Bishop could absorb an energy blast directed at him, and re-channel it as his own weapon. But there was far more to Bishop's power than that.

As the Beast spoke, and now, as Magneto droned on, outlining plans and responsibilities that Bishop vowed would never be fulfilled, he had siphoned energy from the very restraints meant to prevent him from using his power. Slowly, he drained the restraints on his hands and neck, absorbing the power into his every cell until he fairly shone with its radiance.

"Now, then, my friends," Magneto crowed. "What say you?"

"All hail Magneto the Emperor!" screamed a near hysterical Unuscione from the platform where she looked at her Lord with adoring eyes.

"All hail Magneto the Emperor!" the crowd repeated, enthralled.

A light burst of energy shattered the restraints on Bishop's hands, and he tore the metal ring from his neck with ease. Without a moment's hesitation, and before anyone could shout a warning, he gathered up all the power he had absorbed. With a scream of rage, he let it loose in one concentrated burst.

"To hell with Magneto!" he screamed.

Magneto was buffeted by the blast, and actually knocked from his feet. When he spun to face Bishop, already rising from the platform, an infernal hatred raged in his eyes.

"Why must you X-Men always interfere?" he cried. "Don't you know when you are beaten? It is over, Bishop. Over. I have won. Mutantkind has won a great victory today, and you should all be rejoicing. Instead, you make an unending nuisance of yourselves. I have kept you alive to witness my victory, in hopes that one day you, all of you honorable men and women, shall realize your errors and come 'round to the truth."

Magneto floated above the platform in a sphere of magnetic energy. It pulsated with his every word, and hovered just before the spot where Bishop stood, already nearly deflated of energy, exhausted before the fight even began in earnest. He had given all he had, and Magneto had been more than up to the task.

"I begin to wonder whether I should make an exception in your case, man of tomorrow," Magneto said. "Perhaps you should die after all."

Bishop had little power in reserve, not enough to do more than further annoy Magneto. But he was not beaten. The X-Men were a team, after all. Where one could not claim victory, there were always others.

Tensing, he feinted to the left, and Magneto sent a bolt of magnetic force in that direction before he realized that Bishop had run to the right. Three steps and Bishop stood behind Storm. He reached up and grabbed her restraints, his hands erupting with the last vestiges of energy he had stored. The restraints fell away even as Bishop fell to the ground, weakened but searching for a weapon even then, searching for another way to fight.

Though it was entirely possible he would not need to fight at all.

Storm was free.

SANCTUARY

• • •

Those who loved her knew Storm as an eminently calm and reasonable woman. When she had lived as a goddess on the African plains, those who worshipped her had considered themselves lucky to be subjects of such a benevolent deity. But, like the weather she controlled, Ororo Munroe was capable of great peace, and of the mad, chaotic devastation of the storm.

The X-Men had welcomed Magneto into their lives and he had betrayed them. Now, he had taken his mad scheme much too far, and in its wake was the promise of death and destruction on a massive scale. He might well have ruined the future for all mutants. Before he brought the world to war, he had to be stopped.

Storm was aware of all of these things. But at the moment Bishop set her free, she was not conscious of them. Rather, she thought only of Magneto's betrayal of her and her trust. Of being wrapped in that metallic shroud by a man who knew exactly, precisely what it would do to her psyche. She was vulnerable in that way, and Magneto had violated her as surely as if his attack had been more intimate, more physical.

"Magneto!" she screamed, bearing herself aloft on a chill, angry wind.

Down came the storm.

Ororo did not concentrate. Instead, she allowed her righteous fury to tap into her mutant powers, channeling the energy of that anger into the atmosphere. In seconds, the sky darkened and it seemed as though dusk had come to Times Square. Thunder clouds, black and pregnant with moisture, were spontaneously generated above.

Lightning crashed down at her command, striking the

platform nearly one hundred times in less than a minute. Fire broke out on the wooden dais, and in several places, it collapsed beneath the Acolytes. Storm saw Bishop, now bound once more, fall through to the pavement below. It barely registered.

"You must be stopped, Magneto!" she screamed between the whipcrack booms of thunder. "For the sake of us all!"

Far below where she floated amongst the clouds, which had now blocked the sun so thoroughly that it might have been midnight rather than noon, Storm could see Magneto and his Acolytes scrambling. She had created a cloud base low to the ground, effectively fogging in Times Square so that none of them could see more than ten feet in front of them. Fortunately, part of her mutant ability to control the weather had been enhanced perception in such cases.

"Find her!" Magneto shouted. "Kill her if you must!"

And so his true colors were revealed, Storm thought. For all his talk of "rehabilitating" the X-Men, he was just as happy to kill them in the end.

The thunder increased in intensity. No longer did it sound like a distant explosion. It was closer, a deep bass rumble that pounded the ears and buffeted the body as violently as the wind itself. Each thunderstrike was longer than the last, until it sounded as though the sky was being violently rent asunder. Storm brought her wrath down upon the crowd. She willed the black clouds to open wide, to pour out their wet burden onto the streets below. But when it fell, it fell not as rain, but as sleet and hail. Ice pelted Magneto's followers, driving them from the street.

SANCTUARY

Finally, though she herself remained nearly immobile, held aloft by gentle winds at cross currents, Storm lashed out at Magneto's hordes with the wind itself. Fifty, sixty, eighty mile-per-hour winds whipped through Times Square, and the pieces of the platform began to blow away. At one hundred and ten miles per hour, it began to tear itself even further apart. Those people not already inside were beginning to grab hold of things to keep themselves from blowing away. Some already had. Storm vowed that the only thing left standing in Times Square would be the Blob. Then she reconsidered. Perhaps, she thought, it was time to test Fred Dukes' claim that there was nothing on Earth that could move him against his will.

The more destructive forms of precipitation did not reach her, but Storm allowed the rain to drench her entirely. Her hair hung, heavy with it, and partially across her face. With a toss of her head, Ororo whipped it away, sending a spray of water falling on its way with the rest. No longer did she control the storm, she had become the storm.

And she reveled in it.

• • •

Magneto was astounded. Never in his wildest dreams had he imagined Storm capable of the power, the fury that now raged around him. Not only was his public address over, but if he was not able to stop her immediately, Storm might well be able to end the dream of Haven before it had ever truly begun. For the first time, Magneto wondered if Ororo Munroe was, after all, the most powerful of the X-Men.

"My Lord," Unuscione cried, holding on to what

remained of the platform with her exoskeleton, barely able to keep herself from being swept away by the winds. "What can I do? How can we kill this woman?"

"How, indeed?" Magneto said aloud, his words torn away by the wind. Just as he himself would have been carried away if not for the bubble of magnetic energy he had drawn around himself. He pondered Unuscione's question, even as the Acolyte herself was pried loose by the storm and blown, cursing Storm all the while, across the street and through one of the huge windows of the Marriott Marquis, which had already been shattered by the wind.

Magneto knew the answer already, though. Despite his words, he did not want Storm dead. He had always had more respect for her than for most of her comrades, and this display only heightened that respect. Storm could be of great use to him in the future. Of course, if she forced his hand, well then he would have to kill her.

Still intent upon that train of thought, Magneto began to rise up through the fog, wind, and hail. The ball of magnetic energy that surrounded him glowed green and its surface steamed away the impact of any precipitation. He was surprised to find that it took far more effort than usual to keep his course and maintain the integrity of the force shield. The hurricane threatened at any moment to tear away his focus, to hurl him to the pavement, or into the side of a building or a billboard.

Several moments later, he broke through a low cloud and saw her there, at the eye of the storm. Magneto took a moment to admire how beautiful she appeared then, in all the glory of her mutant power. She was a shining example of the magnificence that was the genetic x-factor, the reason why humans must give way to mutant rule. There was a grandeur about her that took his breath away.

Then she saw him.

Immediately, Storm lashed out at Magneto with every ounce of her power. The tempest that had raged in and above the street now seemed to turn, like some predatory animal, and use him as its focus. Magneto was unprepared for its effect.

Hurricane force winds battered his force shield, and it vibrated under the attack. He poured everything into maintaining the shield, then began to muster up enough extra to launch a counterattack. In an instant, the shield was struck three times by lightning.

Magneto cried out in pain, entire body quivering as if he had been electrocuted, which, in some sense, he had. The shield lost its resolution, and he began to fall, whipped into some kind of aerial maelstrom by Storm's power. The breath began to leave him.

"Command: seize alpha mutant designate Storm," he said, wheezing the words into a comm unit on his gauntlet.

Then he felt himself snagged, almost grabbed by hands made of nothing but the gale. His helmet had long since blown off, and his white hair was now soaked with rain, his uniform drenched, and he shook his head to clear the momentary disorientation he had experienced.

Storm was beckoning him, drawing him toward her with the weather at her bidding. He saw her, finger pointed at him in accusation, or perhaps in some kind of mute command. Then he remembered the lightning, and wondered when it would strike. It was a novel moment, as Magneto wondered if he might actually die, if

Storm could bring the lightning down on him and stop his heart.

He had no desire to find out. In an instant, Magneto surrounded himself with yet another bubble of magnetic energy, stronger than before. When he used his mutant power, Magneto could tap into the electromagnetic field of the entire planet. Charles Xavier might have been the most powerful mind on Earth, but for sheer power and potential devastation, Magneto knew that he was unmatched. Every time he had faced the X-Men he had lost because of outside intervention, because he had been surprised, or because of his own, foolish hesitation. Surprise had been the only reason Storm had survived the current battle as long as she had.

Summoning his mutant power, drawing up magnetic energy like a fisherman drawing in his nets, Magneto reached out for Ororo Munroe. If she did not surrender, he would destroy her. As an example to other rebellious mutants, he would impale her on the same spire from which the well-known ball dropped on New Year's Eve.

Magneto found himself saddened by the thought.

* * *

When Storm observed Magneto's swift recovery, she was quick to realize that she had lost her advantage. Instantly, her rage dissipated, to be replaced by survival instincts and deftly honed battle acumen. He would summon all his strength for an attack now, she knew. There was every chance he had been serious in his order to kill her. She had never been successful in repelling one of his magnetic attacks, only in evading them.

But evasion was not going to be a possibility. She was already drained by the incredible amount of energy she had put into the storm. No, there had to be something . . .

Then she had it. Ororo cursed herself for never having thought of it before. The perfect, perhaps the only, defense against Magneto that the X-Men had. It would have been far easier if Iceman had been with her, but they weren't even certain what had happened to him. The Acolytes claimed that they had killed Bobby. Storm didn't want to think about that. Nor did she have the time.

Magneto was mustering his strength, so Storm did the same. While he was, most probably, summoning all the power he could to destroy her, she enacted a desperate plan to save herself from that attack.

Diverting some of her attention from the storm, from her attack on Magneto, she drew all the moisture in the air around in front of her, using the wind to sculpt clouds that had not been there a moment earlier. The sky was clearing already, the sun breaking through and shining down. Many citizens of Magneto's new empire crept from their hiding places or went to help one another up, tending to those wounded during the tempest.

Four feet from where she floated on the air, Storm created a blizzard from thin air. She concentrated her power on that spot, used the winds to whip up a circular motion, keeping as much of the generated snow from falling to the ground as possible. By the count of six, there was a gossamer layer of snow swirling together to form a weather wall between herself and Magneto.

At the count of seven, he reached out for her with his magnetic power. And he was rebuffed. Storm could barely make him out through the curtain of snow she had conjured, but she did not see him to sense his frustration. Like all the X-Men, Storm had received a college-level education at the Xavier Institute, once called Xavier's School for Gifted Youngsters. That education included the basic natural sciences. Electromagnetic energy was radiation. Snow absorbed radiation, such as the sun's heat, like a sponge. The blizzard she had created assimilated and diffused Magneto's blasts.

Try as he might, Magneto would not be able to break through the snow barrier as long as she could continue to generate it. The question was, which of them would become exhausted first? Ororo feared that she knew the answer. Just as she was attempting to determine her next move, she heard Magneto's voice very faintly over the roar of the storm.

"... far more clever than ... credit for ..." she heard. "... nearly as clever ... you thought ..."

The last part, she heard clearly.

"Look up!" Magneto shouted.

Surprised by the tone of victory in his voice, Storm could not help but obey. She looked up, through the heavy blanket of snow and clouds that she had called down on the city in her wrath. Only then did she notice that the sun was no longer breaking through the clouds. But it was not her doing. Something else was blotting out the sky above her. Something huge.

The Sentinel's eyes glowed red.

"Alpha mutant designate Storm, surrender now to avoid painful apprehension procedures," the Sentinel commanded in its flat, emotionless voice.

Realizing she had lost, Storm attempted to retreat.

She did not get very far.

CHAPTER 17

"**W**e have hope now, Charles, that is what is truly important here, isn't it?" Valerie Cooper asked.

Xavier still felt some of the revulsion that had crept into his psyche when he lowered himself to steal the Sentinel override command codes from Gyrich's brain. The feeling lingered within him, never quite disappearing, the way the acrid odor of sulfur remained after a match had been extinguished.

"Indeed," he answered at last. There was no reason for him to burden Cooper with his troubles. In any case, a woman of her pragmatism would not understand them.

"We do have a chance at this, now," he agreed. "Perhaps the only chance we'll get. Once I have communicated the override codes to the X-Men, and redirected them to find the Alpha Sentinel, we'll have done all we can from here. What we need now is some visual cue to identify the Alpha Sentinel."

"Of course," Val said, a bit cynically. "That would be nice, wouldn't it? Thing is, you're not supposed to be able to identify the Alpha Sentinel. That would make things too convenient for someone, like us, who is trying to put the damn thing out of commission."

Xavier frowned. The X-Men certainly had their work cut out for them.

"If you'll excuse me, now, Valerie," he began.

"Do you want me to go?" she asked, very respectfully.

"Not at all," Xavier answered. "Just bear with me. For a moment, it will seem as though it is I who have left."

With that, Xavier cast his mind out over the island of

Manhattan. He concentrated on midtown and began moving south. With the millions of minds on the island, it would take a few moments longer than usual to identify the X-Men's thought patterns. But, as he had once explained to Cyclops, mentally recognizing an individual mind was no more difficult than visually recognizing an individual face. In many ways, in fact, it was easier.

Professor Xavier had taught and trained the X-Men, some for many years. Some of the lessons he imparted to them had to do with the mind, and the protection of its secrets. Their thought patterns were as familiar to him as the faces of children he had never had. When he reached out with his psi power to scour the island in search of them, it was with the utmost confidence.

Indeed, he found them. One by one, he made contact with the X-Men. One by one, he found them unable to respond, or communicate in any way. They were unconscious, had somehow been sedated. At least, that was the case with Storm, Bishop, and the Beast. Iceman had been knocked unconscious, and was far from where the others were being held.

Held. The thought came to Xavier so easily, but he knew it was the only solution. The X-Men had been captured by Magneto, were his prisoners even now. Xavier could only thank God, in that moment, that they were still alive. As long as they lived, there was still hope. But it seemed, at that moment, a slim hope indeed.

Valerie must have noticed some disturbance on his face, for distantly Xavier heard her call to him.

"Charles, are you okay?" she asked.

He might have replied, but instead ignored her question. For there was one X-Man he had not yet found.

Xavier scanned the island again, searching frantically

for Wolverine. He could imagine only two reasons why he might not be able to find Logan. The first, that he had already left Manhattan, did not seem very likely to Xavier. The second, that Logan was dead, he dared not seriously consider. Therefore, he reasoned, there must be a third.

Taking a deep breath, Xavier scanned again. If Wolverine had been part of the melée where his teammates had been captured, and had left the battle of his own volition, he would most certainly be making for the city limits, and reinforcements. Xavier knew Wolverine would choose the most direct route, through one of the tunnels. With great care, he reached out with his mind, as if slowly dragging a mental net over the area of the city between Times Square and the two tunnels.

Finally, Xavier sensed Logan's mind. His psi-scan had not initially pinpointed Wolverine because the man had gone primal, had descended into the predatory persona that seemed to overcome him when stalking his prey.

Wolverine, he thought, and he could feel Logan's instinctive response to the psi contact.

You got beautiful timin', Chuck, Wolverine thought in return. *Where were ya when we needed ya?*

We have no time for such foolishness, Logan, Xavier chided, knowing that Wolverine's jibe was insincere. *The others have all been captured, as I'll assume you know. Now that I am aware of your predicament, you don't need to be concerned with calling in reinforcements. I'll do what I can. In the meantime, you must find the Alpha Sentinel and reprogram it with the following override codes . . .*

When Xavier was through communicating the codes,

he could feel Wolverine's anger and hesitation. He did not want to leave his friends in Magneto's hands for any longer than necessary.

You can't get them out by yourself, Xavier thought. *Taking out the Sentinels is more important right now. You'll just have to leave the other X-Men to me.*

Instantly, contact was broken. Xavier's eyes began to focus once more, and he saw Val Cooper staring at him, her curiosity etched in her face.

"The X-Men have been captured," he said, and watched as Cooper sighed and buried her face in her hands. "Wolverine remains free and has begun the search for the Alpha unit."

After a moment, Cooper looked up, her brows knitted with concern.

"Well, Charles, any ideas as to what the hell we do now? I'm fresh out, I'm afraid," Valerie said gravely.

"I know," Xavier answered. "I told Wolverine to leave rescuing the X-Men to me. But I'm not even sure where to start. He may very well be our only hope, now. One man against a city filled with humans who hate him, and mutants out to destroy him."

"Of course," Val said, trying to lighten the mood, "every day is like that for Wolverine."

* * *

Amelia Voght did not want to see the X-Men killed. Not that she had any great love for Xavier's puppies. Or any sympathy for them. But there was something about the purity of their optimism that she saw as valuable. Magneto clearly did not want them dead either, and that made her think that perhaps he had seen the same value in their continued existence. It also didn't hurt when one considered that, if the X-Men could be convinced to support Magneto, they would not only have much greater firepower in their arsenal, but many other mutants who supported their efforts and not Magneto's might come around. There might be thousands of mutants who would join the cause if the X-Men were among Magneto's followers.

Not that Amelia thought there was a chance in hell of that ever happening. But still, she didn't want to kill them. Not that she ever wanted to kill, but this was something else entirely. The purity of their efforts, sure, that was part of it. But maybe, just maybe, she had a soft spot still for Charles Xavier. And if the X-Men died, as far as Amelia was concerned, much of Xavier's soul would die as well.

On the other hand, there was Wolverine.

He was different from the rest of the X-Men, somewhat less pure. He was more like her. The other Acolytes worshipped the ground Magneto walked on, thought of him as second on to God, infallible as the Pope—if you believed in that kind of thing. In their own way, they were pure as well. Though some of them, Amelia wouldn't mind seeing killed. Ironic, sort of. She didn't want the X-Men to die, but Unuscione? That was another story entirely.

But she and Wolverine were two of a kind. He didn't really walk the path of righteousness that Xavier had laid out for the others. Wolverine was jaded, had seen too many battles, seen the inside of too many human beings, friends, lovers. Voght didn't really know him, but she knew his dossier front to back, same way she did all the X-Men. Yes, Wolverine was different. He'd left the X-Men and returned several times, never completely satisfied with what Xavier had to offer. He was their friend, and loyal teammate, to be certain. But he knew the way the world worked was more complicated than either Magneto or Xavier had ever imagined.

Voght was the same. She chose to follow Magneto, but she knew full well that he was as fallible as the next man, and that she was the only one of his followers who was willing to point that out to him. Idly, she wondered if Charles Xavier, her old lover, had anyone around to do the same. She doubted it. In fact, in that way, she wondered if Xavier wasn't even more of an insufferable egotist than Magneto.

Amelia Voght had seen more than most of the other Acolytes. She understood Magneto better than the rest, knew he was slightly mad, and followed him anyway. Was, in truth, even somewhat attracted to the man.

Of all of them, enemy or titular friend, however, Voght could only claim a real feeling of kinship for Wolverine. She wished she had been able to meet him under different circumstances, wished she was not given the responsibility of hunting him down. But that was the way it had come down, and now, despite the kinship she felt toward him, Wolverine had become the one X-Man she would not hesitate to kill. For a very simple reason.

He frightened her.

Voght would pit herself against any of the X-Men, or the Acolytes, against Xavier or Magneto if it came to that. She would not run from the Sentinels, or the U.S. Army, but the idea of hunting Wolverine had given her fits of trepidation she had not felt since childhood.

After all, this was not a normal human being. This was a savage animal, with human—or more than human—cunning. Unlike the other X-Men, he would not hesitate to kill if it became necessary. In fact, Wolverine's dossier suggested that he had often reveled in killing.

She swallowed her fear. It would not do to have any of the other Acolytes know, or even sense it enough to speculate, that she was afraid of Wolverine. Her leadership, indeed even her life, might be in jeopardy because of it. Amelia stepped carefully, eyes and ears on alert, as though she were hunting the most vicious grizzly that urban forest had ever known. In many ways, she was.

Cautiously, Voght stepped from the shade of an Italian restaurant and quickly crossed the avenue in front of her. She had long since lost track of her precise location. A moment to check the street signs might be the moment she compromised her personal safety. Glancing north for Wolverine, she saw Harlan Kleinstock rushing across the street, and wondered if he were frightened as well. Or simply too stupid to be properly aware of the danger.

It didn't seem right that it was day, that the sun shone so harsh upon her shoulders. It was too warm, too bright for that most dangerous game, the hunting of a human being.

There were several humans on the street ahead, speaking outside the glass doors of an old office building. After a few moments, one of them looked up, then motioned quickly to the others. In a heartbeat, they had retreated inside the building, and when Amelia passed the glass doors, she didn't even see them inside.

There was a noise behind her, panting, the pad of bare feet, and Amelia spun around ready for a struggle to the death.

It was a dog. The mangy mutt stopped in its tracks,

surprised by her quick movement, then gave her what passed for a canine dirty look and crossed to the other side of the street.

Enough of this foolishness, she told herself. By thinking so much about Wolverine, rather than about actually finding him, she might well be endangering herself further, leaving herself open to attack. She shook it off, looked up and down the street, and continued the hunt.

* * *

As Bobby Drake began to wake, his first moment of awareness was consumed by pain. His head, his skull really, hurt so much that he did not dare even move for several moments. When he opened his eyes, sunlight forced them shut again, and he winced with the additional pain of the glare. It felt as though someone were trying to crush his skull like a walnut, that the thin shell would give way at any moment.

"Oh this sucks," he muttered to himself.

Then he remembered it all. Colorado. Magneto. The Sentinels. Manhattan. Getting shanghaied by the Blob and his cronies. He had to get up, he knew, get moving and warn the rest of the X-Men. The temptation to just lie there and whimper was great, but Bobby quickly overcame it. He might have been the joker on the team, but he knew how to play when the stakes were high.

His eyes fluttered open again, and he held his forehead with his left hand, as if trying to hold it together, and began to sit up, blinking back the light. As he looked at the ceiling above him, the windows to his left, he realized suddenly that he'd been moved. He'd been outside after the attack.

"Oh, perfect," he sighed. "The tastefully appointed dungeon of Magneto, Master of—"

"Not another move, Ice-Boy!" a male voice rasped.

Bobby spun toward the harsh voice, wincing again at the pain in his head, and was startled at the number of people in the room with him. He'd thought himself alone, but there were eight or ten others, humans, in a semi-circle by the door. They were armed, several had guns, and none of them looked particularly friendly.

"That's Ice*man*, buddy," Bobby said, eyes narrowing as he glared at the man who'd spoken. "And you'd best get out of my way before somebody gets hurt. We've got a situation here, as if you didn't know."

"Oh," the man said, smiling thinly. "We know. See, we're not sure if you're part of that situation or not. And until we are, you're not going anywhere. You make one wrong move, and you'll be nothing but ice chips. Maybe we'll make margaritas out of you."

Bobby considered the man's words a moment, surveyed the weapons in the room, then let out a deep, relaxing breath.

"Come to think of it," he said. "A margarita would taste pretty good right now."

"I don't think you're funny," the man growled, and thumbed the safety on his automatic pistol.

* * *

In the small office they had commandeered, Trish Tilby and Kevin O'Leary sat in silence. He had tried to get her to talk about what was bothering her, but Trish hadn't been in any mood. And anyway, she wasn't so sure she knew exactly what she was feeling.

Yes, mutants were a menace. Magneto had proven that.

Yes, she was getting the story of her life.

Yes, she wanted more than anything to live long enough to tell it.

But then there was Hank, and that put the whole situation in a new light. Hank McCoy was kind, brilliant, amusing, and above all, gentle. He was not, nor did Trish believe he ever could be, a menace. There should not only be a place for him in the world at large, but a prominent place. If not for his fur, for the obvious changes his mutant genetics had wrought upon his body, he was the kind of man who became a university president, or a presidential cabinet member.

Trish had no interest in rekindling a relationship with the Beast, but she still cared for him greatly. After watching him today, feeling the extraordinary guilt that overwhelmed her when his eyes fell on her, she knew that no story was worth allowing him to remain a captive. The world needed him. By extension, the world needed the X-Men.

She wanted to live, yes indeed. But Trish Tilby knew that she would not be able to live with herself if she did not at least try to help Hank and the others escape. Magneto frightened her. The thought of a world ruled by him frightened her even more.

The question was, what could she really do? After all, she was only human.

* * *

Harlan Kleinstock was getting impatient. The whole thing was stupid as far as he was concerned. They should have just hurried to the tunnel entrance, along the quickest route, and waited for Wolverine there. As soon as they got back, he and Sven would have to have a talk with Unuscione about what to do with Amelia Voght. Not that Harlan had anything major against Voght, but she just wasn't cut out to lead them. Harlan didn't want to question the wisdom or the will of Lord Magneto, but hey, everybody made mistakes.

On the other hand, Harlan was enjoying the hunt. He seriously doubted Wolverine would be able to escape, and he and Sven had a score to settle. Blood stained the front of his tattered uniform from the superficial cuts Wolverine had given him. They wouldn't kill him, or Sven, but they were humiliating. That called for pay-back.

On a lighter note, going after the little X-runt also gave him the opportunity to scope out some parts of the city he wasn't real familiar with. Despite the pollution, which Magneto had already said he was going to do something about, the city smelled good. Mainly, it was the food. Harlan didn't think there was anyplace in the world you could get food like you got in Manhattan. Indian, Thai, Chinese, French, Japanese, Italian, Greek, Mexican, Brazilian, Portuguese, Cajun, and plain old American, all within a few blocks of one another. Harlan Kleinstock loved to eat.

He took a deep breath, inhaling all the food smells along with whatever else the city had to offer. It was clear that the city was beginning to function again, and Harlan was almost lightheaded as he realized that he was one of its bosses. A car drove by when he was halfway down one block, and the human behind the wheel sped up and cowered inside, trying not to be noticed.

It felt good.

SANCTUARY

There was a Greek deli up ahead, on the left, and Harlan could smell the heady aroma of roasting lamb. The place was open for business. Harlan had to admire that. He stopped outside the deli and considered running inside, demanding a souvlaki, for nothing of course, and then continuing with the hunt. Voght would be pissed, and he knew it was not the most responsible thing to do, but . . .

Nah, he decided. He didn't want to chance missing Wolverine.

For a moment, he stared through the plate glass window at the shabby tables and chairs, the sodas and juices lined up on the counter top, the dark-haired, white-aproned man who stared defiantly back from behind the counter. A smile spread across his face as it finally began to really sink in that, if he'd actually had the time, Harlan could have gone in there, taken what he wanted, done whatever he wanted. And nobody would be able to stop him.

"Sounds good," he mumbled to himself, then resolved to finish Wolverine as quickly as possible and bring his brother back to this deli for lunch.

"Smells good, eh, bub?" a voice growled somewhere . . . above him?

Harlan looked up just in time to see someone jumping down on him from the roof of the deli. He had no time to move, so he reacted instinctively, falling backwards and using both hands to fire at his attacker with a double bio-blast from his hands. Trashed by the blast, his opponent fell with a dull, wet thud on the pavement by Harlan's feet. When he sat up, he was stunned to find his brother, Sven, lying on the pavement unconscious. His uniform was blackened by the bio-blast, and there were slashes on his chest where claws had criss-crossed to form an x-pattern hacked through clothing and flesh.

"Oh my God, Sven," Harlan gasped.

He went to his brother and felt his pulse, which seemed fine. He tore away Sven's tunic to get a better look at the slashes. They were not life-threatening. In fact, he had probably done more damage to Sven than Wolverine had.

There was a great, metal, clanking commotion from above, and Harlan's fury was finally released.

"Wolverine!" he screamed, and leaped to his feet, ready to destroy the mutant who had made him hurt his own flesh and blood. Harlan looked up, determined to rip Wolverine apart.

That was when the air conditioner fell on his head.

The Kleinstock brothers lay on the pavement, side by side. Blood trickled from Harlan's left ear.

* * *

Needle's biggest mistake was that, passing a subway station entrance, she didn't bother to turn around and look down the steps. When Wolverine pounced on her, she had no time to react. He drove her to the sidewalk and she wailed in agony as half a dozen of her needle teeth actually snapped as they hit the ground.

She tried to get up, but he slammed her face against the sidewalk again, keeping her from seeing him. That terrified Needle even more. She could feel his breath, hot on her neck as if he were going to tear her throat out with his teeth. Needle recognized the irony in that thought, but didn't smile.

There was a wet click, then a chunk of cement hit her face as three adamantium claws buried themselves in the sidewalk just to the right of her face. Then his voice, little more than a growl.

"Far as I can tell, girl, your biggest sin right now is bein' just plain dumb," Wolverine whispered in her ear. "Magneto is playin' big kid games, now. You don't got the guts to play, you'd best get out now. Otherwise, I'll have to show you what it means to lose."

Then his weight was off her.

After a few moments, Needle began to believe that he was actually gone, that she was not going to die that day after all. She didn't get up, though. She lay on the pavement for more than an hour before she even dared to stand. When, finally, she looked around to see that nobody was watching her but a grey tom cat, she began to walk toward the Lincoln Tunnel.

Her parents had been frightened of what she'd become, but they had never turned their backs on her. Maybe they'd let her have her old room back.

* * *

Wolverine padded silently across the top of a brownstone, determined to take out the Acolytes stalking him before setting off in search of the Alpha Sentinel. The Kleinstocks were powerful, but they were also not very bright, which had made them easy targets. Needle was little more than a girl, feigning a ferocity that was not in her heart in order to survive among more dangerous predators. Logan had saved Senyaka and Voght for last. Each was more clever, more experienced, more dangerous than the rest of their comrades. Except perhaps for Unuscione, who was not part of their little hunting party.

Crouched low, he moved along the roof. While New York streets were so close together that most buildings backed up directly, and often connected, to their rear neighbor, that wasn't always the case. Particularly with older structures. Wolverine grumbled quietly at the discovery that this was one such building. There was a gap of perhaps fifteen feet between the edge of the roof where he stood, and the building behind it. Which would not have been much of a problem were it not for the two-story drop that accompanied it.

Fifteen feet across, twenty or so down. There was no way in hell Wolverine was going to make that jump without making some noise. If Senyaka was close enough to hear the impact of his landing, Wolverine would have blown his cover. Not that he couldn't take the cowled psi-punk without the benefit of surprise, but it would be easier if Senyaka didn't have time to warn Voght.

"What the hell," he growled, and shrugged.

Wolverine backed up fifteen paces, ran to the edge of the roof and dove out over the gap. Even as he arced through the air, pulled his legs up under him and executed a forward aerial roll, he caught the stench rising from decades of garbage that had been dumped between the two buildings. It was far from pleasant.

He came out of the roll with his feet angled toward the opposite roof. With the additional distance of the drop figured in, clearing the gap was no problem. Wolverine landed hard. His jaws clacked together as his feet touched down, and he allowed momentum to carry him into a somersault, then back to his feet. Crouched in defensive position, he listened intently for any reaction to the noise he'd made. When he heard nothing, he moved quickly to the edge of the roof and peered down to the street below.

Nothing. Scanning west, however, he quickly spotted Senyaka moving cautiously along the sidewalk, ducking in and out of alleys and doorways. From there, it was a simple matter to follow along the tops of the buildings until he came to the first small alley. Wolverine dropped down to the fire escape, moving quickly but quietly, and edged out onto the street perhaps twenty yards behind Senyaka.

The Acolyte never heard him coming.

Honor was everything to Wolverine. He had learned it well during his time in Japan. He had attacked Needle from behind in order to heighten the girl's fear of him and drive her away. Senyaka was not an honorable opponent, but Wolverine would still not deliver a killing blow from behind. Which didn't mean the claws were off limits. Not at all.

Snikt!

Wolverine's claws slid from the adamantium sheaths inside his forearms with an audible click, and Senyaka was already turning when he ducked in and slashed the Acolyte's rib cage under his left arm.

"Wolverine!" Senyaka said, grimacing in pain. "That's the last blood you'll see, runt!"

A psionic whip shimmered into existence in Senyaka's right hand, and he cracked it against the ground, sending up sparks. Wolverine could see that he'd already won, though. The way Senyaka held his left arm tight against his side, the fight was over before it had really begun. Which meant that Senyaka would never get to warn Amelia Voght that Logan was coming.

"You wouldn't last an hour in the North country, bub," Wolverine snarled.

Senyaka cracked the whip toward him, and Wolverine

allowed it to wrap around his left arm. He grunted with the pain he'd known was coming, even as he slashed the psi-whip with the claws of his right hand. Senyaka howled.

"You've tried that trick before, boy," Wolverine said. "You'd best start payin' attention. I ain't always gonna be here to show you these things."

Senyaka was doubled over in pain, and when Wolverine approached, he looked up in fear. The look changed quickly to one of pleasure, of satisfaction. Logan thought it was a gag, the old look-behind-you trick, but then the wind shifted, and he caught a familiar scent coming up behind him.

He started to turn, ready to slash his attacker, but he was too late. Amelia Voght hit him high and hard, riding him down the street. Her hands grasped either side of his head, thumbs at his temples. She was faster than he'd expected. He started to bring his claws up, even as Senyaka's newly remade psionic whip coiled around his throat, choking off his air supply and sending a current of agony running through him.

"Don't even think it," Voght barked, staring into Wolverine's eyes as he struggled to cut her. "I feel even a pinprick from those claws and I will teleport your head right off your body."

Wolverine hesitated, claws just inches from Voght's heart. He could kill her in a single beat of that heart, but there was no doubt she had the ability to take him with her.

Voght seemed to read his mind.

"Don't think I won't," she said coldly, eyes locked on his.

And he knew she would.

SANCTUARY

Wolverine stared into Amelia Voght's eyes, struggling to think of an escape despite the little oxygen reaching his brain. Senyaka's whip coiled ever tighter around his neck. The animal in him wanted to struggle, to reach for the whip, to kick, to claw. But the human wanted to live.

His last cognitive thought was of how much he despised Amelia Voght.

Then Wolverine, the last, best hope for the X-Men, drifted into oblivion.

EPILOGUE

S cott Summers was breathing a hell of a lot easier now that they had entered Earth's atmosphere. The battered *Starjammer* cruised through American airspace, cloaked from radar detection but not from visual sightings. It would probably, Scott mused, result in dozens of UFO reports.

"Glad to be home?" Corsair asked.

"You've no idea," Scott answered, and smiled.

"Oh, I think I do," Corsair responded wistfully, and not for the first time, Scott had to wonder why his father did not simply return to Earth for good. One day, he hoped, they would be able to roam the Alaskan wilds around Scott's grandparents' home, fishing, camping, whatever a retired father might do with a son he'd never really known. One day.

"As for me," Corsair continued, "I'm just glad to be alive."

He looked at Scott intensely for a moment, and Scott was tempted to turn away but did not.

"I mean it, son. Thank you for my life," Corsair said.

"And I thank you for mine," Scott responded warmly. "Dad."

A moment later Jean Grey rushed into the cabin. Her face was blanched white, her expression one of horror and disbelief.

"Jean?" Scott asked, even as he rushed to her side. "What is it?"

"I've been trying to contact the Professor telepathically ever since we entered Earth's atmosphere," she said, the words tumbling out of her in a torrent. "I finally found him."

Jean brought a hand to her face, then, letting out a

long breath that seemed as much emotional strain as it was relief to be sharing the information.

"I don't understand," Scott urged. "What is it? Has something happened to the Professor?"

"I'm not sure I understand it all myself," she said. "Somehow, someway, the worst has finally come to pass. Magneto has conquered Manhattan island. It's overrun with mutants and Sentinels. And the other X-Men have already been captured."

"Dear God," Scott whispered.

"Ch'od!" Corsair yelled, jumping up and running to the cockpit. "Chart a new course. Get us to Manhattan as quickly as possible!"

Scott took Jean's hands in his own, and held them tight.

All-New, Original Novels
Starring Marvel Comics'
Most Popular Heroes

__FANTASTIC FOUR: TO FREE ATLANTIS
  by Nancy A. Collins   1-57297-054-5/$5.99
Mr. Fantastic, the Thing, the Invisible Woman, and the Human
Torch—the Fantastic Four—must come to the aid of Prince Namor
before all of Atlantis is destroyed by the fiendish Doctor Doom.

__DAREDEVIL: PREDATOR'S SMILE
  by Christopher Golden   1-57297-010-3/$5.99
Caught in the middle of a battle over New York's underworld,
Daredevil must combat both Kingpin, his deadliest foe, and
Bullseye, a master assassin with a pathological hatred for Daredevil.

__X-MEN: MUTANT EMPIRE: BOOK 1: SIEGE
  by Christopher Golden   1-57297-114-2/$5.99
When Magneto takes over a top-secret government installation
containing mutant-hunting robots, the X-Men must battle against
their oldest foe. But the X-Men are held responsible for the takeover
by a more ruthless enemy...the U.S. government.

__X-MEN: MUTANT EMPIRE: BOOK 2: SANCTUARY
  by Christopher Golden   1-57297-180-0/$5.99
Magneto has occupied The Big Apple, the X-Men must penetrate
the enslaved city and stop him before he advances his mad plan to
conquer the entire world!

           ® ™ and © 1995 Marvel Entertainment Group, Inc. All Rights Reserved.